T0365160

THE Dolomite
CHALLENGE

TOM JOYCE

BALBOA.
PRESS

A DIVISION OF HAY HOUSE

Balboa Press books may be ordered through booksellers or by contacting:

Balboa Press
A Division of Hay House
1663 Liberty Drive
Bloomington, IN 47403
www.balboapress.com
1-(877) 407-4847

Because of the dynamic nature of the Internet, any web addresses or
links contained in this book may have changed since publication and
may no longer be valid. The views expressed in this work are solely those
of the author and do not necessarily reflect the views of the publisher,
and the publisher hereby disclaims any responsibility for them.

The author of this book does not dispense medical advice or prescribe the use
of any technique as a form of treatment for physical, emotional, or medical
problems without the advice of a physician, either directly or indirectly. The
intent of the author is only to offer information of a general nature to help
you in your quest for emotional and spiritual well-being. In the event you use
any of the information in this book for yourself, which is your constitutional
right, the author and the publisher assume no responsibility for your actions.

Any people depicted in stock imagery provided by Thinkstock are models,
and such images are being used for illustrative purposes only.
Certain stock imagery © Thinkstock.

Printed in the United States of America.

ISBN: 978-1-4525-8017-3 (sc)
ISBN: 978-1-4525-8018-0 (e)

Balboa Press rev. date: 8/23/2013

CHAPTER ONE

Vienna West Train Station. Monday, August 25, 1947.

An officious young Viennese man, a clerk in the British Burn Center at the Vienna General Hospital, was standing with awkward stiffness in front of a woman and a man sitting on a wooden bench. The clerk's attention was focused on the woman. When he spoke to her it was in English prefaced by the conventional Viennese words used to address a woman doctor.

"*Frau Doktor Marbach*, I wish you a good three day visit in Paris. Captain Burke is already in Paris. I am sure that with him on the job this will be a holiday for you."

Frau Doctor Marbach was a doctor in the British Burn Center, but she was also a major and since she was wearing her major's uniform the young clerk might have addressed her as "*Frau Major Marbach*." Sitting beside her on the wooden bench in the West Train Station of Vienna was her husband, Vienna Police Inspector Karl Marbach.

Two years ago, Pamela Marbach came to Vienna with the Royal British Medical Corps. That was August of 1945 and the war in Europe was over. The first week she was in

1

Vienna, she met the police inspector. They were married less than one month after the day they met.

Now, two years later, Pamela Marbach was still with the Royal British Medical Corps in Vienna. Because she worked in the British Burn Center in the Vienna General Hospital many people assumed she was British, but she wasn't. She was an American. She joined the Royal British Medical Corps in early 1942 after her first husband, a man to whom she had been devotedly married for almost twenty years, was killed on Bataan in the early days of the war in the Pacific. His death had left her consumed by a desperate need to get into the war and serve the best way she could—as a doctor. But back in 1942 the U.S. military wasn't giving commissions to women doctors. So, like a small number of other American women doctors, she joined up with the British, got a commission with the Royal British Medical Corps. That meant there wasn't much likelihood she would serve in the Pacific, but at least she would be able to serve. She ended up practicing her profession on the battlefields of North Africa, Italy, France and, finally, Germany. For what she did on battlefields she was awarded the Distinguished Service Order (DSO), a combat medal valued just under the Victoria Cross. There weren't many doctors who got a DSO, but several high level officers agreed that this woman doctor had earned the DSO.

Now, in 1947, Pamela Marbach was married to the police inspector, but she knew she would always grieve for the husband killed in the Pacific. She could dissolve into tears whenever she thought about that good man. Sometimes she wondered if she was unique, after all this time, painfully aware of herself as a widow while totally and completely in love with the man who for the past two years had been her husband, her lover . . . her everything.

In the West Train Station, the young clerk was continuing to stand with awkward stiffness.

"Thank you," Pamela Marbach said. She didn't address the clerk by name. She was embarrassed that she couldn't recall the clerk's name. She knew it was bad manners to not know his name, that in Vienna it was especially bad manners to not know the clerk's name.

The officious young clerk made a slight bowing motion and, with a stiff, awkward walking style, went on his way.

Police Inspector Karl Marbach took advantage of an opportunity for some playful humor. "His name is Julius Barwick," he said in the English he usually spoke when alone with his wife. "If you couldn't remember the name Julius Barwick, you might have addressed him as Herr Clerk."

"Oh, pooh," Pamela Marbach said.

"Oh, Pammy," Karl Marbach said with a distinctive Viennese inflection incorporated into the English. He used Viennese inflections whenever he addressed his wife by her name. He usually called her "Pammy," but sometimes he called her "Dr. Pammy." He used one set of Viennese inflections when he called her "Pammy," and a slightly different set of Viennese inflections when he called her "Dr. Pammy."

He liked calling his wife "Dr. Pammy." He liked hearing those words in his head. He knew that the British nurses in the burn center called her "Dr. Pammy," and that even though most of the patients in the British Burn Center were Europeans who didn't speak English, a lot of them spoke the words "Dr. Pammy" when she tended to them.

Karl Marbach raised a finger, debated a moment, finally said, "That young clerk mentioned Captain Burke and said something about a holiday. You have never introduced me to Captain Burke, but I hear he is most handsome. Who is this handsome Captain Burke who is asking you to join him in Paris for what might turn out to be a holiday?"

With humor in her voice, Pammy said, "Oh, Karl, don't be cute. Captain Burke is an idiot and he's at least a dozen years younger than me."

Pammy was in her mid-forties. She fretted about the dark circles under her eyes and she had always thought her cheeks were too round. Most certainly, she had lost the freshness of youth, but in recent years—during the war and now afterward—she was finding that men seemed much more likely to convey appreciation for her as a woman than had been the case when she was young. She liked the feeling of being appreciated by men, didn't take advantage, but liked it.

Pammy stared at Karl. She knew that before the war one of his lovers was a popular Vienna Volkstheater actress named Constanze Tandler who was killed by the Nazis. Often, especially at informal gatherings, when she was nearby, but not included in a conversation, she heard people talking with Karl fervently speak the name "Constanze." But Karl never talked with her about Constanze Tandler. Indeed, he made a point of never talking about any of his former lovers with her. She knew there had been quite a few former lovers. Viennese friends had advised her, sometimes seriously, usually with humor, about the large number of Karl's former lovers.

Pammy knew Karl'd had a lot of former lovers, but she knew he was faithful to her. She knew he was faithful to her because, at the beginning of their life together, he had told her he would be faithful. And he never lied to her. He never lied about anything. Not to her. Not to anybody as far as she could tell. He never lied about the smallest thing. On trivial things, day-to-day trivia, she might lie, but he never did. Sometimes she would tell a lie or do some fibbing to avoid talking about something she didn't want to talk about. But not him!

Pammy continued thinking about Karl and his aversion not only to lies, but even fibs. She thought about how it was that she might tell someone that something they had bought or acquired was excellent when it was just mediocre. But Karl never did that sort of fibbing. Oh . . . he was just impossible!

She studied Karl. She noted that at this moment he was intently reading one of the English language magazines he had purchased for her to read on the train trip to Paris. On the cover of the magazine was a picture of American President Truman. She wanted Karl to put the magazine away and pay attention to her. In recent weeks she had become aware of a wall growing up between them. They'd had an unusual number of arguments, all of them—one way or another—connected with her son's upcoming wedding in the States.

Pammy sat up straight on the wooden bench. She regarded it as unfair of Karl to be obtuse about how important it was for her to attend her son's wedding. Of course, there would be a lot of expense and, even with two incomes, finances were a problem for them in 1947 Vienna. She knew it was awful that Karl would have to stay behind in Austria while she was gone for a couple of weeks, but she was determined to go to the wedding. This was something they very much needed to talk about it, yet every time she brought the subject up he turned it into an argument.

Pammy held a newspaper in her trembling hands. Her hands were trembling because she was angry. She didn't like being angry. If there was one thing she really hated it was to be angry. She grasped the newspaper fiercely, held it up close to her face, and started reading. As always these days the news in the newspaper was frightening. Why wouldn't it be? A darkening cloud was spreading a shadow over Europe. In recent weeks, Communists had killed priests in Yugoslavia and a death sentence had been announced for the anti-Communist leader Nikola Petkov in Bulgaria. In Hungary, things were awful; Communist threats had forced Deszo Sulyok, leader of the Liberty party, to flee. And in Vienna this spring there had been food riots that for a while threatened to result in a Communist overthrow of the government.

Pammy put aside the newspaper. She had stopped reading when she came to an article dealing with the possibility of a famine. A famine, if it came, could change everything forever. Communism would flourish if there was a famine. Yes, thought Pammy, the future was forbiddingly dark, but she couldn't do anything about the terrible things happening in the world. She couldn't even do much about her own personal troubles. She stole a glance at Karl. At the very least, there was one piece of business they ought to talk about before she left on this trip to Paris.

She kept her voice firm. It was vital to her now to talk to Karl about Leo Lechner, one of her patients in the burn center.

"Karl, I had another long talk with Leo Lechner. I know you don't like him, but this is important to me. I want you to see Leo. It would mean a lot to me if you would agree to see him."

A terse reply was delivered. "I knew Leo Lechner when he and I were police officers working together before the war. I had no use for him then and I have no use for him now."

"Was Leo Lechner a monster?" Pammy bristled irritably. "Did he do something awful to you?"

"To me personally Leo Lechner never did anything I can complain about."

"Then . . . ?"

"leo Lechner was like all the other young Nazis. The only difference was that he was more energetic preaching Nazi nonsense than were most of the other young Nazis. He went to extremes telling everyone about his devotion to Hitler and National Socialism."

Pammy was silent for a moment. How could she explain? Words seemed futile. She was a Jew—proud of being a Jew. She hated Nazism with a fury that her sometimes Catholic husband couldn't possibly imagine, but Leo—the mutilated former Nazi—had managed to touch her with the sincerity of his repentance.

"People change," Pammy said, keeping her voice level and firm. "Leo has been through a lot. I have feelings for him. I think maybe you would, too, if you got to know him again."

"I hear Leo was badly burned."

Pammy spoke her reply abrasively. "I work in the burn center!"

7

"If it's important to you, I will see any of your patients, even a miserable rat like Leo Lechner."

"Leo is no rat. If he was when you knew him many years ago, he has changed. Sometimes people do change."

"Why is it that you and I never bicker? Do you ever wonder about that?"

"What in the world do you mean saying we never bicker? That's what we're doing right now."

"Oh . . . ?"

"And this bickering could turn into a fight. Have you forgotten all those dishes I broke yesterday? You're lucky I didn't break some of them over your head!"

"I have never been able to understand your incredible proclivity for breaking glassware."

Pammy felt her temper flare, but in the next moment the soft, gentle voice of Karl captured her total attention.

"Pammy . . . Pammy. You were right picking fights with me recently. You were most certainly right to insist you were going to go to America to be at your son's wedding. That's two months from now." A dramatic pause. "Things are fixed. We will be going to America together."

For a moment, Pammy had trouble taking a breath. Karl was saying he would be going with her to her son's wedding in the States. It was difficult for her to keep her voice under control. "You'll go with me? But you're an Austrian citizen without a passport. How . . . ?"

Aware that they were in the very public West Train Station, Pammy resisted the impulse to shout. Instead of shouting, she bolted into an upright sitting position on the wooden bench and spoke in a clear, direct manner. "If you didn't mind me going, if you . . . if you were working on a way to come with me, why did we have to have so many fights?" A strong anger threatened to ignite within her, but when she looked at Karl's face all of the anger drained out of her. She listened as he spoke.

"Pammy, oh Pammy. You needed to get angry about something. A woman with all of your determination needs to know she can get angry when she is in the right, or even if she just thinks she is in the right." A pause. "Besides, I needed time to see what could be worked out."

Pammy felt overwhelmed, but this was the train station and that meant she couldn't shout, couldn't do any serious hugging and kissing, so she settled for saying with laughter in her voice, "I am going to check this out with your nephew, the priest. I'm not sure you are allowed to go to a Jewish religious service, a Jewish wedding."

Karl touched a finger to his nose. "I suppose they'll be breaking glass and everything. I say . . . is that where you get your disregard for glassware?"

"You're a *beast*! I may let you accompany me to the States, but I'm not sure I'll let you come to my son's wedding." Pammy laughed in the way she knew Karl liked to hear her laugh, in E-flat. Laughing in E-flat, she snuggled her head tight against his chest. She didn't care if they were in a public place. She needed to snuggle up close.

With Karl's arm around her, Pammy listened while more English was spoken with the Viennese accent. "It is grand when you laugh in E-flat."

Karl often said that laughter in E-flat was his favorite female sound. Pammy wondered if any of his previous lovers had laughed in E-flat. Probably one or more of them had, but there was no way he would talk about that. He never discussed anything about his former lovers, not their names, not anything about them. He never said anything, no matter how vigorously he was prodded to provide some details.

While Pammy laughed more of her E-flat laughter, she heard Karl say to her, "I hear there are marvelous mountains in America. Maybe I'll climb one of your American mountains."

Pammy stopped laughing. "You are much too large a man to be a mountaineer. I have climbed with you. I have seen how you climb and I have seen how the good mountaineers climb. The best of them are compact, not big characters like you."

"Compact?"

"Yes, like the French climber, Henri Sampeyre."

Karl examined that remark for a moment. When he spoke he identified the Frenchman by the first name. "Henri telephoned me that he will be in Vienna next week. I told him he is invited to dinner whenever he shows up."

"*Yes! Oh, yes!*"

"That Frenchman certainly has a way of impressing women."

"Henri is a lovely, lovely man." Pammy made a cooing sound, then said, "Oh . . . be still, my heart."

"Compared to Henri, am I too large or too old?"

"Mostly too large."

"Mostly?"

Pammy didn't want to talk any more about Henri Sampeyre, not after learning Karl would be going with her to her son's wedding. She felt like she was filled with words, words that demanded an outlet, but she didn't speak. She remembered the time, three months ago, when her son, Sammy, came all the way to Vienna from the United States to introduce his mother to his bride-to-be, the young woman named Jennifer. Twenty-two-year-old Sammy was initially wary of Vienna Police Inspector Karl Marbach, but early on the day Sammy and Jennifer showed up in Vienna, before wariness had a chance to get entrenched, Karl took Sammy out "to see the town." Just the two of them together. No women included.

When Karl and Sammy returned late in the day, they were bonded together. Some of the bonding came from the alcohol they had consumed, but it was a firm and eternal bond. It didn't matter at first about the bond. Pammy made a big fuss. She broke a lot of glassware while expressing her displeasure. She tossed dish after dish from the kitchen cabinet onto the floor. While glass was still being broken, Sammy smiled sheepishly, kissed his bride-to-be and trundled off to his solitary bed in his private bedroom.

Then, when Karl had attempted to clean up the broken glass, he cut his hand and the bride-to-be became his tender nurse. The blood from the cut could barely be seen on the handkerchief feverishly administered by the moon-faced young woman named Jennifer. For Pammy the final outrage came when Karl croaked that he was beginning to feel a little faint. There had been nothing for her to do but retire for the night. So she went to their room. A few minutes later, when Karl had still not come up to their room, she went to the bedroom door and hollered for him until he came up to bed.

That was how the first day ended. On the day that followed there was a worse problem. Pammy had found herself filled with reservations about Jennifer. She told Karl that the young bride-to-be was too immature, too girlish to be getting married to Sammy. She had actually said that and she had totally believed it.

But, thought Pammy now, things had quickly changed. And it was all Karl's doing. He arranged a mountain climbing venture. A climb up the Dolomite Alps. Before doing the climb, he spent two days teaching Sammy and Jennifer how to do mountain climbing.

Then, the four of them used a cable car to get to a starting place where they began a five-hour climb high up into snow and ice. The weather turned bad, but the group kept going until they were only a dozen meters down from the top.

It was then that Karl, leading the climb, signaled for Jennifer to come forward. He took a few moments to whisper something to her and then shoved her upward.

On her own, Jennifer made her way the rest of the way to the top. When she got to the top, she jumped with joy and hollered for the stragglers to catch up.

Pammy had enthusiastically joined in the joy expressed by Jennifer. She returned from the climb with a profound love for the woman who was going to be Sammy's wife. Not someone who was too girlish, but a wonderful young woman who had climbed a mountain, met the challenge aggressively, even pushed her way to the top ahead of the others. A young woman ready to be a wife.

Now, in the West Train Station, Pammy felt good knowing that a way had been found for Karl to accompany her to the wedding in America. But how had he done it? Passports were almost impossible for Austrian citizens to obtain. It seemed impossible. How had he gotten a passport? It was like a miracle!

Pammy knew Karl well enough to be certain that whatever had been worked out, she would be a long time learning all the details. She told herself that it was just like him to wait until a few minutes before the departure of her train for the Paris trip before springing this marvelous surprise. She would be a bundle of excitement until she got back from Paris. She knew he must have planned it that way. That would be just like him. Yes, most certainly, that was just like him!

Giddy in her happiness, Pammy stared intently around. Many times she had been in the West Train Station. For the past year, at least once every month or two she'd had to go to Paris or some other city.

She directed her total attention to Karl and immediately realized something was happening. The handsome face that could conceal so much was concealing nothing. Karl was staring far back toward the rear of the train station and his entire body had become tense. At first, she couldn't tell what it was that had captured his attention. All she could see was that there were a lot of people in the train station, a bustling crowd. But continuing to follow Karl's line of sight, she saw two men greeting each other. She couldn't tell who had been the one to arrive and who was doing the welcoming. After a moment, an American soldier with a camera came over and took a picture of the two men. These days, the Americans and Russians were taking pictures of all the people arriving in Vienna by train. The British were more selective. They photographed only the ones who might be Jewish. The French made their presence known, but seldom did any photographing at all.

Pammy was startled when Karl suddenly got to his feet and said, "Something important is going on here. I have to run."

"Important? What?"

"There are some people here who practice the profession of burglary."

"Burglars?"

"I have to run."

"Burglars? . . . What about me?"

"I have to run."

And Karl did run. While Pammy sat hopelessly on the bench, Karl ran off on some sort of police chase. He was off on one of his police chases and for Pammy there was the awful feeling of being left alone, waiting totally alone for the train to Paris.

She was angry, but she couldn't hold onto the anger. It evaporated. Joy replaced the anger. In this crazy mixed up world Karl and her were going to be together at Sammy's wedding to the marvelous young woman named Jennifer.

CHAPTER TWO

I t was early in the morning and Police Inspector Karl Marbach was standing at the bus stop in front of the Excelsior Hotel in Vienna. Beside him was Captain Ted Millican, U.S. Army 970th Counter Intelligence Corps (CIC).

Police Inspector Marbach was in the employ of Vienna Kriminalpolitzei (Kripo). He had been working on burglary cases recently, but Kripo coordinated with CIC and he had been asked, as a favor to CIC, to go to the on-going war crime trial of Otto Skorzeny and meet with Hitler's famous commando, the man who led the raid that freed Italian dictator Benito Mussolini in 1943. Marbach had been told by CIC that Skorzeny wanted to talk with him, but he had been provided with no suggestions about what he might talk to Skorzeny about. He didn't see any point having the meeting, but he knew that all bureaucracies can be less than half bright at times, and that he had no choice except to be accommodating to CIC.

Captain Millican, in his late twenties, about twenty years younger than Marbach, had the kind of young American service man's face that wouldn't look out of place on the cover of *The Saturday Evening Post*. Back in the States—in Cleveland, Ohio—Millican had a wife, Sally, and a kid named George who would be going to kindergarten in two and a half years. Millican's wife wanted him back in Cleveland on the police force, or in any job at all as long it was in Cleveland, but she had agreed he could take some time to see what a career in the post-war army might have to offer.

How much time? Maybe a year.

On Millican's uniform were captain's bars and seven medals for valor. The new commanding officer of 970th CIC had issued an order that CIC officers and enlisted men, when in uniform, were required to wear insignia of rank and all of their ribbons and decorations. This was new and unexpected requirement. Millican hoped it wouldn't last long. When the enlisted personnel did their CIC work while in uniform having rank showing made the work unnecessarily difficult, especially when they had to question officers. But Millican was an officer. His concern with the new requirement was that he didn't like being required to wear all of his impressive array of medals and decorations. The only medal he liked wearing was the Combat Infantryman's Badge (CBI). The CBI bonded him with others who had been in combat. He liked having the CBI, but the only time he liked to wear it was when he was in the company of others who had been in combat and who knew in an intimate way what it meant to have the CBI.

A bus finally growled to a stop in front of Millican and Marbach. They got on board, found a couple of empty seats, and tried, with limited success, to make themselves comfortable.

Marbach leaned toward Millican who had his face buried in an American newspaper. "Any stories about Skorzeny?" As usual when they worked together, Marbach spoke English with his American friend.

Millican winced while testing the resilience of the bus seat. Settling himself on the seat, he passed the newspaper to Marbach. "There's an article about Skorzeny on the front page. You oughta read it."

Marbach accepted the newspaper and read out loud the title of the front page article: "*Nazi Commando Chief Otto Skorzeny: the most dangerous man in Europe.*" Identifying Skorzeny as "the most dangerous man in Europe" was routine. All the newspapers and magazines identified Skorzeny that way. Marbach continued reading aloud from the article. "Adolf Hitler's most famous commando, the man who rescued Italian dictator Mussolini from a heavily guarded prison in the mountains is now on trial for war crimes."

Marbach stopped reading aloud when, with a grinding of outraged gears, the bus began moving. Its destination was the town of Dachau, fewer than 20 kilometers away, about half an hour by bus. On the outskirts of the town of Dachau was the former concentration camp where the war crime trial of Otto Skorzeny had been going on for almost a week.

Shifting around on the uncomfortable bus seat, Marbach spotted another interesting article on the front page of the newspaper. "There's a story here about you Americans sneaking Nazi war criminals into your country."

"I read it," Millican said, making a dismissive motion with his hand.

"Is it true?" Marbach asked. He enjoyed pursuing mischief with Millican. They had been friends since the beginning of the Allied occupation of Austria in August of 1945, and teasing each other was one of the things that bonded them together.

Millican sighed. "I asked you to come along with me today, but I only did that because I was told to. Frankly, I think it's silly for you to come all the way here from Vienna to have a meeting with Skorzeny just because he wants to talk with you. If he's as smart as everyone says, he must know that afterward you'll be telling CIC everything the two of you talk about."

"I agreed to come along because you said that's what CIC wanted. I knew Skorzeny in the old days. In 1938 he performed occasional services for Kripo, but we were never close, and I can't imagine what he'd want to talk to me about."

"It's a crazy world," said Millican.

Marbach smiled. "Tell me, my young friend, are you Americans going to put Otto Skorzeny where he belongs? Are you going to hang him?"

"How the hell do I know? Well . . . yes. Of course we'll hang him. At the Battle of the Bulge, his guys wore G.I. uni-forms and killed G.I. prisoners. Skorzeny deserves the rope."

There was silence. During the silence, Marbach thought about newspaper stories he had read, a few of them even in American newspapers, suggesting that the war crimes case against Skorzeny might not be as strong as it looked, but he kept those thoughts to himself.

During the rest of the bus trip to the town of Dachau the only talk between Millican and Marbach was of unimportant things, like how uncomfortable the bus seats were.

When they got off the bus, Millican and Marbach looked around. The town of Dachau was almost totally unmarked by war.

Without wasting any time, they got onto another bus—actually just a converted panel truck—to go the rest of the way to the place that used to be a concentration camp.

This was going to be Millican's first visit to the Dachau camp, but he'd been in other places of infamy. He'd seen the Dora camp, and, near the end of the war, as a company commander with the 71st Division, he had been one of the first American soldiers to enter Mauthausen, the horror camp in central Austria. Millican knew about horror, but, nevertheless, his stomach tightened sharply when the panel truck got to the Dachau camp and the passengers were let out.

With Marbach beside him, Millican walked through the gate and halted in a large yard. Standing side-by-side, they watched while a dozen Polish soldiers marched by wearing their blue and black uniforms. The marching Polish soldiers were part of the security detail at the Dachau Camp.

One of the marching soldiers called out in Polish, "Is that you, Karl Marbach? What are you doing out of uniform? You are Austrian, but you fought beside us in the war. You should be marching with us now."

Marbach delivered a loud greeting in Polish, lifted his hand and provided a smart salute, placing two fingers just above his right eye. Millican, standing beside Marbach, recognized the Polish salute, knew what it meant: the two fingers tight together, one for honor and one for Poland.

Marbach's salute was returned by all of the marching Polish soldiers, all twelve of them. Several offered Polish words of greeting. Marbach yelled back in Polish that he would be seeking out company later in the day. Immediately, one of the Polish soldiers shouted instructions that told how to find a barracks hut being used as a drinking place by the Poles. Another marching Polish soldier shouted that Poles could be found drinking and sharing good company in that barracks hut at any time of the day or night: twenty-four hours a day, seven days a week.

When the twelve Polish soldiers finished marching past, without a word to Marbach, Millican led the way to War Crimes Enclosure 29, the building where matters relating to the trial of Otto Skorzeny were being coordinated.

Millican and Marbach walked inside.

A burly American sergeant approached, conveying an air of weary resignation. After observing routine military protocol, the sergeant said in rough-mannered English, "Today's session won't start for another hour. If you guys want some chow, the officer's club is just two buildings from here. They're still serving breakfast there."

Millican glanced at Marbach, who signaled with a return look that he wasn't interested in having breakfast.

"Thanks, Sarge," Millican said. "We don't need any grub, but if there's still an hour before the trial begins for today, what are the chances of letting my buddy, Police Inspector Marbach, see Skorzeny? It's important to CIC for this guy to talk with Skorzeny."

The American sergeant shrugged. "Well, maybe that's good for CIC, but Colonel Durst has the call. He's Skorzeny's defense lawyer. I can check with him if you want."

"Thanks, Sarge. I'd appreciate that."

The sergeant turned away, walked over to a desk near the door and picked up a telephone. He was close enough for Millican and Marbach to hear him say, "Get me Colonel Durst, will yuh, honey?"

A moment later, all informality vanished. The sergeant came to attention as he talked into the telephone. Even though it was just a telephone conversation, the sergeant behaved almost as though he was standing face-to-face with Colonel Durst. The word "sir" was used repeatedly.

After the call was completed, the sergeant relaxed, hung up the telephone, walked back to where Millican and Marbach were waiting, and said, "Colonel Durst is coming here. It looks okay. He didn't sound any more hard-assed than usual, but to play things safe, I better call the court president and let him know about this."

Scratching his head, the sergeant turned back around, returned to the telephone and put through a call to the court president, the officer in charge of the trial. The sergeant remained relaxed during the conversation with the court president. He only used the word "sir" at the beginning and at the end of the telephone call to the court president.

Marbach found it interesting that the sergeant displayed rigid formality with the defense attorney and a relaxed manner with the court president.

Less than five minutes later, Marbach and Millican were talking about a matter of no consequence when Colonel Durst made his appearance. The stern-faced colonel stared at the captain bars on Millican's collar. "I didn't think you CIC wore rank on your uniforms, Captain."

"Well, sir, it seems that no longer applies to 970th CIC," Millican said.

"You brought this Vienna police officer here," Colonel Durst said to Millican, gesturing in an off-handed way at Marbach.

"Yes, sir," Millican answered.

Colonel Durst pointedly ignored the presence of Marbach. He spoke to Millican as though Marbach wasn't present. "What does the police inspector want to talk to my client about?"

"Nothing important, sir. They used to work together. They're both Austrian."

"Bullshit," Colonel Durst said.

"Well, CIC thinks that maybe Skorzeny—"

Colonel Durst icily interrupted. "During a discussion yesterday, I advised my client to not have this meeting with the police inspector, but my client was insistent." The icy voice continued. "So the police inspector can have his meeting, but not this morning. It will have to be later— maybe this afternoon or possibly tonight. Now, if you'll excuse me, Captain, I have some preparations to make for today's session. The prosecution is going to bring up some business about the use of poison bullets."

Marbach leaned forward. He hadn't heard about a poison bullets charge against Skorzeny.

Colonel Durst continued to ignore the presence of Marbach as he said to Millican. "Former SS Major Stephan Kaas will be testifying for the defense today. Herr Kaas was in charge of Vienna Kripo—the Vienna criminal police—in 1938."

Millican shook his head, but he didn't ask why Kaas, a civilian who sometimes worked secretly as a CIC contact, was testifying for Skorzeny, a man the U.S. said it wanted to hang. He wondered if Marbach knew Kaas sometimes worked for CIC, but kept that thought to himself. The two of them were friends, but there was a lot they didn't share with each other.

"Herr Kaas is an impressive character," Colonel Durst said, making a point of studying CIC Captain Millican closely. "I've had several discussions with him. He'll be a good witness. He is big and tough and honest-looking. He's got a whole basket load of medals he earned fighting the Russkies . . . and he's been denazified. I wish I had more witnesses with his credibility."

"Colonel," Millican said, "Any help you could provide to arrange for Police Inspector Marbach to talk with Skorzeny would be appreciated."

The reply was spoken brusquely. "I already said I'll make the arrangements. But it can't be done this morning. When something can be arranged, the police inspector will be notified."

Marbach decided to intrude his presence on Colonel Durst. "If I may inquire, Herr Colonel, how does the case look for Skorzeny and the other defendants?" Eight other prisoners were on trial with Skorzeny.

Without answering Marbach, Colonel Durst turned around and walked away.

"So that's Skorzeny's lawyer," Marbach murmured just loud enough for Millican to hear.

"He's an odd duck," Millican said. "I think Skorzeny might have gotten himself a less hard ass lawyer."

Marbach shrugged.

"I'm headed for Czechoslovakia," Millican said. "I was told to bring you here, but now I've got other things to do."

At that moment a corporal approached with news that a couple of bunks had been located for them. Millican quickly explained that he wouldn't need a bunk, bade farewell to Marbach and headed for the camp gate. He was off to do work he regarded as more important than anything involving Marbach and Skorzeny.

Marbach stared at Millican until the camp gate closed behind his American friend, then he headed for the building where the war crimes trial was being held.

CHAPTER THREE

Marbach attended the war crimes proceedings until the trial finally adjourned for the day. When he returned to War Crimes Enclosure 29, he learned that Skorzeny was going to be meeting with some American newspaper people and that it looked like the meeting was going to last for hours and hours. That was troubling news, but instead of just sitting around waiting, he decided to go looking for the barracks hut being used by Polish guards. He quickly found the hut, renewed some old friendships and made a few new friends.

There was a lot of drinking and laughing until, a couple of hours later, feeling the effect of drink, he bade farewell, found the building in which there was a cot that had been assigned to him, got into the cot, and immediately fell asleep.

It was an early morning hour when Marbach was shaken awake by two affable American MPs. "You can see Otto Skorzeny, sir," one of the MPs said in passable German.

"Now?" mumbled Marbach.

"If you want to see him, sir."

"That's what I came here for."

Marbach dragged himself off the cot, put on his clothes and went with the two MPs on a short walk to a nearby building. Inside the building, in a narrow hallway, one of the MPs opened a door identified as "Cell 199," made a hand gesture, then silently stepped back into the hallway.

Marbach walked inside Cell 199 and the door quickly clanged shut behind him. He looked around. He was in a very large cell. There was a bed in the cell. Not a cot, but a bed. That was only one of the unusual things in Cell 199. There were also two upholstered chairs and a bookcase and a desk.

Marbach edged around, stopped behind an upholstered chair that would not be out of place in a comfortable living room, and faced the occupant of the cell.

Skorzeny was a muscular man, not quite forty years old, about half a dozen years younger than Marbach. They were both big men, but Skorzeny was taller and heavier. A savage dueling scar ran a ragged journey across the left side of Skorzeny's face. His blue eyes stared defiantly as he said, "It has been a long time, Herr Police Inspector."

Marbach extended his hand and an awkward handshake was completed. After that, Skorzeny gestured toward one of the upholstered chairs.

Marbach sat down on one of the upholstered chairs and watched while Skorzeny settled himself in the other upholstered chair.

They sat facing each other.

Skorzeny spoke first. He spoke quietly, but his voice had the hint of a powerful force held in restraint.

"Before we get started, I ask for your word that you will tell no one except American CIC that you found me anywhere but in a very modest cell shared with three other prisoners."

Marbach delivered an angry reply. "I won't agree to anything until I know why I am here and what this is all about."

Skorzeny's face was resolute. "Before we discuss anything, I must insist on this point of elementary courtesy. Information about my accommodations here must be kept private."

Marbach bristled angrily, but he knew that the tiresome trip from Vienna to Dachau would end up being a total waste of time if everything ended now because of the relatively unimportant business of cell accommodations. After reviewing the situation for a moment, he said, "All right. You have my word. I will say nothing about how comfortable the accommodations here are."

"Excellent," Skorzeny said. He added, "How are things in Vienna?"

"Times are hard . . . very hard."

"That must please the Jews," said Skorzeny in a matter-of-fact voice.

"Go to the devil," Marbach said, rising to his feet.

Skorzeny also got up, but then shrugged expressively and sat back down.

Marbach sat down.

"I didn't mean anything," Skorzeny said. "I have never been an anti-Semite. Not even . . . well, I apologize. If I'm big enough to apologize, you ought to be big enough to accept my apology."

Marbach ignored the suggestion to accept an apology. He asked, "Why was I asked to come here? What do you want to talk about?"

Skorzeny's face registered perplexity. He whispered, "This cell has recording devices." His voice rose to a normal level as he continued. "I need your help, Herr Police Inspector. I am asking for your help."

"What do you want?" Marbach asked, using his normal level of voice.

"In the old days you were careful what you talked about and how loud you spoke," Skorzeny said in a voice barely above a whisper.

Marbach didn't lower his voice as he said, "Why the hell did you arrange to have me come here?"

"Shut up!" barked Skorzeny angrily. He stood up for a moment, then shook his head and sat back down.

Marbach edged around in his chair. "If we aren't going to talk about what you want to talk about, let's talk about what I would like to talk about. What can you tell me about Nazi escape routes? Nazi rat lines? What can you tell me about Die Spinne?"

Skorzeny glared angrily. "You fool!"

"Are you unwilling to talk about escape routes?"

"I have nothing to do with such things. How could I? I am a closely guarded prisoner."

"What do you think about escape routes?"

Skorzeny's voice was menacing. "I know what I read in newspapers. My God! What kind of man are you? Do you want the refugees using those escape routes to be swallowed by the Soviet Moloch?"

"I read newspapers, too. There are stories that link you with Die Spinne. Stories that say you haven't been closely watched by the Americans."

Skorzeny jumped to his feet. "There are fleeing Czechs, Poles, Hungarians, Austrians . . . tens of thousands of innocent refugees who will suffer a terrible fate if they fall into Soviet hands."

Remaining seated, Marbach stared hard at Skorzeny. "Among the fleeing refugees are countless numbers of fleeing war criminals."

Skorzeny sat down again. When he spoke, his voice was low, almost a whisper. "The Communists are plotting to take over the entire world and all you can think about is capturing as many as possible of those whose only crime is that they fought the Soviet."

"Quatsch!" The word for "nonsense" was uttered by Marbach like a defiant challenge. He continued in an angry voice. "Innocent refugees deserve all the help they can get, but that doesn't justify escape routes that can be used by war criminals."

Skorzeny froze for a moment, then made a shrugging motion. He spoke in a normal level of voice. "This is no time to discuss politics. I asked to see you because of a favor you might do for me. I hope you will set aside any unimportant political disagreements. My request of you is for something totally personal. If you help me with my personal request I will make it worth your while."

Marbach kept his face expressionless.

Skorzeny sat erect in his chair. "Have you met my American defense counsel? . . . eh, Colonel Durst?"

"Yes."

"Not very friendly, is he?"

"Colonel Durst impresses me as someone who focuses on getting done what he wants to get done."

"I will be acquitted. The war crime charges against me are ridiculous. You were in court today. You saw my defense counsel refute that charge about me issuing poison bullets during the battle of the Ardennes, poison bullets with a red ring around them."

Marbach made a noncommittal nod.

Skorzeny placed a look of triumph on his face. "You were there. I know you saw it. That idiot prosecutor got a rat who was my supply officer to testify that I issued Russian poison bullets, Russian red-ringed bullets, to my men prior to the battle."

Skorzeny leaned back in his upholstered chair before continuing. "You saw that and you saw the clever way Colonel Durst demolished that nonsense by pointing out that German waterproof bullets also had red rings. He made a complete fool out of that supply officer when he held up Russian poison bullets and German waterproof bullets for everyone to see how similar they look with the red rings. Now it looks like the Americans will drop the ridiculous poison bullet charge."

Marbach nodded. "I know. I saw it."

"All I want is justice," Skorzeny said. "My conscience is clear."

Marbach kept silent.

Skorzeny seemed bothered by Marbach's silence. He stared hard and said, "I performed services for Vienna Kripo in 1937 and 1938. So much has happened since those days. I was just hired muscle, but I performed important services. Some of those services I performed for you and some for Commander Stephan Kaas. I know why you turned against your former comrades in Kripo in 1938. In your place, I might have done the same thing. That was a rotten piece of business, the killing of those two women . . ." Skorzeny's voice trailed off.

"One of the women was Constanze Tandler," Marbach said, staring hard at Skorzeny. "The name of the woman murdered with Constanze Tandler was Marianne Frisch."

Skorzeny shook his head. "I am sorry . . . I mean that sincerely. I am truly sorry for what happened to Volkstheater Actress Constanze Tandler and to the Jewess. I hope you believe me. I was sorry when they were killed and I am sorry now."

Marbach didn't like it that Skorzeny had used the word "Jewess" to identify Marianne Frisch, but he said nothing as he slowly rose to his feet.

Skorzeny also stood up. After getting to his feet, he reached out a hand toward Marbach.

The hand was pushed away.

The two men stood toe-to-toe.

"I have a problem," Skorzeny whispered. After a moment, he added, "In Vienna."

"Get American CIC to help you with your problem in Vienna," Marbach said, not in a whisper.

"There is urgency," Skorzeny whispered. "CIC was supposed to take care of this thing, but weeks have passed and they haven't been able to do anything. Their excuse is that they have to be careful in Vienna. They can't afford to draw onto themselves unwanted attention from the Soviet. CIC agreed to let me ask you to handle it."

Marbach stared disdainfully at Skorzeny.

"You have a debt to me," Skorzeny said, no longer whispering.

"I don't have any debt to you," Marbach said in his ordinary tone of voice.

"Fräulein Anna Krassny," Skorzeny replied in his whispering voice.

Hearing that name caused Marbach to stiffen. "What about Anna?" he asked. Now he was also whispering.

"Stephan Kaas got Anna Krassny out of Mauthausen in 1938," Skorzeny whispered. "I was the one who arranged the escape. After that, I got her to Czechoslovakia. That is the truth. You can ask Stephan Kaas."

This was the first time Marbach had heard about Skorzeny playing a part in Anna's escape from Mauthausen. She was a friend of Marbach's now living in Vienna with her Polish husband. Never had she said anything to Marbach about Skorzeny playing a part in her escape from Mauthausen, but there are some things even good friends don't share. Marbach regarded what Skorzeny was saying as something that made sense. Pieces of a long ago puzzle had fallen into place.

Continuing to stand in front of Skorzeny, Marbach nodded and whispered, "All right, there is a debt I owe you."

"I release you from the debt," Skorzeny said in his normal tone of voice. "I shouldn't have mentioned it."

Marbach made an angry sound.

Skorzeny kept silent. He sat down in his upholstered chair.

Marbach took a breath and began walking in a circular path within the large cell. There was a debt and he was resolved to not waste time getting the debt behind him. He stamped his feet on the floor. He stamped loudly.

At first, Skorzeny looked puzzled, then he realized the purpose of the foot stamping. He got to his feet and, in the next moment, the two men were standing side-by-side stamping their feet. The loud stamping noise would keep any recording device from picking up what they were saying as long as they spoke in relatively quiet voices.

Stamp! Stamp! Stamp! . . .

Under the cover of the noise being made by the stamping feet, Skorzeny said in a very low voice, "In Vienna is a woman named Lisa Beck. She has to get denazified in order to have the life she deserves. If she gets linked with me, denazification will be denied her. I want things to be good for her."

Out in the hallway, heavy boots could be heard, along with loud American voices.

Skorzeny continued loudly stamping his feet as he softly said, "I am going to tell you where a pile of Eichmann's gold is hidden. Not the main place where Eichmann's gold is hidden, but ample enough. You will get a reward from the Allied Forces for showing them how to find the Eichmann gold. A generous reward. I want you to give the reward to Lisa. Keep a share for yourself, of course. Whatever you think is fair."

Stamping heavily with his feet, Marbach spoke in a voice he was sure only Skorzeny would be able to hear. "To hell with any share for me, but I'll do what I can. Give me the woman's address."

Skorzeny spoke the address while continuing to stamp his feet.

Marbach was stamping his feet and staring at the cell door when it swung open.

Four American MPs charged through the cell door with wooden clubs in their hands.

Marbach raised his arms. He hoped that raising his arms might pacify the MPs, but it didn't. They charged at him and Skorzeny, making use of their wooden clubs. In a quick shuffling movement, one of the MPs got behind him and a sharp blow hit him on the back of the head.

Marbach drowned in engulfing darkness.

When the darkness passed away, Marbach found himself alone in a room that was strange to him. He was lying on a U.S. Army cot. Taking his time, he put his feet on the floor and slowly rose from the cot. He moved around, found a towel and applied it gingerly to his bruised face. Damn that Skorzeny, he thought. He added additional curses for the Americans MPs and their wooden clubs.

Moving gingerly, Marbach limped to a wash basin. He was applying a very wet, very cold towel to his face when someone opened a door and walked up behind him.

He looked over his shoulder. Colonel Durst was standing behind him.

Colonel Durst said in excellent German, "I'm sorry, Herr Police Inspector. I just learned what happened. I will bring charges against the MPs for what they did."

Marbach stopped applying the towel to his face. "I hope you don't cause any trouble on my account. Skorzeny and I got carried away with things. I've handled enough prisoners in my day to know that we . . . to know that I was out of line."

Colonel Durst walked back to the door. But before opening the door he turned around and his stern face broke into a grin. "Aren't you getting a little old for brawls with soldiers?"

"I'm certainly feeling my age right now," Marbach said, yielding a grin to the American colonel before returning the towel to his face. He didn't cover his eyes with the towel. He watched while the colonel left the room.

Marbach thought about what he was going to do when he got back to Vienna. First, he would have to report to CIC about his meeting with Skorzeny. He would have to tell them about Lisa Beck, but he was pretty sure they wouldn't object to him giving her the reward for Eichmann's gold. If they did, so be it.

CHAPTER FOUR

Camp King. Wednesday, September 14, 1947.

T wo weeks after being found innocent of war crimes by a U.S. military court, Otto Skorzeny was tied to a chair in a small room inside a building on the U.S. Army post at Camp King, near Oberursel, Germany. His hands were secured to the back of the chair with handcuffs. Standing in front of him was Captain John Simpson, U.S. Army Criminal Investigation Division (CID), the investigative arm of the military police, a unit distinctly separate from CIC.

Usually there was very little coordination between CIC and CID, but on this occasion a CIC agent was in the room. Captain Theodore Millican hadn't been informed why he was here. All he knew was that he was ordered to be present and that afterward he would deliver a report to his CIC superiors.

"You damned Kraut," Captain Simpson shouted before throwing a poorly placed punch that hit the powerfully-built Skorzeny on the side of the head. The blow caused more distress for Simpson's fist than for Skorzeny's head.

Millican's trained eye recorded that Simpson didn't know much about throwing punches.

Simpson held his pain-filled fist up against his chest. "Even CIC is fed up with you," he shouted at Skorzeny. "You're no longer a special character. Everything you told CIC about escape routes was bullshit! Now you're under CID authority and you're going to tell us about the Die Spinne escape route that's taking SS thugs to safety. We know about Die Spinne. We know all about it."

"If you know all about it, then there is nothing I need to say," replied Skorzeny with scorn in his voice. He was capable of speaking competent English when it served his purpose.

Simpson stepped back and stared at the husky man secured to the chair.

Skorzeny stared at Simpson, and very deliberately put a look of contempt for the American officer on his face.

Simpson immediately stepped forward and threw another punch at Skorzeny, but once again Skorzeny shifted around and took the blow not on his face but on the side of his head.

Millican watched while keeping thoughts about how to throw punches to himself.

Skorzeny shrugged indifferently, moved his powerful body as though seeking a more comfortable position on the chair.

Simpson took a couple of steps away from Skorzeny and gingerly nursed his fist.

Millican kept silent. Back in Cleveland, Ohio, when he was with Cleveland police, and sometimes during the war with military prisoners, he had been present when hitting was done. In his experience, hitting prisoners had two big negatives: number one, too often there was just determined silence and, number two, when there was talk more often than not it amounted to screwy nonsense or deliberately phony leads that just wasted a lot of time. He believed that better than hitting was to get a prisoner to start talking. First, get a prisoner to talk about anything at all and then, at appropriate points, unobtrusively ask carefully crafted questions and listen closely to everything the prisoner might say.

Millican watched Simpson turn back around, advance again on Skorzeny and deliver a flurry of ineffective blows. Millican saw that Simpson's problem was that he didn't know how to judge the bobbing motion of Skorzeny's head. The husky German kept lifting his head up and down and moving it slightly from side-to-side, while keeping his eyes riveted on the one assaulting him. The maneuvering kept Simpson from landing many punches directly on Skorzeny's face.

Give the devil his due, Millican thought, only a very tough character could use his head that way.

Simpson's blows continued, at first in frenzied bursts and then more and more slowly until—exhausted-—he let his aching hands drop down to his sides.

"You damned scarface," Simpson said weakly.

Skorzeny laughed.

Simpson's pain-filled hands hung helplessly at his sides.

Skorzeny released loud peals of laughter.

Millican decided to end the nonsense. He walked over to Simpson and said, "Let's get you a cup of coffee. This Kraut'll keep for a while."

Skorzeny's roaring laughter followed them as they left the room.

Millican took Simpson to where the injured hands could be tended, spoke conciliatory words and returned to where Skorzeny was waiting, still secured to the chair. Millican had a wet towel in his hand. He dropped the towel onto Skorzeny's lap, stepped around behind, and unlocked the handcuffs.

After his hands were freed, Skorzeny leaned forward, rubbed his raw wrists, picked up the wet towel and vigorously wiped his face and head.

Millican lit a cigarette and passed it to Skorzeny.

"My thanks to you, Herr Captain," Skorzeny said after taking a few quick puffs.

"All you're getting from me is a cigarette," Millican said.

"To hell with the American army." Skorzeny rubbed his wrists some more and added scornfully, "No American is a real soldier."

"To hell with you," Millican said. As a police officer in Cleveland, Ohio, a wise senior officer had taught him that when dealing with people being questioned, there are times to be passive and times to talk tough. He decided that right now was a time to talk tough. "The army I served in kicked Nazi ass," he said to Skorzeny. "And we kept kicking Nazi ass until you characters gave up."

"Germany was overwhelmed, but we were never out fought."

"Bullshit!"

"What were your battlefields during the war?"

"I was in North Africa and Sicily. After that, from Normandy on, I was with the 2nd Infantry Division."

"The 2nd Infantry Division? Ach, so. Yes . . . Yes, the 2nd Infantry Division. We fought you in the Eiffel Offensive—The Battle of the Bulge, as you call it."

"The 2nd Infantry Division whipped Nazi ass," Millican said.

Skorzeny heaved a huge sigh. "Nonsense. Anyway, that is in the past. What happens now?"

"Do you want some coffee?" Millican decided that at this moment it served his purposes to switch from being tough to being conciliatory.

"If you have coffee," Skorzeny said, making a loud sighing sound, "I will drink it."

"Maybe you're hungry. If you're hungry, we've got ham sand-wiches. What do you prefer, white bread or dark?"

Skorzeny shrugged indifferently.

Millican went out into the hallway and said to an enlisted man, "Pignatelli! Get some damned coffee in here. And bring me a couple of ham sandwiches on white."

"Dark bread," Skorzeny shouted from inside the room.

Millican smiled and amended the order. He said to the one named Pignatelli, "One on dark and one on white." Then he returned to the room.

A few minutes later, when the coffee and sandwiches arrived, Skorzeny picked up his ham sandwich and began hungrily chewing. Millican took his time, pumped a generous amount of catsup onto the ham in his own sandwich and began eating. He had calculated one small sandwich wouldn't be enough to satisfy Skorzeny's hunger, that probably it would just make him hungrier.

Skorzeny wolfed down his sandwich, stared at his empty plate and kept silent.

Millican slowly took small bites out of his ham sandwich on white bread. He took note of Skorzeny's reluctance to ask for another sandwich. In Skorzeny's place, he knew he would behave the same way—not ask for any favors.

"I have been acquitted," Skorzeny said, poking at the crumbs left from his sandwich. "I should be set free. I am innocent. Why am I not released?"

"You're a saint. Go file a protest."

"What good would it do for me to file a protest? . . . And to whom?"

Millican shrugged and slowly chewed what remained of his sandwich.

Skorzeny said, "You Americans should have joined forces with the German army and crushed the Soviet when there was a chance to do that in 1945."

"We were fighting Nazi Germany."

"You are a fool," declared Skorzeny.

Millican decided to first put Skorzeny off balance, then pile on pressure and hope for the breaks. Maybe something interesting might be learned. In order to put Skorzeny off balance he said in a friendly voice, "I didn't like seeing that jerk beat on you."

Skorzeny nodded agreeably.

After seeing the agreeable look, Millican promptly went on the offensive. "But that doesn't mean I give you respect."

Skorzeny jumped to his feet, kicked back his chair and spat on the floor.

They stood facing each other. Millican hadn't intended for this business with Skorzeny to end in a brawl, but sometimes it is difficult to know whether things are being pushed too far or not far enough. For Millican, what mattered right now was that it looked like there was going to be a fight and he had long believed that if there has to be a fight, the thing to do is get in the first punch. He crashed his left fist hard into the exposed mid-section of Skorzeny. Then, taking the briefest part of a moment, he balanced himself, weaved back and forth, stepped forward and pushed his right fist hard against Skorzeny's jaw. After that he stepped back and watched.

Skorzeny collapsed onto the floor, where he lay for a few moments before slowly lumbering to his feet. Steadying himself, he shook his head, mumbled a curse in German, stood absolutely still, and said in English, "Give me a moment."

Remaining on guard, Millican poked around in his shirt pocket. "Here," he said. "Have another cigarette."

Skorzeny stepped forward clumsily and allowed a cigarette to be placed in his mouth.

Millican remained on guard while lighting the cigarette. Studying Skorzeny, he said, "I could get you another ham sandwich if you want it."

"Keep your damned sandwiches . . . and keep your damned cigarettes." Skorzeny pulled the cigarette from his mouth, stared at it with distaste, looked as though he was going to throw it on the floor.

Millican said, "Don't waste a perfectly good cigarette."

"I was acquitted," Skorzeny said. He didn't throw the cigarette away. "I should be released."

"That's not my department."

"I was beaten by your captain."

"And by me."

"Your captain didn't do much. As for you, well, you caught me off guard."

"If you have your wind back, we could go round two."

Skorzeny shook his head. "I think not. Maybe some other time. I find that I respect you even if you are unprofessional enough to speak in a boorish manner to me. I am hoping that maybe we can exchange favors."

"What favor could you do for me?"

Skorzeny looked around within the cell. He didn't say anything. Both men were wary of recording devices. Skorzeny thought about the foot stamping business he had done with Karl Marbach, and began forcefully stamping his feet.

Millican didn't need an invitation. He quickly joined the foot stamping activity.

As the loud foot stamping continued, Skorzeny said to Millican in a quiet voice, "I can tell you where some of the Eichmann gold is. That doesn't compromise my honor. Eichmann and his ilk have dishonored me and my comrades."

Millican stamped hard with his feet. "How much gold and where do I find it? And what do you want in return?"

Skorzeny stared approvingly at Millican's foot stamping activity. "I say to you that it took three military trucks to deliver the gold. Ach . . . so I tell you where it is. I tell you that you will find not just a small amount of the Eichmann gold, but a whole lot. It is within a gypsum mine named Niedermair, just outside Mödling." Skorzeny quietly continued. He explained how Millican would be able to find the Eichmann gold.

Both men kept up foot stamping activity.

While stamping, Millican said, "If the gold is there, I'll find it. What do I do for you in return?"

"There is urgency. A woman in Vienna needs help. Her name is Lisa Beck. Police Inspector Marbach has helped, but she needs more help."

"Tell me about the help Police Inspector Marbach has provided."

Skorzeny increased his foot stamping activity. "Karl Marbach and I were police colleagues before the war. A couple of weeks ago I gave him information about where to find some of the Eichmann gold. He got a reward. I have learned he gave all of the reward to Lisa."

"I'll check what you are telling me with the police inspector."

"Of course, but keep in mind that there is urgency."

"Give me the woman's full name."

While continuing with the foot stamping, Skorzeny whispered the name, "Lisa Beck" and then said aloud, "Between you and me."

Millican stamped his feet, but kept his voice low as he decisively said, "All right, but between you and me, where do I find her?"

Skorzeny whispered the address.

"I'll do what I can," Millican said.

The foot stamping came to a halt. There was nothing more to say.

CHAPTER FIVE

MGB Headquarters, Vienna, Austria.

S oviet Major Konstantin Gorshkov was sitting behind a desk in his spacious office within a baroque Viennese palace occupied by the Soviet secret police. Gorshkov had been with the Soviet secret police in the mid-1930s, when it was NKVD, and he had remained with the secret police when NKVD became NKGB. More recently, in 1946, he had been with the secret police when NKGB became MGB. He had performed intelligence work for the secret police in various localities. Now he was serving in Soviet-occupied Vienna.

Gorshkov aggressively addressed himself to office work. He turned over one piece of paper after the other, finally stopping when he came to a report dealing with SS Major Otto Skorzeny having been declared by the Americans to be innocent of war crimes. Gorshkov believed "decadent" was too good a word for the Americans. He was convinced that the religion of Americans was capitalism, and that the capitalists practiced their religion by trafficking in evil. He had been taught in official Soviet classes that there was a natural affinity between capitalism and fascism, that there would be a final struggle to the death between the Soviet Union and capitalistic America, that the struggle between good and evil would be followed inevitably by the triumph of the Soviet.

Gorshkov studied the Skorzeny report, especially the part stating that Vienna Police Inspector Karl Marbach had been enlisted by the Americans to help get Skorzeny set free. Gorshkov scowled while continuing to read the report. It included personal history information about Police Inspector Marbach. It recorded that Karl Marbach had joined the Russian army after the fall of Poland in 1939, then, near the end of the war, he had deserted. According to the report, the one who was Police Inspector Marbach had recently visited with Skorzeny at Dachau and afterward the Americans had reported the discovery of some of Eichmann's gold, a share of which was provided to Police Inspector Karl Marbach.

Gorshkov regarded what he was reading as documentation of abomination. Having no reason to doubt anything written in an official Soviet report, he indulged a feeling of rage for the police inspector, whom he saw as an enemy of the people, a cur who deserved a traitor's fate. For evil people like Police Inspector Karl Marbach, Gorshkov believed justice must be ruthless or there is no justice.

Gorshkov became conscious of pain in his stomach. He told himself he had been foolish to get so worked up about the police inspector. Now he had a problem with his stomach.

The pain in his stomach was bad and getting worse. He decided to take a drink of the great Russian beverage: Angelic Water. He probed one of the drawers in his desk, found the bottle of Angelic Water, lifted it to his mouth and drank swallow after swallow.

Relief came almost immediately. There was still an unpleasant pain in his stomach, but now it was bearable and getting better by the moment. With great care he returned the bottle of Angelic Water to the desk drawer and again applied himself to his work.

He put to one side the Skorzeny report and picked up another report, one filled with documentation showing the extent to which the Americans were helping Nazi war criminals escape justice. He read how the Americans, with lust-filled energy, were grabbing up enormous amounts of Nazi loot, all sorts of treasures. The report stated that the British and French weren't much better, but that the Americans were the truly evil ones.

Gorshkov's attention was captured by a file lying on his desk, a file containing information about a new Nazi ratline, a new Nazi escape route called Odessa, an escape route that might become much more dangerous than Die Spinne. It was clear to Gorshkov that the new ratline had to be smashed. But as important as it was to smash the new ratline, it was also important to capture Karl Marbach, bring the dog to justice, see to it that the dog was executed.

There was work to be done, but Gorshkov was sure he would be able to handle it. His stomach was feeling all right. Russian Angelic Water had once again worked its magic.

CHAPTER SIX

L isa Beck, sitting in a chair, faced the sleeping form of Otto Skorzeny. She watched while he rolled over and stretched out his arm to the place where she had been lying until a few minutes ago. His face was close enough for her to touch. She studied with fascination the famous scar running down the left side of the face she felt was the most magnificent face she had ever seen, anywhere, at any time. She withheld her hand. She never dared to touch the scar without first getting permission.

Lisa wasn't tall or short, fat or skinny, pretty or ugly. But, barely into her thirties, she was confident of her ability to be good for a man, even a man like Otto Skorzeny. She'd had a lot of experience being good for men when proper remuneration was provided.

While Lisa continued to stare, Skorzeny suddenly came awake. He rubbed his hand over his face, opened his eyes, stared at her, smiled, then made a waving motion with his arm. He wanted her to turn away while he got out of bed.

Lisa understood why Skorzeny wanted her to turn away. Long ago she had learned that the best of men—for her that meant the toughest—were often embarrassed to be seen undressed by a woman. She got out of her chair and kept her back to Skorzeny while he walked on bare feet into the bathroom.

The bathroom door closed.

After a couple of minutes, the toilet flushed, then water was run in the wash bowl. Lisa wished she could watch Skorzeny shave, but she knew he wouldn't tolerate that. Many of the men who slept with her liked to have her watch them shave, but never this man.

Finally, when the shaving was done, Lisa watched while Skorzeny came out of the bathroom pulling tight a robe. He took note of her presence with an agreeable nod, then picked up trousers and a shirt, returned to the bathroom and once again closed the door behind him.

While waiting, Lisa looked around until she spotted Skorzeny's shoes and socks. She picked them up and placed them on a table near the bathroom door.

When Skorzeny came out of the bathroom for the second time, he retrieved the shoes and socks, found a chair and silently finished making himself ready for whatever awaited him this day. He didn't say anything until he finished tying the shoe laces.

"All right, Lisa," Skorzeny said when he was ready.

She stepped forward, kissed him on the forehead and led him to the kitchen table.

A few minutes later they were seated across from each other at a table sipping coffee and eating small pastries.

"How long can you stay?" Lisa asked.

"I must return to Germany this evening."

"So soon?"

"The Americans insist."

"No one knows you are here in Vienna. No one knows where you are except the Americans. The Communist newspapers say that you are in the United States."

"The Communists tell many lies. Some Communist lies are useful to me."

Lisa laid her cup of coffee on the table. "I have the money from Eichmann's gold. A police inspector brought some. And an American brought even more. Of course, all the money belongs to you. I haven't spent any of it on myself."

"I will put the money to good use."

"Can I go with you to wherever you are going?"

"I need you here."

Lisa answered quickly. "I will do whatever you say."

"I have placed much trust in you."

"I will never betray you or Die Spinne."

"Die Spinne is important, but there is going to be a new operation. Odessa will be greater than Die Spinne." After saying that, Skorzeny stared intently at Lisa. "You must never repeat the name Odessa."

"I never will! I swear it! I never will!"

"Good. Now I will tell you about Odessa . . . it is necessary for me to tell you about Odessa. It is a mistake to tell the wrong people what they don't need to know, and just as big a mistake to not tell the right people what they need to know if they are going to do what you want them to do as well as it needs to be done."

"You can trust me."

"So I tell you that Odessa will begin as just another escape route, but it is going to grow into a powerful world force. Ah . . . that is in the future. Right now it is only an escape route, an escape route with a number of sanctuaries. The sanctuaries are called relay stations. They are located at intervals of eighty kilometers—one from the other—stretching from northern Germany through Austria to Italy. When everything is operating as I intend it to operate, this new escape route will set important forces loose. National Socialist Germany is going to be reborn. We don't have Hitler anymore. He is gone. But Odessa will help to bring about a new National Socialist Germany."

Lisa felt thrilled. "I will never betray your trust." She continued. "What do you want me to do with the box of papers hidden in the closet?"

"I have to get those papers to Italy. They contain information about the sanctuaries that will be used by this greatest and most important of all escape routes, this foundation stone for the new and powerful National Socialist Germany."

Lisa was filled with joy. She had to struggle to contain her emotions.

Skorzeny smiled. "I may ask you to help get the Odessa papers to Italy."

"You have only to ask."

"Odessa will take many of the heroes who were part of the first great struggle against a befouled world to where they can be part of the second great struggle, the one that will succeed. The world will be ours. It will be a good world dominated by National Socialism."

"Ask anything of me."

"You are good."

"Maybe not so good."

"You are good."

"I've been to bed with . . . many men."

"That isn't important."

"Do you like me?"

"Very much."

"I am not pretty."

"I appreciate you."

"What kind of women do you like?"

"Women like you. Good Aryan women."

"I am pure Aryan."

"I know."

"I hate Jews."

"For me it is different," Skorzeny said, after reflecting for a moment. "I do not hate Jews. It is just that I never forget they are not human. Jews are like dogs. Some dogs and some Jews are all right. But no dog and no Jew is human."

"More dogs are good than Jews are good."

"True."

"There is time before you have to go. I could be good for you."

"There is time."

"Let me pleasure you."

"Yes . . ."

CHAPTER SEVEN

P olice Inspector Marbach walked quickly on the Ringstrasse until he got to a side street leading to the former SS barracks now being used as headquarters by Field Security Service (FSS) the counterintelligence arm of British Army Intelligence.

It wasn't difficult for Marbach to get admitted to the building. He was a frequent visitor. Once inside, he was taken under escort to a familiar room where he settled into a chair. He had to wait only a few minutes before Colonel Larkswood showed up.

Marbach got to his feet. "How are you, Herr Colonel?" He spoke the greeting in English, using only the British officer's title, not his name.

"Karl, I didn't expect you here today. It is good to see you." Colonel Larkswood used Marbach's first name. The British colonel was much less inclined to formality than was the Vienna police inspector.

Colonel Larkswood looked not much more than thirty-five years old, even though he was well into his forties. The colonel was tall, with presentable good looks, a fussy manner and a high intelligence.

TOM JOYCE

Before there was time for Marbach to say anything, a sergeant pried open a door and inquired, "Will you be wanting coffee, Colonel?"

"Quite so. Quite so, Sergeant. And plenty of cream for my friend here."

"A cup of gold," Marbach said, relishing the thought of a cup of real coffee with real cream.

The coffee was served a few minutes later on an elaborate tray held by the proper-looking British sergeant. By that time, Marbach and Colonel Larkswood were sitting at opposite ends of a small sofa.

After the sergeant left, Colonel Larkswood said, "I know Pammy has gone off to Paris. You, of course, are invited to dinner tomorrow night with Sophie and me. The women arranged it. I trust this fits with any plans you might have."

"I look forward to having dinner tomorrow with you and Sophie."

"Now, is it reasonable for me to assume you came here to register another of your complaints against His Majesty's forces for turning Russian refugees over to the Soviet?"

"No, but I must say that's a wicked piece of business. Even the American President Truman has said that he is opposed to forced repatriation."

"I'm not very proud of myself these days," Colonel Larkswood said, closing his eyes.

Marbach knew the British officer to be a good man. One week ago, Colonel Larkswood went face-to-face with his Soviet counterpart after British soldiers had led a group of Russian refugees to the place where they were scheduled to be turned over to the Russian army. The refugees were Russians from the Ukraine who, during the war, had

54

elected to resist Soviet authority. Now there were tens of thousands of Russians like that in Italy and more than a few in Germany.

At the last moment, just before custody was about to be transferred, Colonel Larkswood had marched down the row of twenty or more refugees, spoke to two or three of them, and declared the entire group to be German and, therefore, legitimate refugees. After placing all of the refugees on the "disputed list" he had allowed them to leave the area, go wherever they wanted. There was talk that Colonel Larkswood might be court-martialed for what he did that day.

Marbach's wife had told him that the British colonel had privately admitted to her that none of the prisoners were German, that all of them were Russian people. She said Colonel Larkswood had told her that he did what he did to save his soul, or perhaps only to save his sanity.

Marbach told himself that this British colonel was a good man. He stared at the cup in his hands and said, "This is excellent coffee."

"You're always welcome to drop in for more of it."

"Before I forget, I should have said this first thing, thank you for taking care of my passport problem and for providing British air service for Pammy and me to the United States."

Colonel Larkswood made a dismissive motion with his hand. "You embarrass me. The important thing is that you are coming to dinner tomorrow."

"I don't care much about eating with you," Marbach said in a bantering voice. "But I do look forward to seeing my friend, Sophie."

The married British colonel's mistress was a friend of Marbach.

"Of course," Colonel Larkswood said.

"How is Sophie?"

"Fine."

"Tell me . . . I know I'm intruding, but Sophie is my friend. When are you going to marry her?" This was a ticklish subject, but Marbach, acting on impulse, intruded his concern.

Colonel Larkswood became very serious. "I do love Sophie, that's for certain."

"Then marry her."

"Oh, be fair. You know I am already married."

"Get a divorce."

"It isn't that simple. I have to talk to my son. I have to explain it to him."

"Your son? But he is in college! Most certainly your son is old enough to be able to handle this."

"Teddy is very close to his mother. I need to talk with him . . . and explain things."

Marbach hadn't planned to bring up his concern about Sophie at this time, but now that it was out in the open, he spoke firmly. "You need to explain to Sophie. If you only love her a little bit, turn her loose to find happiness. But if you truly love her, then pledge yourself to her and get the damned divorce."

Colonel Larkswood glared angrily, made a motion as though he might be ready to throw his cup of coffee up against the wall, but after a moment he shook his head, grasped the cup tight in his hands and began a litany of explanations for why he couldn't marry his beloved Sophie:

he was Church of England; his wife was a fine woman; a very fine woman; and there was his son. This could cause an awful breach with his son.

When Colonel Larkswood stopped talking, Marbach said, "If you truly love Sophie, marry her. She needs to be married to a man she loves. That man happens to be you. Marry Sophie or be damned." Marbach had never before so forcefully pressed his views about Sophie's needs to Colonel Larkswood, but she was a friend, a much-valued friend and a couple of days ago she had said she wanted to be married, very much wanted to be married to this British officer. Marbach knew that if that didn't happen soon Sophie was going to be miserable, even more terribly unhappy than she already was.

It was a welcome relief for both Marbach and Colonel Larkswood when there came a knock on the door.

"Come in," Colonel Larkswood said.

Captain Jenkins, a young British Officer, entered the room.

There was the required protocol of military ritual, then the British captain, standing erect, spoke in clipped speech, beginning with a word Marbach found offensive. "The Yids are stirring up trouble at Bad Gastein. There's a rumor they plan to bomb one of our trains again. The Austrian Ministry of the Interior isn't doing anything. I'd like to take some of our lads and have a look around."

The young British captain stopped talking. He had made his point. A month earlier, the Zionist Irgun had bombed a British military train in Austria. Tension between the British Army and the Jews in Austria, exacerbated by what was happening in Palestine, was a serious problem.

"Take some lads and look around," Colonel Larkswood said in a weary voice.

"Yes, sir."

Captain Jenkins saluted and left.

Marbach was angry that nothing had been said by Colonel Larkswood to admonish the junior officer about using the offensive word "Yid." He made a gesture with his hand that he knew the colonel would recognize as a signal of his displeasure.

Colonel Larkswood said lamely, "Captain Jenkins is not really a bad sort. He's no anti-Semite. It's just that, like a lot of our chaps, he's a bit testy because of the bomb incidents. There was the bombing of that military train and then there were those bombs that went off in the Hotel Sacher. It's all a big mess."

Marbach recalled Pammy's reaction to news of the bombs exploded in the Hotel Sacher. With the occasional vulgarity that always amazed him, she had declared her verdict on bombs and bomb scares: "Those fuckwits in the Irgun are doing more to undermine the cause of Jews than the fucksters in the British Foreign Office."

Marbach smiled ruefully as he thought about what Pammy had said. But after a few moments he stood up. It was time to leave. He had some work he had to get done today for Kripo. He said, "I better go. Tell Sophie I'll send someone over with chicken for dinner tomorrow. We can have some Backhendl."

"I say . . . you always seem to be able to find marvelous chicken for the Backhendl. Not like the scraggy stuff I always have to settle for. Which market do you use? Is it in the Inner City?"

"I shop the black market."

"The black market . . . you . . . you bloody rogue." The British colonel made a wailing sound, then raised his hands in hopeless resignation. "Well, at least we shall have some good Backhendl tomorrow night."

CHAPTER EIGHT

M arbach left British FSS headquarters, stood still for a moment, checking the area around him, then walked to a telephone booth and quickly put through a call.

A familiar voice came on the line.

"Detective Rolf Hiller."

Without identifying himself, Marbach said into the telephone mouthpiece, "If you have enough United States occupation scrip to cover it, I'll let you buy me some mid-morning breakfast at a place where the table cloth is green."

The reply was stated crisply. "You'll pay for your own mid-morning breakfast. I use American script for my own purposes."

The telephone conversation continued. Because countless ears monitored telephone calls, Marbach and Rolf kept their office telephone conversations obscure. This time, like always, when the communication concluded there were routine farewell greetings and telephone disconnections at both ends. The important thing that had been communicated between them wouldn't likely be understood by any eavesdropper.

They would be having mid-morning breakfast together, as they often did, at the Café Florian, located near the Vienna police headquarters building.

Fifteen minutes later, when Marbach got to the café, Rolf hadn't yet arrived, but a frail-looking young priest was sitting at a table in the rear. The frail-looking young priest was Marbach's nephew.

"Father Anton," Marbach said when he was only a few steps away from the table. "I thought you were going to be in Linz this week." His nephew was sitting alone, no dish of food in front of him, only a glass half-filled with water.

"I got back last night," Father Anton said.

Marbach stood still for a moment, stared at the empty table top and asked his nephew, "Are you fasting?"

"Yes."

"In your condition?"

"Yes."

Father Anton wasn't just in bad shape. He was dying. He could still move around, but five years in a concentration camp had taken their toll. Father Anton's stomach couldn't hold much food. Doctors said his condition would keep getting worse until he died, possibly in a year, maybe sooner.

Marbach sat down at the table with Father Anton, but before there was time for more than a few words to be exchanged, Rolf entered the café. Rolf, in his early forties, had the husky frame of a peasant. One of Rolf's distinguishing features was a wide empty space between his two front teeth.

"Grüss Gott, Father Anton," Rolf said, using the Viennese God bless you greeting. Rolf pulled a chair over to the table and sat down. "How good to see you. I didn't expect you back until next week."

Rolf also took note of the presence of Marbach, but provided a greeting that was absent words, a barely perceptible lift of the hand. He received in reply a similar gesture. They were close friends, but they made it a practice to always be reticent, avoid indicating that they were anything but casual acquaintances when they encountered each other in any public place, even ones they frequently visited.

"I came back early," Father Anton said to Rolf.

A waiter approached. Marbach lifted his arm and with no words, just a gesture, signaled that he and Rolf wanted their usual mid-morning breakfast and that Father Anton would have nothing but water.

Father Anton held his glass of water with both hands and spoke in a low, soft voice that could barely be heard by the other two at the table. "In Linz I learned about a new escape route that will be used to get countless Nazis to freedom."

Marbach frowned. When he spoke, his voice was also kept low enough and soft enough so that it would not be able to be heard by anyone at any nearby table. "There are a lot of escape routes. What's one more escape route? You need to take better care of yourself. You need rest."

"I will soon be getting plenty of rest."

Rolf leaned back in his chair. "What did you learn about the new escape route?" Like the other two at the table he was making it appear to anyone who might happen to look their way that he was not talking about anything important.

Father Anton kept his voice low. "Otto Skorzeny has started something that is intended to become more than just another escape route. It is intended to be a vehicle to renazify Germany."

"Is it really that big?" Marbach asked.

"It could become that big."

"What is the money source?"

Father Anton took a series of deep breaths, then managed to say, "Skorzeny has Eichmann's gold. Not just that small share you found, but the whole treasure. All of it."

Marbach edged forward in his chair. "Even locked up by the Americans, Skorzeny calls the shots because he can deliver financing."

Rolf, with a bored look on his face for the benefit of any onlookers, said, "The one who has the keys to the treasure box controls the kingdom."

Father Anton lowered his head almost to the table top while taking in deep breaths of air.

Marbach and Rolf both looked with concern at the young priest. They waited patiently until he managed to get his breathing under control.

Finally, Rolf said, "Skorzeny has been held by the Americans since the end of the war, yet he is able to lead a Nazi underground movement. What is the matter with the Americans?"

There was no answer to Rolf's question.

"Tell us about this new organization," said Marbach.

"It is called Odessa," Father Anton replied. "The word Odessa is made from letters. The letters stand for Organisation der ehemaligen SS-Angehörigen."

"Odessa," Rolf murmured.

There was a short interruption while the waiter delivered coffee and plates of sausage and cold cuts for Marbach and

Rolf. After providing the two mid-morning breakfasts and filling Father Anton's water glass, the waiter left.

"How much of this Eichmann's gold is there?" Rolf asked.

"Enough to make Odessa a fantastic escape route," Father Anton answered.

"What more can you tell us about this Odessa?" Marbach asked.

Father Anton spoke slowly, his voice distressingly weak. "For Odessa there will be ports of call—relay stations— each of them manned by at least three people. The people responsible for operating each port of call will know only the locations of the two nearest ports of call. They will know the one that delivers to them and the one to which they deliver. It's . . ." Father Anton's voice became too weak to continue.

Marbach leaned forward. "Take your time. No need to hurry. Can you tell us how you learned about . . . about this Odessa."

Father Anton managed to get his voice back. "I learned about it from a Franciscan friar." Father Anton stared hopelessly, then said, "The family of the friar is Neumayer."

Marbach made a murmuring sound that became a curse.

"We know the Neumayer family," Rolf said to Father Anton.

Father Anton looked at Rolf, then pleadingly stared at his uncle. "I know what the elder Neumayer did and what his son did. The son is now Friar Paul. He led a sinful life, but he is now trying to atone for his sins."

There was a long period of silence. All three of those at the table knew that in 1938, shortly after the Anschluss, the man now presenting himself as Friar Paul had been an eager young Nazi, and his father had played a critical part in the events that led to the killing of Marbach's lover, Constanze Tandler.

Marbach broke the silence. "If young Neumayer . . ." Very quickly, Marbach corrected himself. "If Friar Paul is honestly struggling to redeem himself, he will have no trouble from me. I don't put the past behind me, but I will cause no problem for him because of anything you tell us." That wasn't a statement made only to get information. It was a firm commitment, recog-nized as such by all three men at the table.

Father Anton closed his eyes as he leaned forward. "Friar Paul has told me that his father is involved in this evil Odessa thing. That places Friar Paul in a terrible predicament."

Marbach and Rolf avoided exchanging glances.

After taking several deep breaths Father Anton said, "Stephan Kaas is mixed up with Odessa, too."

"Are you sure about Kaas?" Marbach asked. "He works for the Americans."

"He's mixed up in Odessa up to his neck," Father Anton said.

"The world used to be a simple place," Marbach said.

Father Anton nodded his agreement.

"Eichmann's gold," Rolf murmured.

Father Anton said, "Without Eichmann's gold there will be no Odessa."

Marbach and Rolf knew about Father Anton's very personal contribution to Eichmann's gold. Like many others at Dachau, the gold in Father Anton's teeth had been removed with pliers.

In addition to gold from teeth, the treasure called Eichmann's gold included jewelry taken from countless victims. The total value of what was called Eichmann's gold was incredible. In American currency, the standard unit of exchange, it amounted to hundreds of millions of dollars.

Father Anton made an expressive movement with his hands before saying, "The regular SS, men like Skorzeny and Stephan Kaas, don't much like Eichmann. What Eichmann did has now been publicly revealed for what it was. Eichmann is an embarrassment to them in their quest for acceptance in the post-war world."

Marbach stared with concern at his nephew. "You need a good meal in you. Tonight there's a going to be a dinner. You know Sophie. She'll be at a dinner tonight with her British colonel. And I'll be there. If you bring your concertina, we can sing some Schrammel songs. Then afterward we can have a long talk with the colonel about this Odessa thing and Eichmann."

"Not tonight . . . or tomorrow night," Father Anton said.

"Why not?" Marbach asked.

"Because tonight or tomorrow night those Odessa papers are going to be showing up in the Franciscan Printing Shop. Those papers will contain information about where relay stations are located."

Marbach clenched his fists. "If we can grab up those papers and get them into American hands, Odessa will be finished before it gets started."

Rolf rubbed his jaw.

Father Anton looked at the two men sitting at the table with him and said, "When they show up, those papers will only be in the printing shop for a couple of hours. Try barging in at the wrong time and you will give everything away. There will be no chance to get the Odessa papers."

Rolf said, "This is dangerous for you, Reverend Father. Don't take an unnecessary risk. Tell us what you are up to. If you get into trouble you will need help."

Father Anton wearily waved his hand. "We all know that I do not have long to live. It is an unimportant thing that I will soon die. What is important is that if the presence of either of you is detected near me while I am doing what I have chosen to do, it will lead to disaster. The only chance to get the Odessa papers will be lost. If you want to help, don't try to spy on me. Wait until I contact you."

"How long?" Marbach asked.

"Have patience. Sometime in the next couple of days, for the duration of no more than a few minutes, the papers of Odessa are going to be vulnerable to theft. The peculiarities of the situation dictate that I am the only one who can be the thief."

After saying that, Father Anton abruptly stood up, bade farewell to Marbach and to Rolf and left the café.

Rolf heaved a sigh and looked at the door that had closed behind Father Anton. He heaved a second sigh and said, "There is nothing we can do about what Father Anton is setting up, but there is something else going on that might interest you."

"What are you talking about?" Marbach asked.

"There's a flat being used by an American."

"Come to the point."

"The flat is occupied by an American scientist named Dr. Robert Shepherd who keeps company with a woman named Lisa Beck."

"Lisa Beck?"

"You gave me her name. We both know her profession."

"Any sign of Skorzeny?"

"No sign of him, so far as I know. All I have is an address. And a few details about Dr. Robert Shepherd."

"An American scientist is keeping company with Lisa Beck?"

"That's right."

"Where?"

"Just follow me."

The bill was paid and Rolf led Marbach on a short walk.

CHAPTER NINE

A fter leaving the Café Florian, Marbach and Rolf stood together in front of a tall building. Marbach peered upward, all the way to the top of the building, and kept his voice low as he said, "What do we do now?"

With a slight trace of humor in his voice, Rolf said, "We could just wait outside this hotel and see who comes and goes."

Marbach smiled. "If this was the usual sort of criminal case, that might be the thing to do, but for this case I think we might pursue the possibility that the flat occupied by this Dr. Robert Shepherd is empty right now."

Rolf shrugged. "Maybe the flat isn't empty. Maybe the woman named Lisa Beck is inside with the American. Or maybe Skorzeny is in there. Who knows?"

It was routine for Marbach and Rolf to talk things out this way even if they were both pretty sure what they were going to do and how they were going to do it. Marbach pulled a package of American cigarettes—Lucky Strike cigarettes—from his pocket. He had given up smoking, but Rolf smoked. Rolf took one cigarette from the package, wet it on his mouth, then held it in his hand for a moment before putting it in his mouth.

Marbach lit the cigarette for Rolf, and spoke in a speculative way. "I wonder how long this American been occupying the flat."

Rolf puffed on the cigarette. "He's on some sort of scientific project, been here for three months." There was a momentary pause, then words were spoken with emphasis. "The Americans are peculiar about people breaking into Viennese flats occupied by Americans."

Marbach smiled. "If being a burglar makes you nervous you can stay down here while I go up and do the burgling alone."

Rolf stared at Marbach's smiling face, puffed some more on the cigarette, and said with calculated humor, "Dr. Robert Shepherd is my lead. If anyone is going to stay down here, I nominate you."

"Quatsch!" Marbach said.

Rolf chuckled. Then both of them walked to the rear of the building where they found a door that was easily forced open.

Soon they were in the lobby checking the mailboxes. With a jerk of his head, Rolf gestured upward. "Flat 202," he said in a low voice.

"All right."

"What next?"

"We go up there and knock on the door."

Marbach took the lead and Rolf followed him quietly up the stairs.

When they got to flat 202, Marbach knocked on the door. After a few moments, they exchanged glances and

Marbach knocked again. Neither man felt any need for discussion. If there had been a response, they'd have made up an excuse, presented themselves as salesmen and, as discretely as possible, gone on their way. That was a routine they often performed at various places while getting Kripo work done.

This time there was no response.

Rolf put out his cigarette and leaned forward. In his hand was a small, long-stemmed device—a lock pick. He expertly intruded the device into the lock for flat 202, cocked his head and listened closely. A few seconds later, after a clicking sound was made, the door came open.

Marbach and Rolf stepped inside, prepared for any eventuality. They weren't wearing gloves, so they had to be careful what they touched. In the manner of professional burglars, they first confirmed that no one was in the flat and then checked for an escape route. They found a rope ladder in the bedroom that could be dropped out the window. The rope ladder wasn't unusual. These days many elevated Vienna buildings had no fire escapes, just rope ladders.

Marbach returned to the door of the flat and pushed a heavy wooden chair under the door knob in a way that, at the very least, would slow down any unwelcome intruder.

Then began the search for what might be found in the flat. There was no need to talk things out. Without saying anything to each other, they moved in a coordinated manner. Rolf surveyed the living room while Marbach walked into the bedroom, went through clothes in a closet and opened a drawer to a bedside table. Inside the drawer, he found a black leather binder. After reading the first handwritten page in the binder he realized he was reading a private journal. Most of the pages were filled with strange mathematical formulae, but finally there was a page that totally captured his attention. On that page there was mention of a priest named Father Mundt. A couple of pages further on, there was an even more important name: Bishop Hudal, the Vatican Spiritual Director of the German People. And on the page after that was the most important name of all: Dr. Heinrich Emhardt. Marbach stared at that name. He had personal reasons for nursing hatred for that particular Nazi scientist.

"Rolf, come in here."

Rolf stepped into the bedroom.

"Take a look at this." Marbach handed Rolf the journal.

Rolf began reading, but at first he had difficulty figuring out what he was supposed to see. He was confused by the mathematical formulae.

"Keep reading," Marbach said.

Rolf flipped through pages for a few moments, then said, "The name Father Mundt is here."

"Keep reading. It gets better."

After a few more moments of hasty page turning, Rolf looked up. "Bishop Hudal?"

"Keep reading."

Rolf turned the page, read for a moment, then spat out the name "Dr. Heinrich Emhardt." Like Marbach, Rolf had personal reasons for hating Dr. Emhardt. To the world, Dr. Heinrich Emhardt was a Nazi scientist, a wanted war criminal. But that was only rhetoric. For Marbach and Rolf some of Dr. Emhardt's victims were people they had known. For both of them Dr. Emhardt was more than just another name on a wanted poster.

"Do you suppose he's back in Austria?" Rolf asked.

"Look at the numbers under his name."

Rolf stared closely, but before he had time to say anything, Marbach indulged a tease. "Isn't there something familiar about those numbers?"

"One of them is a Vienna telephone number."

"Congratulations."

Ignoring the tease, Rolf said in an accusing voice, "The Americans know where Emhardt is. They even have a telephone number for him, but they let him run free."

Marbach said, "We need time to properly study what's in this binder and in these separate pieces of paper marked Top Secret."

"We are burglars. Burglars take what they find."

"Lots of burglars make messes. I'm going to make a big mess. One that will confuse things."

Rolf went to check the other rooms in the flat. Returning a few minutes later, he watched while Marbach finished making a mess. Rolf knew that the Americans would suspect the Russians committed the burglary and the Russians would suspect the Americans, but because of the mess neither of them would be able to rule out the possibility that ordinary burglars were involved.

After watching for a while, Rolf left the bedroom, went into the living room, reached up, and pulled a ceiling lamp onto the floor. He accomplished that with a minimum of noise. Then he went around creating more confusion for anyone who might investigate the burglary of the American scientist's flat. He pulled out desk drawers, tossed contents wherever they might land, but always with a minimum of noise. He found some classified papers with subjects that didn't seem to be important and scattered them around on the floor.

Meanwhile, in the bedroom, Marbach opened a closet and tossed jackets and coats onto the floor.

When the job of creating a lot of mess was almost completed, Marbach walked into the living room and tossed Rolf a towel. "Don't wipe away everything, just places where you or I may have left some fingerprints. I'll scatter things around a little more."

Rolf chuckled. "I didn't leave any fingerprints, but I'll clean up wherever you may have gotten careless."

A few minutes later, when Marbach and Rolf walked out of the tall building, they had with them a briefcase filled with papers and reports.

They walked three blocks, continually checking to be sure they weren't being followed, then boarded a streetcar that would take them to the relative security of the Café Virgil in the British Zone where they would find out what might be able to be learned from the documents that had been stolen.

CHAPTER TEN

A couple of hours later, Marbach and Rolf were sitting at a table in the Café Virgil. With them was a friend they had enlisted to help them make sense of the stolen documents. The friend, Dr. Nahum Wechsberg, was a small man who, before the war, had been a respected scientist. Dr. Wechsberg had existed from 1941 until the end of the war in the so-called "model concentration camp" at Theresienstadt. His wife had died at Dachau and his two children at Nordhausen.

Now, in the Café Virgil, Dr. Wechsberg was peering at a document through eye glasses that had one frosty lens and a heavy black patch over the other lens. He had one reasonably good eye and one empty eye socket. He had lost the eye during one of the countless beatings he had received at Theresienstadt. With dry humor, he sometimes said it was fortunate he had been in a "model camp". In an "ordinary camp" he might have had both eyes kicked from his head.

"Karl, you and Rolf are absolute rogues," Dr. Wechsberg said as he removed his eye glasses. That act made visible his empty eye socket. His one good eye flashed mischievously.

"You two call yourselves honest policemen, yet you commit a burglary and then you enlist me, a respectable man, to help evaluate your booty."

Marbach smiled. "Herr Professor, I think it is time to sum up what we have here." Marbach believed it was important to show respect by addressing his friend as "Herr Professor."

Dr. Wechsberg said, "I am ready to do the summing up."

Marbach said, "Before that please have some of this marvelous Rotgipfler." Without waiting for a reply, he filled three glasses with an excellent Heurige wine made from Rotgipfler grapes. Expensive Rotgipfler was a bit of an expensive indulgence, but Marbach knew it was one of Dr. Wechsberg's favorite drinks.

"To the man who saved my life, Karl Marbach," Dr. Wechsberg declared exuberantly. Turning toward Rolf while keeping his glass raised, Dr. Wechsberg said, "You should have seen this big ox, Rolf, the day he drove that International Red Cross truck into Theresienstadt one full month before Russian soldiers liberated the camp. On that day Karl brought much needed medicine for people in desperate need."

Dr. Wechsberg continued. "He had a shouting session with an SS officer who wanted to keep the truck out. What an absolute rogue Karl was, pretending to be Swiss. If any Nazis had recognized him, or simply seen through his phony Swiss posturing, he'd have been shot dead on the spot."

The story was familiar to Rolf, but he always enjoyed hearing it, especially the way it was told by the small man with one eye.

Marbach cut off more idle talk. "I think we should focus on the subject immediately at hand."

Dr. Wechsberg moved his fingers tentatively across the many pieces of paper on the table. "All right. Let me see. There is information here about Dr. Heinrich Emhardt, an important scientist, and lots of complicated details about a new ratline. There have been many escape routes—ratlines—for the Nazis, but this new one will become a super ratline. It is clear from what is on some of these papers that high-ranking Americans are giving support to this ratline. In addition, there is also support from the Catholic Church. Bishop Hudal is helping Odessa. That is very clear in these papers. And other clerics are involved . . . Franciscans."

Rolf, a religious man who frequently went to Mass before going to work didn't try to conceal the distress showing openly on his face.

Marbach said, "The Americans supporting Odessa feel justified because the United States needs skills these Nazi scientists have. As for the Church, it thinks there is justification because it is saving some of its faithful."

Rolf spoke in a deliberative voice. "Several priests who risked their lives to get Jews and others to safety are now helping Nazis escape over various escape routes. Trying as hard as I can, it isn't possible for me to understand those priests."

Dr. Wechsberg clasped his hands together. "All I say is that if any of the Nazis using the ratlines are going to be set free, it should be done openly. There should be an explanation. The explanation should be broadcast clear enough to be heard by all those whose loved ones were victims of the Nazi evil."

"Yes," said Rolf in a fervent voice.

Dr. Wechsberg closed his one good eye for a moment. When he opened the eye, he said, "Dr. Heinrich Emhardt was once a student of mine. He is most certainly an evil man. The blood of many people is on his hands. But he is a brilliant scientist. He will be a valuable asset for the United States. If he is allowed to escape justice and go to America, he will be an asset for them in the making of atom bombs."

Rolf spat out angry curse words.

Dr. Wechsberg stared at Marbach with his one good eye. "The information we have here indicates that right now Dr. Emhardt is in Freistadt."

Marbach stared back at Dr. Wechsberg. "Did you find that in the papers?"

"Yes."

Dr. Wechsberg picked up his glass of wine, stared at it and said, "I assume you plan to spoil the plans of the Americans to sneak Dr. Heinrich Emhardt into the United States."

Marbach said, "Among the many victims of Emhardt is one who was known to me."

Rolf leaned forward and said, "More than one of Emhardt's victims was precious to me. There were two precious people. The evil done by this man to my two precious friends—and to many others—demands justice."

"Emhardt must face justice," Marbach said.

Dr. Wechsberg nodded his head. "There are dangerous times ahead for the world. It is possible to understand why some United States persons are anxious to have scientific help from the likes of Dr. Heinrich Emhardt."

Rolf said, "The evil done by this man demands justice. He must face justice. Dr. Emhardt can be found in Freistadt. That is the place to go if he is going to be brought to justice."

Marbach had a troubled look on his face.

Dr. Wechsberg stared first at Marbach, then at Rolf.

Looking at Dr. Wechsberg, Rolf provided the explanation for Marbach's troubled look. "Karl can't go to Freistadt. His presence would cause a lot of excitement. To do this job the way it needs to be done there must be as little excitement as possible. If Karl pushed his nose in there everything would get all stirred up. But I am just an ordinary police detective. I am not an important police inspector. I can go to Freistadt and cause only a small amount of excitement. There is even a good excuse for me going to Freistadt—it's an excuse the great Police Inspector Marbach could never use. The Freistadt police have been asking for someone of my modest status to help them deal with thieves stealing animals from the farms. That isn't the kind of case that the esteemed Police Inspector Marbach would work on."

Marbach grimaced while nodding agreement.

Rolf cast a satisfied look at Marbach and said, "I better get going. I have to kiss my wife and children before I leave for Freistadt."

Marbach gestured at the briefcase containing the documents stolen from Dr. Shepherd's flat. "I better get this stuff hidden in a safe place."

"If I can be of any further service . . ." Dr. Wechsberg didn't complete the sentence. The horror in his life had left him afflicted by occasional bouts of extreme melancholy.

Marbach hoped that some of the good man's melancholy might be alleviated by being told of an event scheduled for the coming weekend. "Herr Professor, my good wife wants you to come to dinner with us on Sunday. The usual collection of people will be there. Pammy will be most upset if you don't show up."

Dr. Wechsberg brightened. "That will be a mechaieh," he said, using the Yiddish word for great joy.

Rolf and Marbach bade Dr. Wechsberg an affectionate farewell and left the Café Virgil.

CHAPTER ELEVEN

Marbach got back to police headquarters late in the afternoon and used his authority as police inspector to record on the official register that Detective Rolf Hiller would be spending a day or two in Freistadt to work on a case involving stolen farm animals. After that was done he went to his office, sat idly at his desk and thought about Pammy. While telling himself it wasn't likely she would be in her Paris hotel room at this time of the day, he picked up the telephone on his desk and asked the operator to begin the complicated process of getting him connected to Paris.

What he was doing amounted to improper use of the official Vienna police telephone, but there would be no terribly serious consequences if he got caught. At worst, there would only be some sort of minor reprimand. He was willing to risk a reprimand just to hear Pammy's voice.

It took almost a quarter of an hour before the telephone connection was finally made to Pammy's hotel in Paris. Marbach came alert when he realized the call was being forwarded to her room.

There was a long minute of silence and he began wondering if there had been a disconnection.

Then he heard the familiar voice.

"Hello? Hello?"

"Hello, sweetheart," he said. Talking in English came naturally, but there was also the consideration that it might help confuse possible eavesdroppers working for Kripo. There was a lot of eavesdropping, and most of it wasn't done with recording equipment. Eavesdroppers would have more trouble understanding English than they would have with any other language.

"Hello, my love," said the female voice.

"Can you hear me?"

"Yes, it's absolutely clear at this end."

"What are you doing in your hotel room? If I was in Paris, I wouldn't be staying in my hotel room at this time of day."

"I can imagine what you would be doing."

Marbach was delighted to hear Pammy's voice, her precious voice. But what to talk about? He decided to indulge some spoof talk. "How are you and your Captain Burke getting along? And how come you've never introduced us. You have never one time introduced me to Captain Burke."

The reply was delivered testily. "Why should I introduce Captain Burke to you?"

"I like knowing your friends."

"Him . . . Him a friend of mine? Sweetie, one thing that you seem to have missed is that while Captain Burke very much likes women, he doesn't much like Jews."

"Then why did he take you with him to Paris?"

"He was afraid of how it would look if he didn't. After all, this meeting deals with burn cases and I'm the senior member of the staff dealing with burn cases."

Marbach decided to go further with the spoof talk, maybe defuse a problem. Often in recent weeks Pammy had berated herself for being a hypocrite, for keeping silent in the hospital when there was invective or hollow humor directed at Jews. Averse to giving ammunition to those who might say she was taking advantage of her senior position and showing how Jewish she was, Pammy tended to let bad things pass. But afterward she was self-critical, sometimes harshly self-critical. Marbach wanted to make her see that she didn't deserve the criticism she was directing at herself.

With calculation, he said, "Americans are hypocrites." He was confident Pammy would think that remark was meant to disparage Captain Burke. The captain wasn't an American, but there were reasons Pammy might think he believed the British Captain Burke was American.

Pammy reacted as expected. She said, "You love to find fault with Americans. Well, Captain Burke is not American. If you knew anything at all about him, you would know he is a British officer."

"Captain Charles Burke of the King's Shropshire Light Infantry," said Marbach in a matter-of-fact voice.

"Why . . . that's right?" Pammy was totally confused.

"I meant you as the hypocrite," said Marbach.

For a moment there was silence.

"I am not a hypocrite!" exclaimed Pammy. "How dare you say that?"

"How many times recently have you called yourself a hyp-ocrite? Finally, I agree, but now you say you aren't."

Pammy's response was spoken forcefully. "Yes, I am a hyp-ocrite. I hate that about myself."

Marbach liked hearing anger in Pammy's voice. The anger was giving her strength. "Now, from the little black book of Captain Burke," he said as though he was reading from a document. "Let's see who is in this little black book. Closing his eyes, he repeated first one female name, then another. He was making up the names.

He was at the fourth name when Pammy joined in the spoof talk. "Oh, who would have ever dreamed Charlie Burke was so successful with women. If I wasn't Jewish, maybe he would give me a good romp in the sack. I wonder how good he would be."

"I think he must be very good in bed."

"Go to hell."

"Now you're angry at me."

"You called me a hypocrite."

"Your anger is good. I want you to have anger. That is why I echo the falsehood that you are a hypocrite."

"Oh . . . Karl, what am I ever going to do with you?"

"Maybe you'll think a bit about this business of who is and who is not a hypocrite. By the way, I'm sorry I had to rush off and leave you the way I did at the station."

"Whatever was that all about?"

"Just routine police work. A burglar. It didn't amount to much."

"Oh, blast! Well, while we're on the phone tell me who you are having dinner with tonight."

"Tonight? Why ask? You arranged it. You arranged things for tonight and tomorrow night. You haven't yet informed me who I'll be having dinner with the night after tomorrow. Tonight you have arranged for me to have supper with Zbik and Anna. Tomorrow night I will have supper with Colonel Robert Larkswood and Sophie."

"His name is Bobby. What can't you call him Bobby?"

"He's your friend. I don't know him as well as you do. Our relationship is more professional than personal. Anyway, that's for tomorrow night. Tonight I will be having supper with Zbik and Anna."

Anna was Marbach's former lover from years ago. Now, Anna was married to Zbik and Anna and Pammy were devoted friends. Pammy and Anna shared a close friendship. Occasionally they made Marbach the target of humor. They sometimes said that there should be an operetta made out of his life and that the operetta should focus on the way his former lovers banded together like sisters. In addition to Pammy, Anna had close friendships with two of Marbach's former lovers. She had even introduced one of them to Pammy. Marbach found it all very distressing. He had a long time rule to never tell anything about any of the women who had ever been in his life to any current woman in his life.

Pammy said into the telephone, "This Paris meeting is terrible. I'm dealing with a bunch of bleeding yobs." The very American Pammy frequently used British slang.

"Is it really going to be three more days?" Marbach asked.

"Yes. Three days for me with a bunch of yobs. This God awful meeting is a total waste of time."

"You can handle it, old girl."

"Forget that. While I have you on the line, tell me how you arranged to come with me to Sammy's wedding?"

"It's also the wedding of my climbing partner. Jennifer and I shared a climbing rope. I regard myself as obligated to stand behind my good friend Jennifer at her marriage."

Pammy yielded laughter that quickly became a crying sound. Finally, in a sobbing voice, she said, "I'll be talking to Sammy on the telephone, maybe even today. Oh, my goodness. Well, the thing is . . . well, one of the things I need to be able to tell my boy is when we'll be arriving in the States and how long we'll be staying."

Marbach felt awful hearing Pammy cry, even though he knew it was happiness that was making her cry. He spoke quickly. "My schedule is no problem. All that matters is how your own schedule works out. Arrange the details to suit yourself. I can get time off in any way that fits your schedule." He paused. He decided this was a good time to let her know who was making the trip possible. "Call Colonel Robert Larkswood if you have any questions."

"Bobby arranged this?" Pammy stopped crying.

"He sure did."

"I'll give him a great big sticky kiss."

"If you do, I'll tell Sophie."

"Precious Sophie. I know how much I owe Bobby for every-thing, but Bobby better do right by my precious friend Sophie."

"Don't meddle."

"Sophie's my friend." Pammy's voice was firm with resolve.

"Let them handle their own problems," Marbach said. He made no mention of his own recent conversation with Colonel Larkswood.

"That I won't do."

"I give up."

"Are you having dinner with your mountain soldier friends the day after tomorrow?"

"I forget. My life was so simple before I got involved with you."

"Any complaints?"

"I don't dare voice them."

"Any time I am out of town and don't schedule dinners for you, all you do is hang out with your mountain soldier friends."

"What is wrong with that?"

"Whatever do you mountain soldiers talk about?"

"We sit around and talk about women."

"I imagine you mountain soldiers sometimes talk about war and battles. Do you talk with your mountain soldier friends about the Ortigara?"

Marbach winced. He took a moment before replying. "We talk about a lot of things, but we very seldom talk about battles that happened in the past."

"Codswallop."

"Don't talk dirty."

"You ass."

"More dirty talk."

"You have never talked to me about the Ortigara. You avoid telling me many things about the war you fought, and one of the things you don't talk about is the Ortigara."

"What do you want to know?"

"Was it really an inferno?"

"It was worse than that."

"When we first met two years ago, because you wouldn't tell me any details, I went to the library and found a book that tells how the Emperor himself gave you the Maria Theresa medal, the greatest medal in the Austrian army. I never told you that before. You have a way of precluding such talk. But now I am telling you I read all about the Ortigara and your medal in a blasted book!"

"What about your own medal? That DSO? What did you do to win the DSO? Have you ever noticed, love of my life, how vague you have always been about your DSO?"

"I told you about it."

"In the two years we've been together, you have mentioned it exactly three times and each time you were vague on the details. I had to learn what happened by talking to British soldiers."

There was a long silence before Pammy said, "I told you more about what I did to get my DSO than you ever told me about what you did to get the Maria Theresa medal."

"For my medal, I climbed a mountain and killed some good men. We killed each other at the Ortigara because we were wearing different uniforms. There is nothing more to be said."

There was silence on the line until Pammy spoke. Her voice made it clear she was determined to hold her own. "For my medal, I stayed with some wounded men. There is nothing more to be said."

Marbach liked hearing the determination in Pammy's voice. "You saved lives," he said. "Everybody was retreating, but you stayed behind and saved lives."

There was a long silence on the telephone line.

Finally, Marbach broke the silence. "How are you feeling?"

"I am fine. When I get home, I'll have you give me a back rub. That's all I need."

"Is your back bothering you?" There had been two really important women in Marbach's life and one of the many things the two women had in common was that both of them had large scars on their backs and both of them got those scars performing acts of heroism. Marbach recalled how Constanze Tandler had often fretted about the scars she got fighting the fascists during the 1934 worker's uprising and now here was Pammy troubled by the scars she got saving the lives of British soldiers in 1943. Such remarkable women, he thought. Both of them. Constanze the wonderment lost to him forever, a woman he would never forget and Pammy who was better than he had ever imagined a woman could be.

Lost in his thoughts, Marbach came alert when Pammy made a sighing sound.

"Anything wrong?" he asked.

Pammy's voice became clear and strong. "I hate to think what might happen to them if Zbik and Anna go to Poland to see if they can help some friends."

"Yes," Marbach agreed. He said nothing more. He saw no point saying what both of them knew. Zbik was a Jew and a Pole. Most of Zbik's Jewish friends said there was no longer a place for Jews in Poland, that the place for him to go was Israel. But Zbik loved Poland. His Polish roots ran deep.

Pammy spoke in a voice so low Marbach could barely hear her. "The Communists are becoming terribly powerful in Poland."

Marbach felt a need to say something, but at this moment the only thing he could think to say was what they both knew. "The Communists in Poland have control of the police and the other major organs of government. Back in January, there were supposed to be free elections, but that turned into a farce. Once the Communists get Stanislaw Mikolajczyk out of the way, they will have a free hand in Poland."

"It will mean the end of the Peasant Party," Pammy said. She didn't say—didn't need to say—that Stanislaw Mikolajczyk was the leader of the Peasant Party, the opposition party to the Communists in Poland.

There was a crackling sound on the telephone line.

Marbach spoke gruffly, "Things are bad. And the Americans are only making a bad scene worse. They are trying to fix things so Germany will be a buffer for them against the Russians. The Americans are even talking about getting the Poles to give some of the Silesian territory back to Germany."

Pammy said nothing in reply. They had talked about all of this many time before.

There was silence for a few moments. Finally, Marbach said, "The Poles know there is no hope for them to obtain meaningful economic aid from the United States. Stupidity on the part of the Americans works to the best interest of the Communists. They are able to move against Mikolajczyk without having to worry about stirring up unrest. The Americans offer Poland nothing while the Russians offer support for claims against Germany. How can Mikolajczyk rally opposition to the Communists when the Americans behave this way?"

"It's awful," Pammy said. "I don't understand why America is behaving this way. It doesn't make sense."

Marbach kept silent.

Finally, Pammy said, "Anna is almost finished with all the treatments I can give her for her burns."

In the closing days of the war, while attempting to flee the Russians, Anna had been in a truck that blundered into a combat area and got shot up by the American forces. She had ended up with bad burns on her face and on various parts of her body. For two years Pammy had been paying for Anna's medical expenses. Anna was getting better and better all the time, but her face was still a little bloated and the skin on her face had pale red streaks in it.

The telephone connection began crackling loudly.

"Are you still there, sweetheart?" Marbach asked anxiously.

Pammy laughed. "Yes, I can hear you."

The crackling sound got worse. It was obvious that the vulnerable telephone connection was about to break up.

Without warning, Pammy whispered, "I love you, my chocolate policeman."

Marbach was surprised hearing himself addressed as the chocolate policeman. He wondered if Pammy had learned from Anna that Constanze used to playfully identify him by referring to the chocolate soldier character in the operetta by Oscar Straus.

But before he could say anything, the telephone connection crackled, made a squeaking sound, and was lost.

CHAPTER TWELVE

M arbach returned the telephone receiver to its cradle. A few moments later he came to attention when the telephone began jangling. He nursed hope that after the disconnection Pammy had somehow managed to get connected with him this fast.

"Police Inspector Marbach here," he said eagerly into the telephone mouthpiece.

But the voice that answered on the other end of the line wasn't Pammy's. It was the deeply pitched, very masculine voice of the Commander of Inner City Vienna Police.

"Karl, I've just had a call from the American intelligence people. I would like for you to come and see me right away. This is important."

"Yes, sir."

Less than a half hour later, Marbach was sitting across a table from the commander. He listened while the commander said, "I know you aren't going to like this. I know I don't like it, but, well, here it is. It seems there was a burglary of a flat occupied by an American scientist. The American CIC is investigating and they have asked for our help."

Marbach kept any reaction from showing on his face.

"There aren't any good guidelines for something like this," said the commander. He paused. "The American intelligence people say it was a burglary by the Soviet. But who can believe the Americans? Aghh . . . the point is Vienna police can't ignore a request from American intelligence, but, on the other hand, it would be a mistake to get in the middle of what could become a very noisy dispute between the Soviet and the Americans."

"What do we know about this American scientist?" Marbach asked.

"His name is Dr. Robert Shepherd. Oh, Hell, I don't know anything more about him than his name. I haven't had time to check into this."

"It sounds tricky."

"The Americans asked for a meeting today at any time we are available in the Café La Meynardie. Don't ask me why they chose that place to meet. Anyway, you are the best one I can send. You know how to deal with Americans."

Marbach decided to ask for the address for the American scientist's flat. Of course, he knew the address, but it was best for him to ask for the address, behave like he was totally ignorant about everything connected with this business.

After providing the address of the flat, the commander said, "Maybe you can get to the Café La Meynardie before the Americans get there. That would be good."

The commander indicated there was nothing more to say and made a dismissive move with his hand. Marbach bade farewell. As he left the commander's office, he reflected that he had known the Commander of Inner City Police for a long time, liked him in a qualified way. He wondered if American CIC knew that the commander was a Communist. Maybe they did, possibly they didn't. And maybe it wasn't important. Marbach knew he wasn't the only one who regarded the commander as more Viennese than Communist.

CHAPTER THIRTEEN

Captain Millican and Sergeant Fay, along with two junior enlisted men, were moving around inside Dr. Shepherd's flat. All four CIC men were in civilian clothes.

"Where is Shepherd now?" Millican asked while looking around at the mess in the flat.

"He's in the toilet throwing up," said Fay in a level voice. Fay was a newcomer to Vienna, but he had a lot of State-side police experience under his belt.

"The bastard," Millican said. "He screwed up real bad. There'll be a lot of hard flak over this. Half the papers scattered around this place are classified. The thieves must have made off with a whole pile of classified stuff."

Fay placed his hands on his hips. "Christ knows how much Top Secret stuff the burglars carried away with them. There's going to be hell to pay for this."

"Have our guys learned anything that might help identify the burglars?"

"Not one damned thing."

Millican and Fay stared at the two junior CIC men, both corporals, both trying to look like policemen while poking around in the flat.

"They're doing their best," Fay said. "It's not like they're trained cops." He continued. "Do you think the Russians did this?"

"I doubt it," said Millican. "They wouldn't leave a mess like this. My guess is this was done by regular burglars. The important thing is that we've got to find out who did this—get any secret stuff back if possible."

Fay shrugged. "I did cop work back in the States, but Vienna ain't my city. I can't speak decent German, let alone the Viennese lingo. Anyway, I just got word from the top cop with Vienna police and learned he is sending a guy named Police Inspector Marbach to meet with us at the Café La Meynardie. The police inspector is gonna be helping us with this case."

Millican smiled. "I was a cop, too, back in the States, and I can speak pretty good German, even Viennese-German, but I can't do proper cop work in Vienna. Not like it needs to be done for a something like this."

"Say, I hear you know this Vienna cop, the police inspector."

"Yeah, I know Police Inspector Marbach. He's a good man. I've known him since August of '45."

"I'm looking forward to meeting the guy. Heard a lota good stuff about him."

Millican rubbed his hand across his face. "Dr. Shepherd is a problem. Have we anyone who can hold onto him for us?"

"Morgan can handle that job. I already called him. He's in one of our places about ten minutes from here."

There was nothing more to say.

Taking the distraught Dr. Shepherd with them, Millican and Fay left the flat, found the place where CIC Agent Morgan was staying, deposited Dr. Shepherd, and hurried off to the Café La Meynardie, where they quickly found a table and sat down. Police Inspector Marbach was nowhere to be seen.

Millican raised his arm and a waiter came over.

"Do you have a copy of *Stars and Stripes*?" Millican asked, in Viennese-German. "And two glasses of brandy?"

After taking the order, the waiter left.

Fay cast a mildly critical look at Millican and said, "Doesn't that copy of *Stars and Stripes* just advertise we're GIs?"

Millican shrugged. He didn't tell Fay that even in civilian clothes no one in this café was going to think they were anything but American GIs.

A few minutes later, the waiter returned with the newspaper.

Millican accepted the *Stars and Stripes*. Quickly, his eyes skipped down to an article posted under a small headline:

RUSSIANS CLAIM SKORZENY IS IN THE U.S.

The Russians are claiming that Colonel Otto Skorzeny, acquitted by a U.S. military court on September 9 of charges he violated the rules of war during the Battle of the Bulge, has been secretly flown to the United States and is now employed as an instructor at a secret army base in Georgia.

But more reliable sources than the Russians say the Nazi commando chief is securely locked up at Camp King outside Oberursel, Germany where he is under "automatic arrest status". He was acquitted of war crimes specific to the Battle of the Bulge, but the U.S. Army still regards Colonel Skorzeny as "The Most Dangerous Man in Europe." It appears likely he will soon be handed over to Poland or Czechoslovakia or Austria to face war crime charges. That is regarded as a quick and efficient way to handle Otto Skorzeny.

"What do you make of this article about Skorzeny?" Millican asked, tossing the newspaper to Fay.

After reading the article, Fay shrugged and said, "The Russkie stuff is dumb."

"Probably. But is Skorzeny being held at Camp King?"

"He is unless somebody's playing games."

"Maybe we ought to—"

At that moment, there was an interruption. A big man with a Tyrolian hat in his hand had walked up to the table.

"Hello. I am sorry to keep you gentlemen waiting," said Marbach. He smiled a friendly grin, shook hands with Millican and Fay, and sat down.

A waiter appeared with a glass of kummel—schnapps—for the police inspector. It was obvious the waiter knew the police inspector, knew what the police inspector would want to drink.

There was no toast. Marbach sampled his drink before asking in English, "What can I do for you gentlemen?"

"Maybe we ought to speak German," Fay said. "It doesn't pay to advertise that the captain and me are Americans."

Millican smiled.

Marbach stared at Fay's American civilian suit, then pointedly at Fay's haircut and said, "You are what you appear to be. In this café, no one cares unless you try to appear to be what you are not. Only then do you draw attention to yourself."

Fay blinked a moment, pushed his hand through his G.I. haircut and grinned.

Marbach grinned back at Fay, then turned to Millican and said, "I heard the sports news on the GI radio today. It looks like the Brooklyn Dodgers will be going up against the Yankees in the World Series."

Before Millican could reply, Fay asked Marbach, "Do you follow American baseball?"

"My dear wife is obsessed with American baseball. We listen to the games on the Munich radio station that plays American programs. During the World Series next week, I'll be rooting for Joe DiMaggio and the Yankees and my wife will be rooting for Jackie Robinson and the Brooklyn Dodgers."

"I've heard about your wife," Fay said. "She's a British doctor. How did someone who's British get interested in American baseball?" Fay paused for a moment. "You don't have to answer that if you don't want to."

"My wife is American," Marbach said with a small laugh. "She joined the British army early in the war. It wasn't till near the end of the war that American women could be doctors in their own army, so my wife joined the British army. They didn't waste any time putting her into their ranks as a doctor."

Fay shook his head. "Well, I'll be . . ."

Millican had known Pammy for the past two years. He lifted his glass. "Here's a toast to a grand woman. Here's to Dr. Pammy."

The three glasses chimed as they were brought together.

After the toast was completed, but before any drinking began Millican said to Marbach, "CIC wants help looking into a burglary that took place today. We need to get an investigation started real quick and we need for it to be kept totally secret."

"Ah . . . a burglary," Marbach said. His eyebrows lifted as though with anticipation at what he was about to hear.

"The burgled flat is over by the Café Neptune. Fay provided the address of the flat.

Marbach made a nodding motion with his head, behaved as though he was hearing the familiar address for the first time.

Millican said, "Some papers were taken. The occupant of the flat is an American scientist named Dr. Robert Shepherd. If the job was done by Viennese burglars, we'll be willing to pay a generous reward for a prompt return of the stolen papers."

"Is it possible the Russians did this burglary?" Marbach asked. He knew he had to ask that question. It was a logical question to ask.

"We're hoping they didn't," Millican said. "The thing is we've got to know if they did. And if there's any chance at all, we need to get the papers back. That's where you come in."

"Ah . . . yes." Marbach planted a look of deep concentration on his face.

Millican lit a cigarette and puffed aggressively. "We need help. Do you think you might be able to get those papers back for us?"

Marbach made a gesture with his hands that signified he was willing to help. "If the Russians didn't do it, maybe I can help. Please tell me what you think I need to know to get the job done."

For the next few minutes Millican and Fay related what they knew about burglary in Dr. Shepherd's flat. It wasn't much.

Finally, summing up, Fay said, "We really don't know a damned thing."

"Did your team talk to the other tenants?" Marbach asked.

"No. You'll be able to do that better than we could."

"How many flats in the building?"

"About twenty . . . I think."

Marbach spoke slowly as though in deep deliberation. "I'd like to use a trusted friend to help with the questioning. Some-one not connected with Vienna police, but a good man. A very trusted friend. Frankly, it is best to keep Vienna police as far away as possible from the flat. Whether or not the Russians did the burglary, they may be watching the place. It is best for the Vienna police to avoid trouble with the Russians."

"What about Rolf Hiller?" Millican asked. "He might be able to pass himself off as a bill collector or something."

Marbach shrugged. "As it happens, Rolf just got an assignment that requires him to be out of Vienna for a day or two."

"I'll trust your judgment about getting one of your non-police colleagues to help," Millican said. "Just be sure whoever you get understands that this has to be done fast, and, very important, it has to be kept secret."

"Yes," Marbach said, sounding like a man resigned to a burdensome chore. "There will be secrecy. The first thing to do is get my colleague into the flat so he can do some checking around. As for me, I'll busy myself checking some of those who have done burgling in that district in the past and I'll check people who occasionally handle goods supplied by burglars. I'll get started immediately. But to be clear on this, what exactly are we are looking for?"

"A notebook," said Millican. "The notebook is very important. Also any papers with Top Secret stamped on them. Actually, any papers taken from the flat are important for us to have."

"Scientific? And all this fuss. May I ask? Does this have anything to do with the conference that has begun here in Vienna? The conference on atomic energy?"

"Shepherd is involved in the conference, but he's not just here for the conference. He is officially assigned to Vienna."

"Is it possible we dealing with atomic secrets?"

Millican looked uncomfortable. "There's a lot of Top Secret stuff that doesn't deal with atomic energy. The important thing is that we need all the stolen papers back, especially those with Secret or Top Secret stamped on them."

"I will get started immediately," Marbach said.

"Money loosens tongues," said Millican. "Offer up to three thousand dollars in American script or cigarettes. That's per each individual you think might have something that ought to be part of the record. More if you think it might help us get something. Your own compensation will be three thousand dollars if you can pull our chestnuts out of the fire and maybe a thousand or so for your colleague."

"Three thousand American dollars? For me?"

"Unless you come up totally dry. I'm sorry, but if you don't come up with something, you'll be lucky if you end up with one package of cigarettes and I'll probably have to provide that out of my own pocket."

"Three thousand dollars is more than my yearly salary."

"If you get those papers back for us, you'll get at least that much, and more if I have anything to say about it. Frankly, friend, we're pretty desperate. But I say again it is vital to keep all of this secret. You and your colleague have to keep this under wraps. We are dealing only with you and your colleague. Do we have an understanding?"

"Yes," Marbach said. "We have an understanding. And I assure you that my colleague will honor our understanding. I guarantee that."

The conversation between the two Americans and Marbach continued. It lasted for another five minutes. Marbach felt it was best to ask standard police questions. He knew Millican was a former policeman and speculated that the other American might have been a former policeman, too.

CHAPTER FOURTEEN

W hile Marbach was talking with the two Americans
at the Café La Meynardie, in another part of
Vienna a man going by the name Friar Paul was
sitting in lonely vigil outside a room in the General Hospital.
Within that room was one patient, Father Anton.

In 1942, the one who now called himself Friar Paul was
Waffen SS Lieutenant Paul Neumayer and his father was
Colonel Count Neumayer, high level SS.

One of Lieutenant Paul Neumayer's assignments, while
he was serving the Waffen SS in France in 1942, had been
to check out what was going on in one of the Franciscan
monasteries. Performing his job with efficient competence,
he had identified three friars who were friendly with Britain.
When he turned in his report to the SS, the three friars
were bundled off to the terrible fate that awaited them in
Germany.

Two years later, in 1944, in the chaos that rose up
after the Allied invasion, the monastery was in ruins, but
Lieutenant Paul Neumayer managed to find a certificate
that, with a little manipulation, appeared to officially
identify him as a Franciscan friar.

By the time the war finally ended, he had become expert at passing himself off as one of countless friars doing service in France and Germany and Austria. Being a friar became his identity. Going from place to place in post-war Europe, he came to believe that if he wasn't Friar Paul he had no identity.

Now, in the Vienna General Hospital, using nervous hands, he fumbled with the rope belt tied around the middle of his brown Franciscan habit. He was trying to pray, but, to his distress, he couldn't. He wanted to pray for Father Anton. If there was anyone in the world for whom he ought to be able to pray, it was Father Anton, but he found it impossible to pray.

Consumed by wretchedness, he buried his head in his hands. He remembered how, with the help of Father Anton, for a short period of time he had gotten free of his feeling of terrible sinfulness, but now the sinful feeling was back, more engulfing than before.

Before encountering Father Anton, he had several times sought out priests to confess his sins. For the confessions, he had always identified himself as Friar Paul and he was careful which sins he confessed and what he told about himself.

Then, a couple of months ago, he encountered Father Anton, and, for some reason it hadn't been possible to lie to Father Anton. The sins were told, everything about himself was told. Father Anton conveyed understanding that the sins were terrible and therefore levied a heavy penance. But Father Anton also said that he understood it wasn't practical or safe, in this dangerous time and place, for a former SS officer to immediately separate from the pretense of being a friar.

The heavy penance imposed by Father Anton involved more than just prayer. There was a requirement to perform a considerable amount of charity work. Much of the charity work was done for Jewish people.

The important thing that Father Anton did was convey brotherly love to a pitiful sinner. He frequently spoke words for which the Franciscans were renowned. Those words brought hope that there might be grace for a sinner in a wicked and evil world. The words spoken by Father Anton had been committed to memory.

God himself loves you. That love is not dictated by logic or calculus. That love is available to you if you will but accept it. All you have to do is embrace God's love. You must find God's love within yourself and pass it on. You must pass God's love on to persons who are strangers to you.

At this moment, Paul Neumayer was repeating those words to himself.

Suddenly there was noise. The door to Father Anton's room was opening.

A nun came walking out.

"Brother Paul," the nun said, using the proper form of address to a friar.

"Yes." Paul Neumayer stood up. His wooden sandals made a loud clacking sound as he got to his feet.

The nun's voice was solicitous. "Brother Paul, you can go in and see the Reverend Father Anton now, but try not to tire him. The poor soul is very weak."

Paul Neumayer made a nodding motion and entered the room. His wooden sandals made an awkward clumping sound. He found Father Anton lying on a bed, looking sick and weak.

Father Anton said, "Come close to me."

Paul Neumayer approached the bed.

Father Anton said, "You look miserable."

Paul Neumayer slipped into a chair next to the bed.

Father Anton held out his hand and closed his eyes.

Paul Neumayer grasped the outstretched hand and listened intently as Father Anton looked at him with sadness while saying, "The thing called Odessa must be destroyed."

Paul Neumayer lowered his head. "I know that Odessa must be destroyed and I know that I must help destroy it. I have already pledged to you that I will do whatever I can to help destroy Odessa. I hold to that pledge."

"Have you contacted Police Inspector Marbach? He can help you deal with the Americans."

"No. I have had no contact with Police inspector Marbach. He despises me. Why shouldn't he despise me? He sees me as one of those who helped get a woman named Constanze Tandler killed."

"You and I have discussed this. From what you have told me it is clear that you had no part in getting Constanze Tandler killed."

"Everyone despises me. I failed . . ." Paul Neumayer's words trailed off for a moment. When he recovered, he said, "I am betraying many Franciscans."

Father Anton closed his eyes. "Odessa must be destroyed."

Paul Neumayer looked at Father Anton lying on the bed. He knew Father Anton had fought against National Socialism for many years.

Father Anton began praying the Hail Mary.

Paul Neumayer realized the Hail Mary was being prayed for him and he buried his tormented face in his hands.

Father Anton continued praying while opening his eyes and staring at the holy cross on the wall beyond the foot of his bed. Paul Neumayer followed the line of sight of Father Anton and joined in the prayer. He found that he was able to pray.

When Father Anton finished the Hail Mary, he said, "Promise me that you will go and see the police inspector, that you won't go anywhere until you have seen him." There was resolution in Father Anton's voice.

Paul Neumayer blessed himself and said, "I promise."

CHAPTER FIFTEEN

ate in the afternoon, Marbach headed for a building in the American-occupied zone of Vienna. As he approached the building, he stared up above the front door at a familiar sign reading MAX HARTMANN PRIVATE INVESTIGATOR. Under the sign were modest sized words: "Discrete Inquiries Treated With Discretion."

An elderly woman with a broom was sweeping the sidewalk.

"Grüss Gott, Frau Gerstecker," Marbach said.

"Grüss Gott, Herr Police Inspector." The conventional Viennese greeting was delivered by the woman in an angry voice, but that was to be expected. Frau Gerstecker was seldom in a friendly mood.

"Do you know if Herr Hartmann is in his office?" Marbach asked.

"That reprobate," came the reply. "You can't expect him to be in his office at a respectable hour after being out with one of his hussies all night. He is upstairs in his apartment."

"Do you know if he has company?" That was an important question to ask.

"If you mean one of his cheap women, the answer is no."

"I would like to see him."

"You know the way." After saying that, the woman aggressively returned her attention to her sweeping.

Marbach went through a door and up two flights of stairs to Max's apartment. He knocked on the door and when there was no response, he knocked louder. There was still no response, so he made use of his skeleton key.

The skeleton key unlocked the door and he entered Max's apartment. He walked into the bedroom and spent a few moments studying the man lying blissfully asleep in the bed. Finally, he shoved roughly. "Wake up, you reprobate. I've got work for you to do."

Max made a groaning sound, opened his eyes, and said, "Oh, Karl, leave me alone. Last night I was with a most wonderful and generous woman. Have mercy. I need rest now."

"Shame on you, Max. You don't understand anything about women. You just use them."

"The way I feel now," Max said, grinning sheepishly, "I am the one who was used." Max was nearly forty, somewhat small for a man who did detective work, but physically fit. In 1939, although born in Austria, Max had enlisted in the Polish army in order to join the best way he could in the fight against Hitler's army.

Marbach dragged the protesting Max out of bed, across the bedroom and into the bathroom. "Come on, scoundrel. A few minutes under that fine shower you always brag about and you should be ready to listen to me."

"Oh, no, Karl. Please—"

Marbach shoved Max under the shower and turned it on. He got a little wet, but Max got thoroughly soaked.

Afterward, while Max was getting into street clothes, Marbach explained that an American's flat had been burgled and he wanted Max to use discretion but find out as much as possible about had happened. This wasn't an unusual request for Marbach to make of Max, who for the past two years had been frequently employed to perform special chores for Vienna Kripo.

Very deliberately, Marbach didn't tell Max that he and Rolf did the burglary. He wanted to find out what Max would be able to learn. If Max wasn't able to figure out who did the burglary, it wasn't likely that anyone else could. Based on past experience, Marbach was confident his friend Max would check with him before conveying whatever he might learn to anyone else, but he made a point of explicitly telling Max to check with him before sharing anything he learned with anyone else.

After sending Max off to do his job, Marbach returned to police headquarters. He retrieved the notebook and papers taken from the American scientist from where he had hidden them inside his office safe and went to his desk. Even in these strange times, it wasn't likely that anyone would break into his office safe, and where else to hide the notebook and papers? He looked at what had been in the safe. It was important to find a quick way to get these things back to the Americans, and, at the same time, convince the Americans that ordinary burglars were the culprits. All of that would involve trickery, but it could be done.

Marbach set aside the notebook and fussed with the papers until he came to a report stating that Bishop Hudal had advised the Americans that sooner or later there was going to be a war between their country and the Russians and that National Socialist scientists—on one side or the other side—would likely tip the scale.

Marbach rubbed his jaw. He wondered if Nazi scientists were that important. Did they matter only a little, or might they be a determining factor as the conflict between American and Russia became more and more intense? These days it was a certainty that the conflict was going to keep getting more and more intense until . . .

Marbach cursed softly, took a breath and directed his attention to a Top Secret paper describing the CIC recruitment of a man named Klaus Barbie. The paper contained a clear statement that Barbie was the former Gestapo chief in Lyons, France and that he was wanted by the French as a war criminal. More important, the paper reported that Barbie was being recruited by CIC because he knew where Nazi scientists were hiding.

Marbach stared hard at what he was reading. It angered him that this Barbie character wasn't being held accountable for his foul deeds.

Marbach continued reading. He spotted a short paragraph describing the fate of one of Barbie's victims when he was Gestapo chief in Lyons:

> Barbie demanded that eighteen-year-old Hildegard Webler give him the names of her contacts in the resistance. When she kept silent, he ordered her to be undressed, and beaten. After she lost consciousness, he had her pushed into a barrel filled with water. When

she recovered, the torture session continued.
Hildegard Webler perished without giving up
the names of her friends.

Marbach closed his eyes, put aside the piece of paper
and said a silent prayer for Hildegard Webler.

CHAPTER SIXTEEN

Marbach got to his feet inside his office, returned the notebook and the pieces of paper to his office safe, picked up a package containing a bottle of Vybrovka, expensive Polish vodka, put the package under his arm, and left for dinner with Anna and Zbik.

It didn't take him long to get to the familiar building in the British Zone of Vienna. He entered by a rear door, walked up the stairway to the second floor, took a moment, shifted the package from one hand to the other and knocked on the apartment door.

"Who is out there?" shouted Zbik from inside the apartment.

"I am out here," Marbach shouted back.

Marbach had known Zbik for a long time. He knew Zbik's father had been one of the original three hundred—the celebrated Kadróka—those who had joined Marshal Józef Piłsudski in the Polish struggle against Russia. The three hundred of the Kadróka grew into a brigade and the brigade grew into the Polish Legion, fourteen thousand strong. Like other Jews who served in the Polish Legion, for Zbik's father it had always been of highest importance to keep faith with Pilsudski. In 1935, when Pilsudski died, Zbik's father was one of the honor guard at the funeral. A hundred Jewish delegations from all over Poland attended the Catholic funeral at Wawel Castle. On the living room wall of Zbik's apartment, beside a picture of Pilsudski, was a picture of the Rabbinate of Rovno who had given expression to his admiration for Pilsudski by asking that all Jewish boys born in Rovno during the month of May be named Józef in honor of the great Polish hero, Marshal Józef Pilsudski.

In 1939, Zbik's father perished in the fight against Hitler's army at Zagnanski Pass.

A few years later, Zbik's mother was put to death in the extermination camp at Sobibor.

Now, standing front of Zbik's apartment door, Marbach's thoughts about Zbik's father and mother were interrupted when the apartment door came open and Zbik stepped forward and eagerly took the hand extended to him. "Yidden Partisaner!" shouted Zbik.

Marbach smiled warmly. He liked being called "Yidden Partisaner" by Zbik. In 1944, Zbik had been the leader of a Jewish partisan unit that had accepted Marbach into its ranks, and Zbik was the one who had mischievously given him what he regarded as the high honor of being called "Yidden Partisaner".

Zbik took the package Marbach was holding in his free hand and withdrew the bottle. "You have brought Vybrovka. We shall have excellent conversation tonight while drinking Vybrovka."

"Yes," said Marbach.

"Anna!" Zbik called out. "A big, ugly man is here to see you. He has brought excellent Polish vodka, so, to be fair, we shall have to feed him."

Anna came out of the kitchen with five-year-old Piotr trotting behind her. The youngster spotted Marbach and gave out a peal of joy.

Marbach grinned at Piotr, then kissed Anna several times on her precious injured face, a beautiful face that had been badly damaged during the war. He stopped only when Zbik, laughing with tears in his eyes, asked if he might be permitted to kiss his own wife.

While Zbik and Anna kissed, Piotr hollered for attention. The young boy wanted to "touch the ceiling" in the living room.

Marbach enthusiastically grabbed Piotr and thrust the small boy high over his head. The ceiling was not very high. There were already many handprints on it, but there was still a lot of space to put more. Helping Piotr make handprints on the ceiling was a ritual that took place whenever Marbach came to visit. It was a ritual playfully encouraged by Zbik and reluctantly tolerated by Anna.

Piotr's hands were dirty, as usual, and the dark marks he made on the ceiling were vivid to see. The boy shouted with triumph.

But there was only a little time to admire the handiwork made on the ceiling. Dinner was ready. It had been prepared by Zbik. On occasions like this, Anna tolerated Zbik taking charge of the kitchen. Her only contribution was to open a bottle of wine.

The meal prepared by Zbik began with chlodnik, a delicious cold soup made of cream, beets, cucumbers and tripe. There were nuggets of chicken in the chlodnik.

After the chlodnik was eaten, little Piotr solemnly lifted his glass of milk and spoke the traditional Polish toast. "Na Zdrowie."

"Na Zdrowie," echoed the three adults, raising glasses of wine.

When it was time to return to eating, Zbik served bigos, a stew with cabbage in it along with small portions of meat.

Additional "Na Zdrowie" toasts were made at various times until the meal was finished.

After pushing away his emptied plate, Zbik reminisced about "The Old Doctor," Janusz Korczak. Zbik talked about a radio tribute done when the great Pilsudski died back in 1935.

"On that radio tribute, 'The Old Doctor' told everyone that even if some said Polish heroes were not supposed to cry, the courageous Pilsudski had cried at times, thereby demonstrating that sometimes it is manly to cry. I shall always be grateful to 'The Old Doctor' for saying it was all right to cry for Pilsudski. Because of him, I will always believe that it is sometimes all right for a man to cry."

Anna stared proudly at her husband, then said to her son, "Piotr, recite for Herr Police Inspector Marbach the statement of children's rights set forth by Janusz Korczak."

Excitedly, five-year-old Piotr began:

The child has the right to be loved.
The child has the right to be respected.

The child has the right to be appreciated.
The child has the right to make mistakes.
The child has the right to have opinions.
The child has the right to protest injustice.
The child . . . has . . .

Piotr shut his eyes. He couldn't remember what came next.

To cover what could have become a painful silence, Zbik began clapping loudly. "Soon," he said to his son in an encouraging voice, "you will be able to recite all the children's rights proclaimed by a great Jewish gentleman who in 1942 showed his love for children by leading two hundred Jewish orphans under his responsibility to the Nazi horror of Treblinka, where he shared with them their fate unto death."

A few minutes later, Piotr reluctantly trundled off to bed and Marbach's bottle of Vybrovka was brought out. The three good friends sat together in the tiny living room drinking the excellent Polish vodka and talking. The talk was in Polish, a language that Berlin-born Anna spoke with excellence. Marbach's Polish was good, but he wasn't as fluent as Anna.

"I am glad Piotr is learning the old doctor's principles," Zbik said. "It does me good to hear them."

"Yes, it is good that Piotr is learning the old doctor's list of children's rights," Anna said. "And, as his mother, it is good for me to hear them, know them . . . I need to be totally aware of those very important words."

After a few moments of silence, Zbik inquired about Pammy and the trip to Paris.

Marbach talked about his wife for a few minutes, but he had something else on his mind. Finally, he came out with it. "I hope the two of you are not really planning to go back to Poland any time soon."

"I won't have Anna or Piotr going to Poland with the Communists so powerful now," Zbik said. "But my place is there. I am a union member. My place is with my union brothers in Poland."

"Most Jews don't feel the way you do," Marbach said, speaking tentatively. This was a touchy subject. Press reports out of Poland were saying that six thousand textile workers were striking and that sympathy stoppages elsewhere had brought the total number of textile strikers to at least forty thousand. It was a strike by workers against a government dominated by Communists.

Zbik stirred angrily in his chair before beginning an angry tirade against the Communist government that was exploiting workers as badly as any capitalist government ever exploited workers.

Marbach let Zbik vent his anger. When Zbik finally quieted down, Marbach said, "Since the end of the war, the only choice in Poland has been between terrorists on the right and a different sort of awfulness on the left. In the middle, as always, are the masses of people who just want a decent life."

Anna made her contribution in a strident voice. "How can the American government be indifferent to the hatred the Poles have for the Germans? Every Pole has lost at least one family member or close friend to the Nazis. No country in Europe was more ravaged by the war. It would not be human if the Poles didn't have anger toward Germans." She paused. "I, a Berliner, say this."

Both men stared at Anna as she continued. "So what happens? Poles go hungry while the Americans send enough food to Germany so that every single German gets at least one thousand eight hundred calories a day. That's the figure: one thousand eight hundred. It's in the newspapers."

Marbach rubbed his hand across his face. The Americans were feeding the Germans in the U.S. Zone of Germany, making sure the Germans were getting at least eighteen hundred calories a day and they didn't appear to be at all concerned about the Poles averaging several hundred calories a day."

Anna declared angrily, "Do the Americans feel they have to occupy a country in order to feed hungry people? I am a German, but I say Poland suffered countless times more than Germany in the war that Germany started. And now the plunderers are treated generously while Poles go hungry. It is wrong. It is terribly wrong . . . *it is wrong.*" Anna's face was flushed as she repeated the words "It is wrong" again and again.

Zbik stared hopelessly around the room before saying, "Two years ago, the monster of National Socialism was destroyed . . . and now the monster of Communism is taking its place."

Anna slammed her emptied glass onto a table. "What the Americans are doing is bad humanity and bad politics. The Poles still see Germany as a threat to them. The only country that says it is ready to protect Poland from Germany is Soviet Russia. The American policy operates as though Americans want to turn Poles into Communists."

A somber mood descended on the three people gathered together in the modest apartment. Finally, Marbach decided it was nearly time for him to go. But, resolved to leave Zbik and Anna in a happy mood, he got up from his chair and retrieved a concertina almost hidden among some of Piotr's toys. Then he began walking around the room, working the concertina, trying to get the tune he was striving for. He kept trying, tried and tried, but the tune wouldn't come.

Anna smiled indulgently as she got up from her chair and took the concertina from Marbach. She quickly began playing a lively mazurka, Polish music in triple meter, but that was only to get started. She knew the song Marbach had been striving for and the mazurka had been used by her to set the mood. Now, with a triumphant thrust of her head, she began the *Pierwsza Brygada*, the song of the first brigade, the Pilsudski march song.

Zbik and Marbach jumped to their feet and began shouting in Polish. They shouted their way through the song.

Anna was not pleased hearing the men shout their way through the song. When they finished shouting the song she stared at them with intimidating disappointment. Then, with a vigorous tossing thrust of her head, she resolutely challenged them to sing the song, not shout it. Once again she began playing the familiar tune.

Zbik and Marbach picked up on what was expected of them. They sang. No more shouting. They marched around in the small apartment and sang:

> The Legions stand for a soldier's pride.
> The Legions stand for a martyr's fate.

The Legions stand for a beggar's song.
The Legions stand for a desperado's death.
We are the First Brigade. A regiment of
rapid fire. We've put our lives at
stake. We've willed our fate. We've
cast ourselves on the pyre.

The two men paused only to empty their glasses of Vybrovka before doing more marching and singing.

Finally, Zbik, with tears streaming down his face, picked up his glass, filled it with Vybrovka and spoke words made famous by Marshal Pilsudski: "To be defeated and not to yield is victory."

Marbach echoed the toast, but spoke it in its entirety: "To be defeated and not to yield is victory. To win and to rest on laurels is defeat."

There was more marching, drinking and singing until Marbach finally said it was time for him to leave. Standing at the door, he reminded Anna and Zbik that they were expected to come to dinner with Pammy and him on Sunday. Then he shook Zbik's hand, kissed Anna's precious injured face, and left.

On the way home to his lonely house, Marbach mumbled Pilsudski's words: To be defeated and not to yield is victory. He didn't add the words that followed. It had been a long time since there had been any chance to rest on laurels.

CHAPTER SEVENTEEN

T he next morning, while Marbach was tending to police business in Vienna, in Freistadt, a small town in north-central Austria, Police Detective Rolf Hiller was behaving like a police detective interested in the theft of farm animals. He poked around the town, asked some of the town people a few questions, got useless answers, and finally made his way to a tavern that, in addition to being an eating and drinking place, provided guest rooms for visitors.

Inside the tavern, he went to a desk where he rented one of the guest rooms, then he went to an alcove where there were four tables. Three of the tables were small and had no one sitting at them. One table was large. There were a half dozen farmers sitting around the large table drinking. Their glasses were filled with the delicious Austrian cider called Most.

Marbach calculated that possibly these farmers might know something about Dr. Emhardt. If so, that would have to be drawn out carefully.

Marbach was figuring how he might introduce himself to the farmers when one of them took note of him and waved him over. He walked up to the large table, identified himself, and explained he was looking into the theft of farm animals.

He was invited to sit down. An empty glass was found, and he drank Most while listening to the farmers express their concern about the theft of farm animals. They wanted to have action taken against DPs—displaced persons. They blamed the DPs for the theft of poultry, pigs and other livestock.

"The DPs must be kept away from here," one farmer declared angrily. "If they are permitted to remain around here my family will go hungry this winter."

Another farmer reached over and grabbed onto Rolf's arm. He said, "As you can see, we are not prosperous men. Last winter brought the most terrible cold weather and snow any of us has ever seen. If the weather this coming winter is that bad some of us will perish. The DPs must be dealt with."

"Have you caught any of them?" Rolf asked, making it clear his question was directed to all the farmers at the table.

"Of course, we catch them," said a farmer who had not yet spoken. "We beat on them, but then we have to turn them over to the soldiers and more DPs take their place. I caught one young DP a few weeks ago. I beat on him with my staff until his head swelled up like a melon. I thought he was going to die. I allowed him to crawl away. But last week he was back. I caught him again. The very same man."

Rolf didn't ask what had happened to the DP the second time he had been caught.

"There'll be famine this winter," the oldest of the farmers declared. "Everyone knows that. We have to protect our families. I hope we can survive."

"I was born on a farm," Rolf said. "I understand." He told himself it was a terrible thing—farmers facing famine in coming months. But the DPs were starving, suffering terribly. What was the answer? He wondered about that: what, indeed, was the answer?

"Something must be done about the DPs," one of the farmers said with desperation in his voice. "It's them or us."

"If the Americans love these DPs so much, let them feed them," another farmer said. "I have one of those DPs tied up in my barn, a young girl, but big enough to try to steal one of my sheep."

"I can take her off your hands," Rolf said, unsure why he said that.

"Turn her over to the Russians," the oldest of the farmers said. "Don't give her to the Americans. The Russians know how to handle her kind. She'll get what she deserves from them."

"I will take charge of the DP," Rolf said.

CHAPTER EIGHTEEN

Rolf picked up the DP. She was young, a Slav, spoke Slovak, a language Rolf was able to understand because of its similarity to the Polish he had managed to learn serving with Poles during the war. The DP said her name was Bozidara Adamovicia. Rolf knew that the name Bozidara meant "Divine gift of God." He couldn't help thinking that this unhappy fräulein, probably no more than eighteen years old, with a dirt-stained face and confused eyes, didn't have the appearance of any sort of gift.

After bidding farewell to the farmer who had captured the fräulein, Rolf took Bozidara with him and went to find American soldiers. He didn't want to turn this fräulein over to the Russians.

It didn't take Rolf long to find a group of American soldiers. "Can you take this fräulein off my hands?" he asked a young American lieutenant.

"No," the American lieutenant said. "Let the Russians have her."

"I'd like to give her a chance."

"Well, I can't take her. Maybe our guys in Linz can help you. Those guys can pretty much do as they please."

Rolf knew that the only thing to do, other than give up Bozidara to whatever awful fate might await her with the Russians, was to take her to Linz. He couldn't make himself indifferent to her fate even if it meant the search for Dr. Emhardt was going to have to be put on hold.

Linz was not far away, only about fifty kilometers, but it was necessary to take a bus. When Rolf and Bozidara got inside the bus station, they found out that the bus schedule called for several stops. The round-trip journey would take three hours. To take that much time troubled Rolf, but he knew that he was committed. He bought tickets for Bozidara and himself and, ten minutes later, the bus trip to Linz began.

Some of the bus passengers regarded Bozidara with hostility. Rolf was distressed when remarks were loudly made about a Slovak being on the bus with respectable folk. He delivered glances of irritation, but that did nothing to stop the hostile remarks. Focusing his attention on Bozidara, he tried to engage her in friendly small talk, but the unhappy fräulein indicated with a weak hand movement that she had nothing to say.

When the bus finally arrived in Linz, Rolf pushed a package containing two unsmoked cigarettes into a pocket on Bozidara's skirt. She looked at him with expressionless eyes while they walked together a few paces to the inspection area where some soldiers and a sergeant were standing.

Rolf passed through the inspection quickly, but Bozidara didn't. "Hey, Mac," the American sergeant said to a corporal. "Look what I found in this one's pocket. Two cigarettes." He grinned an expressive grin as he shoved the cigarettes into his own pocket. "Spoils of war," the American sergeant declared triumphantly. "You won't need these where you're going, sweetie." He rubbed his hand on Bozidara's flat chest. "You ain't got no tits, sweetie. We don't need sweeties who ain't got no tits. The Russkies can have you."

"Can't you Americans take her?" Rolf asked in the best English he could muster.

"She don't belong to us," the American sergeant said.

"Who's in charge here?" Rolf asked.

"I'm in charge," the American sergeant said. "And I say the Russkies can have this titless wonder."

"I'd like to see her not end up in Russian hands," Rolf said, conscious of the futility of his words.

"You ain't got no vote." With those words, the matter was settled. The American sergeant waved his arm at some nearby Russian soldiers and beckoned for them to come over.

Rolf watched helplessly as Bozidara was passed from American control to Russian control. He started to walk away, had taken a few steps, when he heard a sweet-sounding Slovak voice filled with emotion.

It was Bozidara. Her richly Slavic voice called out, "Thank you, Mr. Policeman. I know you tried to help me."

The words affected Rolf deeply. He raised his hand in a gesture of farewell.

The American sergeant spotted the interchange and made a vulgar remark. Rolf stared at the American sergeant and then at the retreating figure of Bozidara. He raised his hand, but Bozidara had her head lowered as a Russian soldier began leading her to whatever sad fate awaited. Rolf let his hand drop limply to his side.

The American sergeant made an obscene gesture with his finger toward Rolf and called to the other American soldiers to join him in laughter.

In the odd way that things sometimes happen, the laughter of the American soldiers caught the attention of Bozidara. She raised her head and fixed her eyes on Rolf. He lifted his arm again. This time he kept it raised.

With eyes no longer expressionless, Bozidara conveyed acknowledgement of Rolf's farewell gesture with a vigorous wave of her arm.

Rolf watched Bozidara disappear. Why do people do ill to such a person? he wondered. Why do so many people find it easy to hurt someone like Bozidara? Is it because it is easier to hurt, or, at the least, cast disdain, than it is to look . . . see . . . feel . . . recognize . . . connect?

CHAPTER NINETEEN

Rolf caught a bus back to Freistadt. It was painful for him to think about Bozidara, but he couldn't manage to put her out of his mind. Late in the evening, he got off the bus in Freistadt and went directly to the drinking alcove in the tavern. He sat at a table, ordered a pitcher of Most, and indicated he had no objection when three farmers came over from one of the other tables and asked if they could sit with him. They were different farmers from the ones he had sat with a few hours ago.

The three farmers were congenial while they complained about DPs and asked questions about what might be able to be done about the theft of farm animals. Rolf muttered innocuous replies.

When the conversation at the table seemed to be exhausted, Rolf asked in a matter-of-fact voice if he was the only stranger in Freistadt.

"A somewhat odd character is staying right here in this tavern," said one of the farmers. "He is renting a room upstairs."

The other two farmers quickly agreed that the man was, indeed, an odd character.

"He is a professional man," the first farmer said.

"He has a lot of money," one of the other farmers said.

The first farmer examined his glass of Most as though searching for an answer before saying, "He's a Berliner."

"From his accent, a Berliner," observed another farmer.

"He writes numbers on pieces of paper," mused the third farmer.

"Probably a businessman," the first farmer said.

"He keeps getting telephone calls from Vienna," one of the other two farmers said.

Rolf clasped his hands around his glass. He wondered, was the man they were talking about Dr. Emhardt?

As tends to happen with idle conversation, the subject shifted and the three farmers began talking about kidnappings being done by Russians.

"The Americans do nothing about the kidnappings," one of the farmers said in a complaining voice. "And the British and the French also do nothing. The Russians take anyone they want. Workers with skills they need, businessmen, good-looking women, fräuleins . . . anyone they want."

One of the other farmers made an angry gesture with his hands. "We heard on the radio that an American was taken from the Inner City in Vienna. The Americans can't even protect their own. If they can't protect their own, how can we count on them to protect us?"

Rolf listened as the three farmers continued talking about the American kidnapped in Vienna, a story that had attracted a lot of attention throughout Austria. Like most good stories that go through a lot of repetition, it had become highly exagger-ated.

Finally, speaking in as mild a voice as he could muster, Rolf offered a correction to what was being said. "That case of the American who was kidnapped ended before it got started. The Russians returned the man a few hours later. They even apologized. They know they can't kidnap an American citizen."

"But it was in the Inner City," one of the farmers said with exasperation. "The Russians took an American from the Inner City into the Soviet Zone and questioned him." With indignation, the farmer raised his voice. "And the Americans let them get away with that sort of thing!"

The other two farmers nodded agreement. All three of the farmers were convinced that the incident had sinister implications.

Rolf raised both hands to indicate he was not in a position to comment further on the case.

"We understand," one of the farmers said.

At that point, the conversation at the table shifted to humorous subjects, foolish talk of no importance.

Everyone was laughing when a fräulein, one who was obviously still in her teens came by and stood at the entrance to the alcove.

"That is Fräulein Kiridus," one of the farmers said. "She will sing if we make it worth her while."

Another farmer added for the benefit of Rolf, "She needs help. She has a child. Two years ago, a local boy who has now gone on his way took her for his pleasure and she ended up with an unwanted child."

After entering the alcove, the fräulein stood in front of the table where Rolf and the three farmers were sitting and began singing. In a fetching voice, she sang old Austrian songs and only occasionally had difficulties with the melodies. While she sang, additional details about her were discretely provided to Rolf by the three farmers: her father was killed in the war; her mother was very sick; her family had a farm, but it was likely her family would soon lose the farm.

While the fräulein sang, one of the farmers found an empty plate and placed an almost totally smoked cigarette on it. These were hard times for the farmers, but the young fräulein was in need and her singing was pleasant. Each of the other two farmers contributed a small amount of tobacco. When it came his turn, Rolf generously pitched one good-sized cigarette butt onto the plate.

The young fräulein continued singing. She began a familiar lullaby:

> Are you asleep, Miriam—Miriam, my child.
> We are but a shore, and deep in us flows
> blood from those past to those who will come.
> All are within us! Who feels alone?
> You are their life—and their life is yours.
> Miriam, my life, my child, go to sleep.

Moved by the song, Rolf pitched another cigarette butt, somewhat larger than the first, onto the plate.

Before there was time for the song to be completed, there was an interruption. A telephone hanging on the wall gave out with a jangling sound. It jangled twice, then stopped. A few moments later, a well-dressed man of middle age entered the alcove and fussed with the telephone. Finally, he dialed a number. He looked like a perfectly ordinary man. For Rolf, the important thing was that he wasn't Dr. Emhardt, didn't match Dr. Emhardt's description in the vaguest way.

But a few moments later when the man concluded a telephone call, he passed within a few feet of Rolf's table and recognition hit with full force. In 1938, in Vienna, the man who had just walked past had been in charge of the Jewish emigration office for the SS. And after that . . .

"Excuse me, gentlemen," Rolf said to the three farmers sitting at the table with him. "That man who just passed the table looks like someone I knew in Vienna before the war. I just can't think of his name. Do any of you know it?"

"That's Herr Otto Henninger," one of the farmers said. "He's a businessman of some sort. He is carrying on with Fräulein Kiridus. I hope he is giving her money. He is too old to be a husband for her. Thankfully, he won't be here long. I hear he is planning to go to Innsbruck."

One of the other farmers nodded agreement.

Pretending that the identity of the man was of only minor importance, Rolf emptied his glass. "This is excellent Most. Will you gentlemen join me in another glass?"

The glasses were filled. There was no toast, but the four glasses were carefully touched together. While he drank, Rolf kept his face expressionless. The man who had just made use of the telephone had been head of Section IV B4 in the Reich Central Security Office. He was the ultimate office manager, an executioner who rarely visited the camps or other places of human destruction under his authority. He was the one who had coined the term "the final solution," the one who had directed with administrative impersonality the murder of millions.

The one calling himself Otto Henninger was *Adolf Eichmann.*

CHAPTER TWENTY

While Rolf was pondering the implications of having spotted Adolf Eichmann in Freistadt, at police headquarters in Vienna Karl Marbach took time from a report he was working on to telephone Private Investigator Max Hartmann.

After indulging conventional amenities, Marbach went to the purpose of his call. "Did you learn anything yet?"

"I haven't had much time. It would be better for you to ask me that question tomorrow."

"What time tomorrow?"

"Ten o'clock. We can have mid-morning breakfast."

"Usual place?"

"Yes. And let us have no misunderstanding. You will pay for what I eat."

"Agreed. I'll see you then."

After hanging up the telephone, Marbach reviewed his situation. It was impossible for him to tell from the sound of Max's voice what, if anything, had been learned about the burglary of the American scientist's flat. If Max had found out who did the burglary, hopefully it would be possible to fix things so that no one else would be able to do the same.

Marbach sat silently at his desk for a moment, then picked up his telephone again and got himself connected to Captain Millican. The conversation was kept short.

"I know you are anxious for a meeting," Marbach said.

"You bet."

"I'd like more time." Marbach didn't need any time, but he felt he would be in better control of this thing if he waited a couple of days before having a meeting with the Americans and giving them their secret documents. If they got assurance right now that they were going to get their stuff back, but that it would take a day or two, this whole piece of business might make more sense to them and they might be less aggressive about demanding all the messy details. On the other hand, giving them everything today could very easily set in motion intimidating demands for every single detail about the burglars.

"We ought to talk," said Captain Millican.

"I know how important this is for you, but I'd really like some more time."

"I have people to report to. My boss, Colonel Crider, for one."

"If it is understood I can protect my source, you can tell your superiors that you will have the stolen documents back real quick. The Russians had nothing to do with the burglary."

"That sounds great, pal."

"I am certain that if we meet the day after tomorrow at noon I will be able to give you each and every scrap of those stolen papers."

"That's great. Usual place?"
"Yes."
"Can I bring my boss?"
"Of course."
"See you."

CHAPTER TWENTY-ONE

M eanwhile, back in Freistadt, for more than half an
hour Rolf had been sitting with the three farmers,
drinking Most and pretending to be attentive to
idle conversation while all the time thinking about what he
would do when the one who was Adolf Eichmann showed
his face again. He knew that Eichmann was in an upstairs
room and would have to walk through the alcove in order
to leave the tavern.

"You'll see," Rolf heard one of the three farmers say, "The
Bolsheviks will soon have total power in Europe. Greece is
already lost. Nothing can stop the Bolsheviks there. Italy
will be next and then France. It won't take more than a year
for Communism to gobble up all of Europe."

The other two farmers nodded rueful agreement. One
of them stuffed a cigarette in his mouth and said, "We'll
have a bad winter. This time there'll be famine. Democracy
doesn't work! When faced with loads of trouble people will
choose to be ruled by those who can make things work. I
used to think National Socialism was the answer. Maybe it
was and maybe it wasn't, but that doesn't matter now. Most

certainly, the masses are going to turn to Communism if only to get enough to eat."

Rolf didn't want to get into a disagreement, so he made his voice sound tentative as he mentioned the massive new aid program proposed by the American whose name was George Marshall.

One of the farmers spoke in a dismissive voice. "The Marshall Plan will never work. I wish it would. I hate the Communists, but the naive Americans made a terrible mistake by asking the European countries to get agreement among themselves about how to divide up the aid. That shows how foolish the Americans are. Such foolishness. There'll never be agreement. A few months from now there'll be no more Marshall Plan."

Before Rolf could reply Fräulein Kiridus emerged from wherever she had gone to and walked past the table toward the exit door. She solemnly passed a quiet greeting.

Close behind Fräulein Kiridus was Adolf Eichmann. He passed no greeting, simply followed the young fräulein out the door. He seemed like just another middle-aged man going out with a fräulein.

"Fräulein Kiridus is a good kid," one of the farmers said. "I hate to see her get tangled up with a man who can't do her any good. How much money is he giving her? I'll wager it isn't much. She needs a young man who will help her take care of her child. It will be better for her when that man leaves Freistadt."

Rolf stood up. "Well, gentlemen, it's time for me to go. I need to walk around a bit before going to bed. I hope we will meet again sometime. I have enjoyed the good company you have shared with me."

The farmers bade farewell and Rolf quickly left the tavern. In the darkened street up ahead, he saw Eichmann and Fräulein Kiridus. He followed at a discrete distance, careful not to be spotted. He was debating the pros and cons of rushing forward and seizing Eichmann when suddenly it was too late. Eichmann and Fräulein Kiridus arrived at a modest-looking house with a battered green roof and quickly went inside.

For Rolf there was nothing to do but take up a position across the road from the house. He quickly found a place behind a flat-board fence where he could keep himself concealed while watching the house and planning what to do next.

He waited while lights went on in one room after another, continued waiting until the lights began going off again until only a bedroom light was on. Finally, the bedroom light went out.

He lit a cigarette and pulled out his weapon, a half-loaded Enfield revolver. Under Allied regulations, Austrian police were permitted to carry only one kind of weapon, the British issue Enfield, a not entirely reliable handgun. Under Allied regulations, it was forbidden for individual Austrian police officers, absent someone in authority giving the order, to load all six chambers of the Enfield revolver. Without explicit permission, only three chambers could contain shells.

To hell with Allied regulations, Rolf thought as he reached into his pocket, withdrew three contraband bullets and filled the three empty chambers of the Enfield.

He stared at his weapon and reviewed the situation. He might leave this place where he was waiting and search for the American Army in Freistadt. Once he found the Americans, he could identify himself as a Vienna police detective and solicit their assistance in a raid on the house.

That thought was tempting, but the temptation was rejected. Even if the Americans could be quickly found, they might require authorization from some higher level authority before coming with him. And even if everything worked out for the best, how long would it take? Indeed, how much time?

Rolf was not inclined to take any chances. Inside the house was a man whose name was synonymous with Nazi evil. Adolf Eichmann was an evil man responsible for the deaths of countless people.

Rolf prepared himself to go into the house. Hopefully, he would capture Eichmann. If he wasn't able to capture Eichmann, he was determined to kill him. Hopefully, Eichmann and Fräulein Kiridus were the only ones in the house. If not, so be it.

CHAPTER TWENTY-TWO

Rolf finished smoking a cigarette in his hiding place behind the flat-board fence, crushed out the cigarette, put the butt in his jacket, took off the jacket, and laid it across his right arm. He was ready to go inside the house after Eichmann. Once inside the house, he could use the jacket to partly muffle the sound of a shot if it became necessary for him to do any shooting.

Rolf tried to imagine what the inside of the house would be like. He was certain he wouldn't have any trouble getting past a locked front door. If there was a dog in the house, he would kill it as quietly as possible. After that, if anything unexpected happened, and the unexpected could always happen, he would make his way as quickly as possible to the upstairs bedroom to make sure Eichmann didn't escape. With any luck, he wouldn't have to kill anyone—or even hurt anyone. The vulner-ability of the young fräulein who had made herself available to Eichmann was vivid to him.

As Rolf thought about Fräulein Kiridus, he found himself thinking about another fräulein: the Slovak fräulein named Bozidara. But he knew this wasn't the time to think about anything except the business at hand: the capture or the killing of Adolf Eichmann. If it was possible to do a capture, he would march Adolf Eichmann—dressed or undressed—back in the direction of the tavern. Two blocks beyond the tavern was the U.S. Army command post in Freistadt.

Just as Rolf was getting ready to leave his hiding place and start toward the house, he heard something that stopped him cold. Far down the dirt road, an automobile was approaching, proceeding at a modest speed on the darkened road. He snuggled back behind the flat-board fence and waited.

The automobile came to a halt in front of the house. One man got out of the car and went up to the porch of the house.

Rolf stared hard as the man got onto the porch and turned around. There was enough moonlight to identify the man. The face was familiar. It belonged to Stephan Kaas. Even after a lot of years, it was still possible for Rolf to recognize Stephan Kaas, the Berliner who, back in 1938, had come down from Berlin to be chief of Vienna Kripo.

Rolf was trying to figure out what was going on when he heard the sound of a second car coming down the darkened road in the opposite direction from the first car. It came to a halt directly across the road from the first car. A man got out, but didn't approach the first car, just stood posted like a guard.

Rolf stared into the empty darkness behind himself and charted an escape route. He needed to know where he might run if flight became necessary. He had just about sorted things out when the front door to the house opened and two figures came out onto the porch. Not a man and a fräulein, but two men. One of them Eichmann. No sign of the young fräulein. She had remained in the house. That was good. Inside the house was the safest place for her.

Rolf peered closely at the second man. It was possible to match the second man with pictures and other descriptive information. The second man was Dr. Emhardt, the despicable Dr. Emhardt. Rolf watched while both men shook hands formally with Stephan Kaas. There was talk among the three men on the porch. Most of the talk Rolf couldn't hear very clearly, but in the cool night air, he was able to distinguish the word "Innsbruck" spoken not once but twice.

Rolf fixed the sight of his Enfield revolver on one man, then the next, and then on the third. There was no way to do a capture. Killing was necessary. If the Enfield did its job, it was close to a certainty that one man would be killed. After that, there was a good chance of being able to kill a second man. With a little luck, possibly all three would be killed.

The thing to do was decide which one to shoot first. But which one most deserved to be killed? The only real choice was between the despicable Dr. Emhardt and the reprehensible Adolf Eichmann. Rolf made his decision quickly. Personal consid-erations made their claim. Dr. Emhardt would be the first target.

Rolf tested the flat-board fence before quietly settling his weapon on it. Taking his time, he aimed the Enfield at Dr. Emhardt and slowly tightened his finger on the trigger. He held his breath, took careful aim, and pulled the trigger.

The hammer of the Enfield clapped down with a sharp, metallic click.

No discharge.

Only a metallic clicking sound. A sound loud enough to be heard all the way to the house.

Nothing but a loud, betraying click.

Rolf pulled the trigger again.

There was another loud metallic click.

With impotent rage, one final attempt was made to fire the weapon, but again there was only the metallic click.

No discharge.

Just the loud clicking sound.

An automobile horn made an idiotic bleating noise, while off in the distance a dog began barking loudly.

Rolf stared helplessly, watched the two cars fill up with men. He saw Kaas wait a moment, look around, pull out a pistol, and fire several times in the general direction of the flat-board fence. One round landed close, but Kaas was only guessing where to shoot.

Automobile engines were racing. After a loud slamming of car doors, the two vehicles took off in opposite directions. Lights were going on in nearby houses.

Rolf slammed his fist hard against the flat-board fence. For an instant he came close to pitching the Enfield revolver away, but he knew that would be stupid. The weapon could be traced to him and who likes answering a lot of questions?

He considered showing himself on the road. He could go to the road and wait for the U.S. Army or the Freistadt police to show up. But he rejected that idea. Instead, he walked quickly but carefully to the rear of the lot, went across a road and trotted down a gully.

A few minutes later, he was far away from the scene of what he regarded as his failure.

When he got to his room in the tavern, he threw the Enfield onto the bed, then washed his face and began shaving. While shaving, he examined his situation. Aggressively enforced police procedure required him to check out at the Freistadt police station before leaving this area and there was an idiotic requirement that the checkout could only be done during day time. It would create serious problems if he didn't wait until tomorrow morning to check out, but it was imperative that Karl Marbach be quickly informed what was going on.

So, what to do? Using a telephone wasn't a viable option. Even a call from the Freistadt police office wasn't safe. Any call made from the police office to police headquarters in Vienna would attract attention. Any call made from any Freistadt phone would be hazardous, yet there was important detailed info that needed to be quickly communicated. Forget the telephone, the best way to handle this was to write out a brief one page report, find someone to promptly carry it to Vienna and place it in the hands of Karl Marbach. The police inspector wouldn't get the message until tomorrow morning, but that would be soon enough. Yes, a written message was a better way to handle this than using a telephone.

Rolf wrote out a detailed report on a piece of paper, put it in an envelope, and pulled a hair from his head which he placed under the seal of the envelope. Placing a hair under the seal of an envelope was something he and Karl Marbach sometimes did so that the one receiving an envelope could be reasonably sure nobody had tampered with it. It was a certainty that this was one of those times Karl Marbach would look for a hair.

Rolf spent an hour wandering around the town. Who to use as the messenger? He didn't like the idea of using one of the Freistadt police officers, but maybe that was the only thing to do.

While walking in the general direction of the police building, he encountered some people sleeping at the temporary bus station. Among them was a young Hungarian fräulein with a small child, a little boy. Taking his time, he introduced himself to the fräulein, talked with her for several minutes. Her ability to speak German was passable.

Finally, he said to the Hungarian fräulein, "I will pay you to get on the bus, go to Vienna, and deliver this envelope tomorrow morning to the Vienna police. I will give you payment in addition to paying the cost of bus tickets for you and your little boy."

"I want a legitimate identification card," the Hungarian fräulein said. She was a DP. The identification card would mean more safety for her and her child than she had known for a long time.

"I can promise that you will get an identification card," Rolf said. He could make that promise and know it was a promise that Karl Marbach would keep for him.

"Then I will deliver your envelope to Vienna police," the Hungarian fräulein said.

"I put trust in you," Rolf said.

"I already said what I would do."

"I will take you to the bus station."

"You will pay for the bus tickets."

"Yes."

Rolf hoped this fräulein would do what she promised. It was clearly in her best interest to do so.

There wasn't time to waste. Rolf gave the fräulein the sealed envelope, then found an extra piece of paper, wrote on it what he had promised in exchange for delivery of the envelope and handed the piece of paper to the woman.

He spoke slowly and deliberately. "Keep the envelope out of sight. That piece of paper says I have promised you an identification card. The piece of paper doesn't have my name or Police Inspector Karl Marbach's name on it, but if you deliver the envelope to Police Inspector Karl Marbach early tomorrow morning when he comes to work and show him the piece of paper, he will honor my promise."

"Police Inspector Karl Marbach," the Hungarian fräulein said, then silently repeated the name. She added: "I will deliver the envelope early tomorrow morning."

"Yes. Don't forget the name. And don't share what I have given you with anyone but Police Inspector Karl Marbach. Not even with another Vienna police officer. That is an absolute requirement. If you share the piece of paper or the envelope with anyone but Police Inspector Karl Marbach, you will get nothing. No identification card. Nothing. Do you understand?"

"I understand." The fräulein said. "Only Police Inspector Karl Marbach."

Rolf took the fräulein and her child to the bus station and bought their bus tickets. Before handing the tickets to the woman, he asked one more time, "To whom do you deliver the piece of paper and the envelope?"

"Police Inspector Karl Marbach."

"Good."

"God bless you."

"Are you sure you will be able to find the police head-quarters building?"

"Yes."

"Give what I have provided you only to Police Inspector Karl Marbach and I promise that you will get your identification card."

"God bless you."

Rolf returned the blessing. Then turned around and walked at a fast pace to his room at the tavern.

Inside his room, it was late and he was exhausted, but he spent an hour tearing the Enfield revolver apart trying to determine why it had failed him. He used a coin to remove the large screw at the front of the trigger guard, removed the cylinder, and then removed various springs and rods. Fussing and cursing, he put the weapon back together again. Maybe it would fire now, maybe not, but it was all he had and heavy fatigue was overwhelming him. He stretched out on the bed fully dressed and fell into a troubled sleep. After a short time, he woke up. Then he fell asleep again and began dreaming. In a dream he found himself walking with the Hungarian fräulein. Not like they were lovers, but like he was an older brother. Then, in the odd way that dreams work, he was walking with the young Slovak fräulein he'd last seen being led away by a Russian soldier. In the dream it was like he was a trusted older brother. Very clearly in the dream the young Slovak fräulein told him about an exciting dance she was going to attend in the company of a marvelous young man. It was a good dream.

CHAPTER TWENTY-THREE

In Vienna early the next morning, when Police Inspector Marbach arrived at police headquarters he found a young Hungarian fräulein waiting for him outside his office. She was holding a small child in one arm. Using her other arm, she pushed forward a piece of paper and an envelope. She had an anxious look on her face.

After telling the fräulein to come into his office and inviting her to sit down, Marbach sat at his desk and read the piece of paper. It stated what Rolf wanted done for the Hungarian fräulein. Without comment, Marbach put the piece of paper off to the side and examined the outside of the envelope. He saw that there was a small intact hair. Reasonably sure no one had tampered with the contents of the envelope from the time it had been sealed, he opened the envelope and read Rolf's report. In convoluted language, with no recognizable names, but with prolonged sentences containing descriptive information, the report conveyed to Marbach that Dr. Emhardt had been in Freistadt yesterday. That wasn't surprising. The important news was that Adolf Eichmann and Stephan Kaas were in Freistadt with Dr. Emhardt and that the three men would be quickly on their way to Innsbruck. Convoluted language and no recognizable names, but for Marbach there was no doubt about what was contained in Rolf's report.

Marbach turned his attention to the place on the piece of paper that specified an obligation owed to the Hungarian fräulein.

He said to the Hungarian fräulein, "You will get what you were promised."

"I . . . I thank you, Herr Police Inspector."

"I thank you for delivering this envelope. I will promptly see about getting you an identification card."

"Oh . . . please. If you can do that . . ." The young Hungarian fräulein began weeping and quickly the child started crying. Marbach stood up, went around his desk, retrieved the child from the fräulein's arms, held him up in the air and started laughing. "Soon, little boy, you will be needing an identification card yourself, but right now we have to get one for your mother." As Marbach continued laughing, the child's crying sounds became laughter.

Carrying the laughing child, who clasped him tight around his neck, Marbach lead the young fräulein to an office where her identification card would be created.

While information for the card was being collected, Marbach doted over the child and provided encouragement to the young mother.

A short time later, the desperately needed identification card—an identification card partly fiction but officially certified as legal—was ready be given to the Hungarian fräulein. Marbach gave the Hungarian fräulein the identification card and then went to his office to make himself ready for his mid-morning breakfast meeting with Private Investigator Max Hartmann.

When ready, Marbach left police headquarters, walked to the nearest tram stop and caught a tram that took him to a tram stop across the street from a café. He got off the tram, did a discrete check to be certain he hadn't been followed, then went inside the café. He immediately spotted Max, went to the table where Max was sitting and sat down.

The mid-morning breakfast began.

"Have some of this awful-tasting ersatz coffee," Max said.

Marbach sipped ersatz (imitation) coffee while noting ruefully that, as usual, Max was looking dapper.

"I thought I might be late for this meeting," Max said in a cheerful voice. "I had a hell of a time shaking off some Russians."

"You were followed by Russians?"

"I'm sure of it. The Russians were watching the flat when I showed up to do my business." Max wrinkled his brow as he drank more of the ersatz coffee. "Oh, this is bad. This coffee is just awful."

"Either drink the coffee or leave it be," Marbach said. "Aside from attracting the attention of the Russians, did you accomplish anything?"

"Well, I can tell you the Russians didn't do the burglary."

"Get on with it."

Max didn't waste any time. "You did the burglary, Herr Police Inspector. You and Rolf. Now . . . really, you should have told me that when you asked me to do this little job for you."

Marbach shrugged. "I needed to find out if I'm in trouble."

Max rolled his eyes up toward the ceiling, then grinned wickedly. "Don't worry. I was able to cover things up."

"Is it totally covered up?"

"I took care of things."

"Are you sure?"

"I wouldn't say it was covered up if it wasn't."

"Good."

"Tell me," Max said in a teasing voice, "How much do you and Rolf make pulling off these petty burglaries? I know a nice little jewelry store you might want to burglarize. It's over in the French Zone."

Marbach suffered the tease gracefully.

Max asked a reasonable question. "Are you going to tell me what this little adventure of yours is all about?"

"Before I fill you in on what is involved here, tell me how you found out Rolf and I did the burglary."

Max grinned. "One of the old ladies in the building gave descriptions that helped me identify you and Rolf. She was impressed by the wide gap between Rolf's front teeth and she provided a pretty good description of you. I also talked with her husband and a few of her friends in and out of the building. I impressed upon everyone I talked to that if the Americans or the Russians ask them questions, they should be careful not to make themselves too interesting. I pointed out what everyone knows these days: that the Americans and Russians can be bothersome pests. The important thing is that I promised a generous reward if no tales are told to the Russians or Americans for two weeks. When I pay that reward—"

Marbach interrupted. "I understand. You can count on me for the money you'll need. Now, just for my own interest, tell me the whole thing. The details you haven't yet told me."

"All right. I will give you the benefit of my years of experience doing detective work. Please listen closely. Maybe you'll learn how a real detective does his job."

Max delivered a loud sigh before continuing. "I talked with many people in the building. A total of three people are the only ones who know anything that might be helpful to the Americans or the Russians. The others in the building are very separate from the three who have a financial interest with me. The others know only silly, unimportant things. To several of these others I told some nonsense that they will be passing on to the Russians, probably the Americans, as well. The Russians and Americans will go crazy chasing false leads. Many of the false leads trace to Vienna police. Of course, none of the leads trace to you."

Marbach stated what both of them knew. "The Russians might make trouble for you. If not them, then the Americans."

"I am prepared."

"I imagine you are. Anyway, not for the first time in our association, I am impressed by how you have handled things."

"There's something else I found out that you ought to know. Actually, it's kind of amusing."

"Go ahead."

"The Americans have made a lot of use of that flat. Before Dr. Shepherd, the American men occupying the flat frequently brought in guests, but always just men. Never any women or fräuleins. What else would the tenants think? They're convinced it's a hangout for a bunch of homosexual Americans."

Max laughed uninhibitedly as he continued. "One of the women tenants described a recent visitor who fits your description. I asked a lot of questions to be sure about this. When the tenant told me the date that visit took place, I knew it couldn't be you. Anyway, she said it was terrible for a man who looks so respectable to be having sex with other men."

Marbach shook his head, tried to keep from laughing, but the effort was futile. There were men highly respected by both Max and him who were homosexuals, but neither of them could keep from laughing at this bit of humor.

For a few moments, there was a sharing of laughter, but even while he was laughing Marbach began thinking about the identity of the man described as looking like him. He and Stephan Kaas looked a lot alike, but he decided there was no point exploring that now with Max.

As the laughter died down, Marbach asked, "So, old friend, there is one more thing I want to hear about. Did you go inside the flat?"

"Yes, but there was nothing to find. American soldiers had cleaned everything up." Max paused for a moment. "I had one very good piece of luck."

"Tell me."

"One of the ladies in the building provided me some very helpful information. She takes care of the laundry for those who need their laundry done. It seems that Dr. Shepherd used to leave scraps of papers with telephone numbers in the pockets of some of his shirts she washed. There were other things in his shirt pockets, but the telephone numbers are what is important. For her own reasons, which are no concern of mine, the woman kept some of those scraps of paper."

With a satisfied look on his face, Max took a piece of paper from inside the pocket of his suit coat, handed it to Marbach and said, "As you can see, the name the name on that piece of paper is Heinrich Hoth and the telephone number is a Freistadt exchange. I made a telephone call to Freistadt. I got hold of a helpful telephone operator and she went out of her way to check telephone records for me. I'll have to look up that woman someday. She sounded like a most appealing woman."

"Get on with it."

"Don't be impatient. Well . . . the agreeable telephone operator told me that her records showed that most of the calls Heinrich Hoth made were to Vienna, but several were made to someone named Natasha Yakovlevna in a hotel in Bratislava."

"Natasha Yakovlevna . . . who is she?"

"In good time. In good time."

It was obvious Max was building up to something and Marbach realized that the only thing for him to do was let Max tell the story in his own way, at his own pace.

"This woman is traveling with Russian papers, very likely using her own name."

"Unless she's working for the Russians," Marbach said.

"She isn't. I checked her name out. Part of being a detective is knowing when to check names. I ran up a small telephone bill, but I learned that Natasha Yakovlevna is a Russian woman married to Dr. Heinrich Hoth."

"Who is Dr. Heinrich Hoth?"

Max answered with a touch of condescension. "Dr. Heinrich Hoth is Dr. Heinrich Emhardt and Natasha Yakovlevna is his wife."

"Dr. Emhardt must be brought to justice," Marbach said.

Max pursed his lips together. "Find Frau Emhardt or Natasha Yakovlevna, whatever name she is using. Find her and you will have a trail to Dr. Emhardt."

Marbach pushed his uneaten meal to the side and placed his tightly clenched fists on the table.

"You take this personally because you're thinking about Charlotte," Max said, referencing a name from both of their pasts.

"Don't you take this personally?"

"I take what happened to Charlotte very personally."

Neither man spoke for a few moments. They were both thinking about Charlotte, a shy, beautiful young Polish woman who'd had promise as a scientist. At different times, both Marbach and Max had loved her. She had yielded her favors to neither of them, but they had both loved her. Charlotte had remained a friend to each of them after the brief, unconsummated love affairs were over. After the Anschluss she fled Vienna, went to Poland, and ended up joining with the Poles in the fight against Nazism. In 1943, she was captured and sent to the Dora concentration camp where men and women worked twelve, fourteen hours a day—sometimes around the clock. Charlotte was assigned to Mittelbau, a place of special horror in the hell of the Dora camp. Dr. Heinrich Emhardt was the one who set the work schedules for Mittelbau. Nine months after entering the Dora camp, Charlotte was worked to death, one of the countless persons sacrificed at Mittelbau because of work schedules ordered by Dr. Emhardt.

Marbach took a moment to recall personal memories of Charlotte. When ready, he said, "Dr. Emhardt has a very valuable skill as an atomic scientist."

"Just a year or so ago," Max said, "I'd have been confident that if they ever caught him, the Americans would bring him to justice. Now, I'm not so sure. Maybe that isn't fair to the Americans, but it's the way I feel."

"Maybe Natasha Yakovlevna is working with the Russians to bring her husband, Dr. Emhardt, into their fold," Marbach said.

"No, if she was working with the Russians, she wouldn't be trying so hard to hide from them."

"Are they looking for her?"

"There's no question about it. I checked the Soviet call-up lists. The Russians are looking for Natasha Yakovlevna and for any woman with the last name of Emhardt. It's one of the call-up orders that calls for violence if the person doesn't yield quickly."

Marbach took a breath. "Tomorrow I have a meeting with the Americans. I'll see what I can find out from them without giving anything away."

"Whatever happens I won't tolerate not being included in the chase after that bastard Emhardt."

"Do you care about Eichmann?"

"I hope Eichmann goes to hell, but the one I really hate is Dr. Emhardt."

"There is a new Nazi escape route called Odessa."

"I'd like to see all Nazi escape routes totally destroyed."

"Skorzeny and others are committed to this new escape route. It is a way for them to save Nazi comrades. They think it is a way to bring the return of National Socialism to Germany."

"I want in on the chase."

"All right, you're included in the chase. Just be sure I can find you when the chase gets started."

"When will that be?"

"I'll know better after my meeting with the Americans tomorrow. I hope to get started right after that meeting."

Max said, "My telephone is answered twenty-four hours a day. I have women who handle my telephone calls for me. I make of point of letting them know how to promptly contact me. I'll be keeping in especially close touch tomorrow. You won't have any trouble letting me know when and where the chase will get started."

CHAPTER TWENTY-FOUR

After leaving Max, Marbach returned to police headquarters where a large quantity of paperwork demanded his attention. Late in the afternoon, after he had just finished signing an unimportant piece of paper, his office telephone began making its characteristic clanging sound.

"Police Inspector Marbach," he said into the telephone mouthpiece.

"This is Anna."

Marbach was delighted hearing Anna on the line. He grabbed tight to the telephone. "It's grand to hear your voice."

"I tried to call you two hours ago."

"You should have left a message."

"There wasn't time. I had to go to the train station. Oh, you beast. I should leave you in ignorance, but I won't. Pammy is back."

"Pammy is back? For certain?"

"For certain. I took her from the train station to your home."

"I didn't expect her back this soon."

"The Paris meeting was terrible, but that was good because it gave Pammy an excuse to come back early."

"Is she really home?"

"Yes and she's with a man."

Marbach laughed. "I trust the man is better looking than me."

"He is a British colonel and, yes, he is definitely better looking than you."

Laughing loudly, Marbach bade Anna goodbye, hung up the telephone, left police headquarters, and hailed a taxicab.

Ten minutes later, after paying his taxi fare, he stood in front of his house. The lights in the house were shining brightly. Through the living room window he could see Pammy walking back and forth in front of Colonel Larkswood, who was sitting in the comfortable guest chair.

Marbach went inside the house, and, ignoring the British officer, drew his wife into a strong embrace that lasted until a droll voice said in English, "You'd think Pammy never took one of these short trips before."

Pammy pushed free from the tight embrace. Then, making a point of speaking English, she said, "Whatever is the matter with you, Karl? Please . . . we have company."

"I'll have a drink," Marbach said, also speaking English.

"How have you been?" Colonel Larkswood said, nursing his glass of brandy.

While Pammy went to fetch a drink for him, Marbach settled into the chair in his house that was reserved for him alone and, with calculation, made what he intended to sound like a casual observation. "I hear an American scientist got burglarized." He carefully monitored the British officer's reaction.

Colonel Larkswood cocked his head. "Oh? You heard about that? Well, it was sloppy stuff."

"Is there anything you can tell me?"

"Are Vienna police working on the case?" An anxious look appeared on the British colonel's face. "Eh . . . don't answer that. The plain and simple truth is that I can't talk with you about the burglary."

Pammy returned with glasses of whiskey and soda for Marbach and herself. Marbach reached out his hand and took one of the glasses. He was disappointed when Pammy didn't touch his hand with her fingers, like she often did.

Pammy planted herself comfortably in a chair opposite the two men.

Marbach stared at the drink in his hand, took a moment, and said, "What an impossible world it is when a civilized Viennese man has to drink a barbaric American drink just to keep peace with his wife."

Laughing softly, Pammy said to Colonel Larkswood, "I tried to get Karl to drink Tom Collins. That was a failure. It's a major victory to get him to drink whiskey and soda. Left to himself, he would just drink kummel, his damned schnapps."

"Tom Collins," mused Colonel Larkswood. "Tom Collins is, most definitely, a barbaric drink."

"You are both peasants." Pammy stared with calculated imperiousness. "Tom Collins is a civilized drink."

"See what I have to put up with," Marbach said.

"Well . . ." Colonel Larkswood didn't complete his thought.

"I didn't spot your broken-down British buzz-wagon anywhere nearby," Marbach said. "How did you get over here?"

"The British buzz-wagon is not a broken-down vehicle," Colonel Larkswood said defensively.

"*British* buzz-wagon. So you say!" Pammy exclaimed, empha-sizing the word *British*. She continued: "The buzz-wagon used by British forces is an American vehicle. It's an eight hundred weight Chevrolet."

Mischievously, Marbach said, "It is difficult to believe that the famous British buzz-wagon is just an American vehicle."

All three of them knew that the British buzz-wagon was an American Chevrolet, but it was fun to exchange humor. They joined together in a sharing of additional humorous topics until Colonel Larkswood indicated with a weary wave of his hand that it was time for him to depart. He'd done his duty keeping Pammy company until Marbach got home.

Marbach accompanied the colonel to the door.

Pammy walked up close to the two men. "Where are you going now?" she asked. It was obvious she wanted to hear the British officer say he was going to see Sophie.

"A British brigadier is flying in at midnight tonight," Colonel Larkswood said. "I promised to gather some of our chaps and give him a proper greeting at the Officers' Club."

There was an awkward silence. It was obvious Colonel Larkswood was not going to be taking Sophie. The British Officers' Club was in the Kinsky Palace and it was prohibited for British officers to take Austrian fräuleins there, no matter how wonderful the fräulein might be.

Pammy didn't hide her anger. "Sophie is coming here on Sunday for dinner. I don't know if I am going to invite you."

"I hope you will," Colonel Larkswood said, looking properly contrite.

"Oh, blast!" said Pammy. "You're invited, but only if you give me a call tomorrow at the hospital. We have to talk about you and Sophie."

Smiling weakly, the colonel slipped through the door.

After the door closed behind the colonel, Marbach walked around inside his house, conscious of Pammy watching him. He took his time looking at unopened mail that had accumulated in the dish placed in front of the stairs leading up to the second floor. There was nothing of interest to him in the mail. He smiled when Pammy walked up behind him, put her hands firmly against his back and started shoving him up the stairs toward their bedroom.

CHAPTER TWENTY-FIVE

T he next morning, Marbach and Pammy were sitting together at their dining room table. Marbach was thinking how lovely Pammy looked eating her favorite breakfast.

Finally, she looked up and stared back at him. He grinned while shifting his attention to the box of Ralston cereal sitting on the table beside her dish.

"Why don't you eat bacon and eggs like other Americans?" he asked playfully. As usual, the conversation was in English.

"Those of us who are *straight shooters* eat our hot Ralston," Pammy said, plunging her spoon deep into the bowl of heated cereal. She enjoyed characterizing herself as a Tom Mix "straight shooter." She was a big Tom Mix fan. Tom Mix had been dead for several years, but his films still routinely played in the Vienna movie houses and a Tom Mix 15-minute radio program sponsored by Hot Ralston cereal was broadcast each weekday by the U.S. Armed Forces Network in Europe.

Pammy enjoyed making spoofing comparisons between Tom Mix and her police inspector husband. Tom Mix, she liked to say, was quicker catching desperadoes than was the police inspector. Tom Mix got the job done in less than an hour and a half in the films and on the radio he was even quicker.

Planted in his chair at the dining room table, Marbach stared at Pammy while her spoof continued with details about how slow he was compared to Tom Mix. When she finished, they got up from the table and walked together into the kitchen. It was almost time to go to work—her to the hospital, him to police headquarters.

Above the kitchen stove was a picture of Tom Mix and surrounding the picture of Tom Mix were Pammy's other heroes: the Army football player Glenn Davis, the Brooklyn Dodger Jackie Robinson, the scientist Albert Einstein and David Ben-Gurion, the chairman of the Jewish Agency for Palestine.

Marbach put his hand on Pammy's shoulder. "There's a new Clark Gable film playing at the movie house. We might see it, if you'd like. It's all about a newspaper man who takes on the Japanese early in the war."

"That's an old film," Pammy said, placing her hand on top of Marbach's. "I'd like to see something I haven't already seen before—or, if not, then one of the Tom Mix films."

"To hell with Tom Mix."

"Don't blaspheme."

"I apologize."

There was laughter between them. When the laughing was done, Pammy drew Marbach into her arms. "I already saw the Clark Gable film, but there's a new western at the kino by the tram stop called *My Darling Clementine*. Why don't we see it? You like American westerns—except the ones with Tom Mix."

"Clementine," Marbach said slowly, enjoying the sound of the unfamiliar name. He moved his hand very tentatively down to the small of Pammy's back. "I'll give you a back rub when I get home from work," he said. "Then we'll go see the movie about Clementine."

Marbach was glad when Pammy let herself be held for several minutes before he finally left for work.

CHAPTER TWENTY-SIX

After getting his morning office work done, Marbach went to a café deep within the American Zone for his noon meeting with CIC. Inside the café, he spotted Millican sitting at a table with Sergeant Fay and a man Marbach didn't recognize. All three Americans were in civilian clothes. On the table in front of the three Americans were glasses of beer.

When Marbach got to the table, Millican and Fay stood up and ritual handshaking took place. The man with Millican and Fay remained seated, extended his hand while leaning across the table. "I'm Colonel Ralph Crider. Very glad to meet you. I'd like to have English spoken during this meeting"

Marbach performed a quick handshake with the seated colonel, then sat down between Millican and Fay.

The colonel asked Marbach, "Do you want anything to eat? Do you want a drink?"

"I'll have a beer," Marbach said in the required English. He discretely surveyed the people sitting at various tables in the café, quickly identifying a man at a nearby table who was a professional informer who sold his services to the highest bidder. He wondered if the man was working for the Americans. Of course, he might be working for the French or the British. Possibly he was working for the Soviet. It was conceivable that the man was working for everyone at the same time: the Americans, the French, the British, and the Soviet.

"Beer is what we're drinking," Colonel Crider said. "It's Austrian beer. Austrian beer makes American beer taste like piss water."

"What did you learn about the burglary?" Millican asked Marbach.

"It wasn't the Communists. Just a couple of small-time burglars," Marbach said. He never liked to lie, but consoled himself with the thought that this was one of those times when lying was necessary.

"Give us their names," Colonel Crider said. "We'll take it from here. We know how to deal with burglars."

"A colleague who doesn't work for Vienna police cleared up the case for me," Marbach said, making a point of looking deeply concerned. He continued, "My colleague had to make some promises to get back what was stolen. I was told that was the important thing: get back what was stolen. My colleague promised anonymity to those who helped get back what was stolen. He also wants anonymity for himself. And he wants payment for what he has done."

"We'll pay," Colonel Crider said. "But give us your friend's name. We'll protect his anonymity, but it's better if we handle the rest of this."

"I cannot give you my colleague's name without first getting his permission," Marbach said.

"Why no names?" Colonel Crider asked suspiciously. "Your guy can go to work for us. A permanent job—money in his pocket."

"A lot of Viennese don't want to work for the Americans," Marbach said, deliberately putting a measure of uneasiness in his voice. "Things become difficult for people who want to live peacefully in this city if the Russians find out that they are friendly with Americans. Family and friends are also put in jeopardy. In this case the burglars are very young. They misbehaved, but it won't happen again. My colleague is insistent on protecting his own anonymity and that of the two very young men. He very much wants to avoid complications. If it is necessary to compromise anonymity, I need to discuss the situation with my colleague. On the other hand, if there is urgency in getting back what was stolen—"

"There is urgency," interjected Colonel Crider.

Marbach said, "If it is possible to not compromise anonymity, what was stolen will be returned to you within a couple of hours. You'll get back everything, absolutely everything that was taken. But the first thing to get settled is the business of anonymity."

"Anonymity is all right with me," said Colonel Crider.

Marbach said, "If there is anonymity, we next need to settle on the amount my colleague will receive for his services. It isn't too much, but you may want to negotiate. He wants eight cartons of cigarettes."

That was a generous payment.

Colonel Crider leaned forward eagerly. "Your colleague can have his damned cigarettes if we get the papers in two hours."

"That can be done if I am able to tell him I will provide the eight cartons of cigarettes today, tomorrow at the latest."

"Give him the damn cigarettes. He can have the cigarettes as long as all of Dr. Shepherd's papers are delivered in two hours."

Marbach said, "If we have agreement, I think it is safe to say you can have the papers no later than two hours from right this minute."

Colonel Crider didn't waste any time. "You got a deal."

Marbach quickly finished what remained of his glass of beer, stood up and said, "You men have important things to talk about and I have work to do. I better get started if I'm going to get Dr. Shepherd's papers to you in two hours."

"Good," said Colonel Crider.

"Take care, pal," Millican said.

There were no farewell handshakes.

Marbach left the café with a sense of relief. If necessary he was prepared to use a couple of very young Viennese burglars who would be able to effectively pretend they had committed the theft, but hopefully that wasn't going to be necessary. If the Americans changed their mind, became assertive about identifying the people involved in this case, that problem would be dealt with at some later time.

CHAPTER TWENTY-SEVEN

Marbach returned to his office, collected the stolen documents, deposited them in a cardboard box that couldn't be traced and called into his office a tough jail inmate with whom he had a long connection. The inmate was instructed that he wouldn't have to return to jail if he acted like an anonymous messenger, delivered the cardboard box to the Americans and avoided any entanglement with the Americans. Marbach emphasized that as soon as the delivery was made the inmate should telephone him from a public telephone booth.

The inmate left and Marbach waited patiently in his office He waited until he received the telephone call affirming that a successful delivery had been made and the Americans hadn't even asked the inmate his name. After that, feeling restless, Marbach left his office and went to the burn center where Pammy worked.

He walked down a familiar hallway, looked inside a room where there were children who had been badly burned during the war. Some of the children had lost limbs.

As always, seeing the damaged children was painful for Marbach. He turned away, continued down the hallway until he got to the ward where the adults were being treated. He went inside, walked from bed to bed, sometimes passing greetings to those he recognized from past visits, or who were patients who looked like they wanted a greeting.

He was talking to one of the patients when Pammy came by the ward. She was pressed for time. She had an operation to perform, but there were few minutes to spare. She stared at Marbach, who was unaware of her presence. He was sitting at the bedside of one of the many burned soldiers, a man with no hands.

While Pammy watched, Marbach took hold of an arm that looked like a lobster craw and talked to the patient about something that seemed to have the man's total attention.

Pammy remained silently watching until it looked like Marbach was getting ready to leave. At that point, she quickly left the area, went to the room where she would be performing an operation. In the operating room, while waiting for the patient to be delivered, she wondered about discussing with her husband what she'd seen him doing. Yes, she finally decided, they would talk about it, but she wouldn't press him too much if he didn't want to talk with specificity.

CHAPTER TWENTY-EIGHT

I n the baroque palace within the fourth district of Vienna, MGB Major Gorshkov was sitting at his desk. Three hours ago, there had been a telephone call on the secret Soviet line between him, a relatively unimportant major in MGB, and Comrade Lavrenti Beria, the third most powerful man in the Soviet Union.

Even now, three hours later, Gorshkov was in a state of exhilaration. It was the first time the third most powerful man in the Soviet had spoken to him. During the conversation, there had been no bullying, no intimidation. They had spoken together over the telephone with an understanding grounded in a common ethnic tradition: they were both born in the land of the Soviet called Georgia. At Comrade Beria's invitation, they had communicated as one Georgian to another about the importance of capturing the Nazi scientist, Dr. Heinrich Emhardt. Comrade Beria had explicitly referred to their mutual Georgian heritage of fearless courage, heroic honesty, raw determination, fierce loyalty and awareness that the greatest rewards go only to those who are audacious.

The private telephone conversation had ended with the immortal words *"Our cause is just."* Those powerful words spoken by all good comrades during the war had recently lost their fervor for Gorshkov. But not any longer. Now the words *"Our cause is just"* were once again filled with great feeling and profound meaning.

Gorshkov affirmed to himself that he would never fail the Soviet and he would never fail Comrade Beria. He was going to do whatever was necessary to capture Dr. Emhardt. That creature properly belonged in Comrade Beria's Sukhumi installation, where, willingly or unwillingly, along with other foreign scientists, he would help build atomic bombs for the Soviet. That was what the great Comrade Beria wanted and that was the way it was going to be.

Gorshkov focused on what Comrade Beria had emphasized during the telephone conversation: the best way to find Dr. Emhardt was to capture the woman identified as Natasha Yakovlevna, who actually was the wife of Dr. Emhardt. Comrade Beria had disclosed what he knew about Natasha Yakovlevna's history. During most of the war, keeping her original family name, Natasha Yakovlevna had lived in the Leningrad. In recent months, she had moved, without attracting MGB attention, first to Poland and then to Bratislava, the Czech city on the border with Austria. By that time the chase after the Nazi physicist had resulted in MGB file checks that surfaced information about the Russian wife, but before action could be taken Natasha Yakovlevna had left Bratislava, crossed the border into Austria and vanished into emptiness.

As he sat at his desk, Gorshkov reviewed the situation. Even before the telephone call from Comrade Beria, just doing his job for MGB, he had learned that more than twenty Russian police and large numbers of the army were scouring Vienna searching for Natasha Yakovlevna. The frightening thing was that that the capitalist forces of America, England, and France, were engaged in an aggressive search for Natasha Yakovlevna in Vienna and elsewhere in Austria.

Gorshkov put a cigarette in his mouth and lit it. Had the Americans already found Natasha Yakovlevna? Had they already brought her into their web of capitalist deceit and treachery? More important, did they already have Dr. Emhardt? Those questions had no answers.

To get answers, immediately after the telephone call with Comrade Beria, Gorshkov had assigned one of the most resourceful of all the MGB agents under his command— Sergeant Dotnara Petrova—to learn what she could and deliver a report in no more than three hours. The time was almost up.

While Gorshkov puffed on his cigarette, the buzzer on his desk rang. It was Sergeant Petrova. She never missed a deadline.

Gorshkov gave the signal for Sergeant Petrova to be admitted, but avoided watching as she approached his desk. He didn't want her to realize how attractive he knew her to be.

"Comrade Major," Petrova said, delivering a crisp salute.

"Sit down, Comrade Sergeant," Gorshkov said, keeping his eyes lowered while returning the salute. He would give anything to have Petrova available to him as a woman.

Petrova sat down and crisply delivered a report covering the burglary and related matters. Her conclusion came at the end of her report: "Of one thing I am reasonably certain, Police Inspector Marbach could give us a lot of answers. He is deeply involved with the American CIC. If the Americans have Dr. Emhardt, or if they have Natasha Yakovlevna, Police Inspector Marbach probably knows about it."

Gorshkov got up from his desk chair and walked to the window. "So we pick up the police inspector and make him talk."

Petrova waited patiently to hear what would come next.

Gorshkov asked, "What do we know about this Police Inspector Marbach?"

"His wife is British," said Petrova.

"British? Are you sure? I thought someone said she is American."

"No. She is a major in the British army. She is a doctor at the British burn center."

Gorshkov accepted what sounded sensible to him. He had one question. "What about the woman . . . the woman named Anna mentioned in your report? What can you tell me about her?"

Petrova took a moment before replying. "Frau Anna Peszkowski lives with her son and her husband. Her husband is Polish. He is a Jew. She was an actress before the war. She was badly burned on her face and parts of her body during the war. The police inspector and his wife are close friends with Anna Peszkowski and her family."

Gorshkov said, "We can't just hope that fate is with us. If we want to catch Dr. Emhardt, we have to make our own fate."

"Yes, Comrade Major. We will pick up Anna Peszkowski."

"Good. As for Police Inspector Marbach, we can make up a charge later, but the important thing is that I want him in my hands before this day is over."

"Today?"

"I want you to head an MGB team and capture the one named Police Inspector Marbach. I want that done today."

"How many agents will I have?"

"I've got eight extra MGB agents you can have. I'll also give you some soldiers to back them up. I want Police Inspector Marbach brought to me alive. We can't touch his British wife, but this Anna Peszkowski has no immunity. Pick her up. The police inspector will tell us what we want to know or he will be responsible for what will happen to the woman named Anna Peszkowski."

"Yes, Comrade Major," Petrova said. She leaned across the desk and said with infectious enthusiasm, "Our cause is just. I will be worthy of our cause."

Gorshkov, conscious of Petrova's marvelous bosom, felt an unbidden emotion.

Petrova stood up and stretched herself into an erect posture. "I will capture the police inspector and I will also bring you the woman named Anna Peszkowski."

"There is danger for you in doing what I have ordered you to do. You could lose your neck if this thing fouls up. The Soviet will be intolerant of failure. I'm almost sorry I brought you into this."

Petrova didn't reply; she stood gallantly at attention.

Gorshkov wondered if there could be any woman in the world as marvelous to look at as Petrova. He said, "Whatever you do and however you do it, I pledge my bond to you."

Petrova saluted smartly.

Gorshkov told himself he would be willing to do anything to get Petrova to be with him in a man-woman way. But he didn't know if she favored him that way. One thing was certain, he would never in any way force his presence upon her. He wistfully watched Petrova leave his office.

CHAPTER TWENTY-NINE

L ate in the afternoon, Police Inspector Marbach walked up to where Private Detective Max Hartmann was standing across the street from the Hotel Jupiter. They didn't exchange a greeting. For a few moments they simply stood silently side-by-side.

Max had sent Marbach a message saying that the Russian woman named Natasha Yakovlevna was staying in the Hotel Jupiter.

"How did you find Dr. Emhardt's wife?" Marbach asked.

"It is what is called doing detective work."

"Where is she?"

"In the hotel."

Marbach looked around. "I will stand watch with you."

"You look like a bum," said Max.

"I don't need to be fancied up to go on a watch with you. Certainly not this watch. This isn't like those cases you spec-ialize in where it is important to look dapper while collecting evidence that disrupts the lives of people who are merely seeking a little love."

"I don't take cases like that anymore. Not very many, anyway."

"You mean you turn some of those cases down?"

"Go to the devil."

"Why be mean and snarly?"

"Because I need to go pee. I'm going to take a long, luxurious pee. I shall get more physical gratification from that pee than you have gotten from the most passionate love making you have experienced in your entire life."

Marbach laughed and made a dismissive motion with his hand before asking, "Are you certain Natasha Yakovlevna is in this hotel?"

"Of course. My guess is she won't be coming out for a while."

"I'll stand watch alone for a few minutes while you get yourself gratified. If the woman comes out, I'll take a quick peep inside that café over there where you'll be going to have your pee. It won't be difficult to enlist someone to drag you out of the toilet while I follow the woman. You will be able to catch up with me."

Max shrugged while turning away. Playing the clown, he walked with exaggerated stiffness to the nearby café. After getting inside, he soon completed the errand that had occasioned his visit, but when that was done he decided to take his time before returning to where Marbach was waiting. Most of the tables in the café were unoccupied. He planted himself at one of the empty tables and ordered a cup of coffee. Not ersatz coffee, but real coffee.

It was dark inside the café, but Max didn't care. He was enjoying his coffee. More than that, he was enjoying the thought of Karl Marbach waiting for him, wondering what was taking so long.

Max looked up when a young fräulein came over to his table. Her voice was filled with uncertainty. "Do you want a little company?"

Max looked at the fresh young face camouflaged under heavy make-up and garish red lipstick.

"I'm just having a cup of coffee."

"I arrived in Vienna this morning. I haven't done this work before. This is my first day working here. I was told to come over and see . . . see if you would buy me a drink."

"Sit down. Eh . . ."

"Christine."

"Max."

"Hello, Max," Christine said as she sat down.

"Max knew the routine. He raised his hand and caught the attention of a waiter. "A drink for the young lady, whatever she will be having."

Christine conveyed a look of gratitude. Max appreciated her good looks, but told himself he was too old for her. He wished now that he had simply returned to where Marbach was waiting for him. If he had, he'd have saved himself some money.

An expensive glass of cognac was placed on the table in front of Christine. "Thank you for the drink," she said in an awkwardly high voice.

Max found Christine to be disarmingly nervous, fetchingly vulnerable. He tossed enough scrip on the table to pay for his coffee and for the glass of cognac. "I can't stay here long," he said. "I have to go back to work pretty soon."

"Are you a businessman?" Christine asked in an anxious voice.

"Yes." Max was glad when she hadn't asked what his business was. He'd have lied, of course, easy enough to do that, but still he was glad she hadn't asked and that he hadn't lied.

Christine began talking about the high hopes she had for herself. It took a long while for her to get it all said. This wasn't where she intended to end her life. She was from a farm family in the Burgenland. She desperately wanted to escape from what life offered her in the Burgenland: the sad fate of being the wife of someone who would be a poverty-stricken farmer all his life.

Max knew what sort of life Christine had left behind and, more important, what would probably be her dismal future. She was facing a cruel and unforgiving world. With that in mind, he decided that when this was finished he would give her some extra scrip to pay for the short time spent in her company.

"Would you like a second drink?" he asked.

"I like you," Christine said. "You're a nice man. Maybe you are lonely . . . I have a baby or I wouldn't be here."

Max didn't want to hear what was said next.

"There's a room upstairs. We could have a party. It doesn't cost much . . ."

Max took a package of American cigarettes from his pocket. There were three unsmoked cigarettes remaining, much more than the established price for sex. He shoved the package across the table to the young woman.

Anxiously, Christine grabbed up the package. "Shall we go up to the room?" she inquired with a small tremor in her voice.

Max stood up, took the hand of the young fräulein and kissed it. "No, Christine," he said. "I have to leave now. I have to go back to work. I wish you well. Most truly, I wish you well."

After saying that, he provided a smile he hoped conveyed his sincere good wishes, stepped away from the table, walked out the door of the café, across the street, up to where Karl Marbach was waiting in what appeared to be an irritable mood.

"It took you long enough," Marbach growled. "I was beginning to think you might be indulging yourself in your usual recreational activity."

"Go to hell."

Marbach ignored Max's bad humor. He asked, "Did you check with any of the hotel staff about the Russian woman's telephone calls?"

Max nodded his head. "Of course. That is just routine detective stuff. I promised my body to the woman in charge of the telephone switchboard in the hotel. A fine looking woman. Some age on her, but a fine looking woman. She has guaranteed that if any calls go through to Natasha Yakovlevna at any hour of the day or night I will be given a full record of the conversation—and any other relevant information."

"Have you ever in your life turned down an invitation to jump into bed with an available woman or an available fräulein?"

Max didn't reply. He thought about the young fräulein named Christine he'd just left in the café.

Marbach picked up on the distressed look on Max's face and teasingly said, "Do you tell all your sins in confession?"

"Yes!" Max declared angrily.

Marbach teased, "Tell me the worst sin you ever told a priest."

Max made an angry, growling sound. "All right, I'll tell you. In the winter of 1943, it was my job to stay alive and fight Nazis. One night I saw a Nazi officer in Warsaw who was wearing a fine overcoat while I was almost frozen to death. After I cut his throat and walked away wearing his fine overcoat I felt incredible joy."

"Don't get complicated with me."

"Who is being complicated?"

"Was killing that Nazi officer a sin?"

"The joy I felt killing that Nazi officer made it a sin."

"So you told that sin in confession. Now tell me—". At that moment, before more could be said, both men became aware of a woman leaving the Hotel Jupiter.

Max gestured. "There's Natasha Yakovlevna. She's that woman coming out of the front door right now."

"The wife of Dr. Emhardt," Marbach murmured.

CHAPTER THIRTY

Careful not to be seen, Marbach and Max followed Natasha Yakovlevna. She walked to a nearby food store and went inside. Unobtrusively peering through the store window Marbach and Max watched her select one slice of bread, one tiny piece of chicken and a plate of vegetables. It was a modest meal even for one person.

"I don't think that woman is expecting any company today," Max said.

"I agree," Marbach said. "But you never can tell."

Max nodded. "You never can tell."

After paying for what she had selected, Natasha Yakovlevna left the store and proceeded to the bus station, where she stayed about fifteen minutes.

After she came out, Max waited a discrete moment and then went inside the bus station.

Remaining out on the street, Marbach watched the woman walk back toward her hotel. He still had her in sight when Max came out of the bus station.

"She bought a ticket to Innsbruck," Max said. "The night bus. Not too many stops. She'll be in Innsbruck tomorrow morning."

"And you'll be on the same bus, looking oblivious to the world, keeping an eye on her all the way to Innsbruck."

"That won't be necessary. I've got a colleague who will be able to take care of things on the bus. I'll ride in a car with you."

"All right."

"It might be more comfortable on the bus, but I always get nervous when you're off somewhere and I'm not around to take care of you."

Marbach laughed. "We have been in quite a few tough spots together, haven't we?"

"When I am with you the most innocent places easily become hell holes."

Marbach shrugged.

CHAPTER THIRTY-ONE

Marbach watched Max leave to go arrange things with the colleague who would be going on the bus to Innsbruck. Then, moving at a face pace, he made his way toward the hospital. He hoped he would be able to see Pammy, perhaps talk with her for a bit. It was important to let her know he would be going out of Vienna for a few days.

Less than fifteen minutes later, he entered the burn center and learned that his wife was working on a case and couldn't be disturbed. She wouldn't be free for at least another half hour.

Debating a moment, filled with a need to do something that would please Pammy, he made some inquiries and quickly learned where former Waffen SS Captain Leo Lechner could be found.

A few minutes later, he entered a large room containing one bed. At the foot of the bed was a tag with Leo's full name on it. The man lying in the bed was facing toward a faraway window.

"Leo?"

"Who is it?" The man on the bed rolled over.

Marbach identified himself.

"You have come to see me?"

Even though he'd prepared himself, Marbach was shocked at the sight of what had once been a handsome man. Now, Leo had only the remains of a face and what looked like claws at the ends of what used to be arms. Leo had no eyes, only empty eye sockets, badly scarred empty eye sockets.

Marbach recalled other sights he had seen in recent years: damaged people, even children, persons of all ages living with the horror of what had been done to them because of Nazism.

Leo, one of the Nazi horror-makers, was now a horror himself.

"I came to see my wife," Marbach said. "She is busy right now. She told me about you . . . so, I thought I'd pay a visit, see if there is anything I can do for you."

Leo's voice was a rasping sound. "Dr. Pammy is a beautiful woman. I don't have eyes to see with, but I can tell she is beautiful. I can tell from the sound of her voice and the feel of her hands when she touches me. I had a beautiful wife . . . once."

"I remember Hilde."

"You must not tell Hilde that I am here . . . like this."

"I haven't talked with your wife, but I know some things about her. She lives here in Vienna."

"You must not tell Hilde anything about me."

"I won't say anything to her without your permission."

"It is important that Hilde doesn't know I am alive."

"Well maybe if she did know—"

"No!"

"If that's your decision, I won't contact her . . . Are you receiving good care here? My wife says you are one of her very special patients."

"She has great kindness, your wife . . . a very special feminine kindness. I feel grateful whenever she is near."

"I am glad she is able to help you."

"I wonder what Dr. Pammy would have thought of me ten years ago, before I ended up looking like this. I used to be proud of how handsome I was."

Marbach remained silent. Ten years ago, Leo had been a very handsome man.

Leo had a question. "What would your Jewish wife have thought if she had seen me in 1938, handsome and resplendent in my SS uniform?"

Marbach wished there was a way to soften the harshness of the truthful answer he felt obligated to give. "She would have despised you."

"Always the honest man, aren't you? You'll never know how much I wanted your respect in the old days. When I finally knew I couldn't get your respect, I hated you."

Marbach shifted awkwardly from one foot to the other. "Let's put the past behind us."

"Is Hilde well? I mean . . . does she need anything?"

"I never looked into her situation closely, but I have my sources. I know a few things about her. She seems to be doing all right."

"Don't tell me anything more. I don't want to know if she has a man, if she is married, has children . . . or anything. Maybe . . . maybe later I'll ask about those things. But these days I need my old memories of her. Not knowing anything about her current life helps me keep my old memories pure and intact."

"I understand. I won't tell her anything without your permission."

"You believe in the soul, don't you, Karl?"

"The soul? Yes, of course."

"Do you know . . . can you believe that I wouldn't trade the cinder of a body I have now for the wonderful body I had ten years ago if it came with the Nazi soul I had in those days?"

Marbach couldn't think of anything to say in reply.

"Do you know what the oddest thing is?" Leo asked.

"What?"

"My mind is awake now. When I was a Nazi, my mind was asleep. Even though I thought of myself as an intellectual, I didn't use my mind to think with. I only used it for Nazi things."

"For a man who was asleep, you were quick on your feet."

"While sleeping, I liked to repeat words I was told should guide me in life. Those words had a powerful effect on me: *Celebrate passion without reflection, action without conscience, and feeling without reason.*"

Leo paused for a moment before continuing. "I used to love speaking those words. We young National Socialists thought we were fully alive, but now I know we were asleep."

"You're awake now."

"Do you think my suffering woke me up?"

"I don't know."

"Suffering doesn't make people better, but sometimes it does wake them up."

Marbach took a wet towel and wiped Leo's mutilated face. He told himself it was just something he would do for any suffering creature.

"Thanks," Leo said. "It is hot in this room. Tell me, is it still August? It is so hot."

"It is September. The weather will soon be getting cooler."

"I have been thinking about the mountains. I like all of the Alps, but most of all, I love the Dolomites. I love the Dolomite Alps."

Marbach did more wiping of the mutilated face.

Leo said, "I remember having friends who told me that there is no sin for those who climb up high in the Dolomites."

Marbach said, "I've heard that, but during the war when I was up in the Dolomite peaks, at the Adamello, the highest spot on the earth where armies have ever fought, I saw a lot of sin."

"I have heard that if someone starts a Dolomite climb in a state of sin and climbs upward keeping himself straight and true, at the top of the Dolomites there will be no sin."

"Yes . . . I have heard that said."

"I did so many awful things. I always had a brain. Why would a man with a fine brain like mine ever have been enthusiastic about anything as awful as National Socialism?"

"You had a lot of company."

"But never you. You were never one of us. You never gave your soul to National Socialism. Like I did . . . like the rest of us did. There weren't many like you. You and those like you were rare. We Nazis regarded your kind as freaks."

One of Leo's clawed hands began trembling, then the entire arm began shaking. Marbach used one of his hands to grasp Leo's arm and with his other hand he grasped the claw at the end of the arm. It took a few minutes for the arm to stop shaking.

After the shaking stopped, Leo said, "There is something under my pillow."

Marbach released his hold on Leo, reached under the pillow, and pulled out a familiar looking medal.

"I'll be damned," Marbach said, wondering why Leo would be keeping the Austrian Eagle medal under his pillow. The Austrian Eagle had been awarded to Leo for service performed while help-ing the fascist Austrian government put down the worker's revolt in 1934.

"You'll never know what the Austrian Eagle meant to me back in 1934," Leo said.

"What about your Iron Cross?" asked Marbach "Where do you keep that?"

"The Iron Cross came to me after I was fully corrupted. I found it easy to throw that medal away when I stopped being corrupt. It was the Austrian Eagle that robbed me of my innocence. I haven't thrown it away. Not yet." Leo began coughing. When the coughing stopped, his breathing became a wheezing sound.

Finally, Leo managed to talk. He said wistfully, "I didn't know Dr. Pammy was your wife when she first tended me. When I found out, for a long time I didn't tell her I knew you. Always when Dr. Pammy came in here she would hold my arms . . . my shoulders. Dr. Pammy touched my body. A burned up freak can still yearn for, desperately need the touch of . . . of a human being."

A door slammed in the outside corridor. In the next moment, a nurse appeared and told Marbach he would have to leave.

Leo said, "Will you bring me some books . . . ?"

"Of course."

"Goethe would be good. I have a friend in the next ward who says he will read to me. I would like to hear him read *Faust*. I remember seeing Constanze Tandler play Margarthe in Max Reinhardt's *Faust*."

Marbach had a mixed feeling. He wondered if Leo had played a part—any part at all—in what had led to the killing of Constanze, his lover all those years ago.

As though reading Marbach's mind, Leo said, "As bad as I ever was, in my worst moment I never did any harm to Constanze Tandler. But anything that has happened to me can't be too terrible for what I did to Anna and to others."

"What did you do to Anna?"

"I took her to Mauthausen."

"You couldn't have stopped Anna being sent to Mauthausen."

"No, I couldn't have stopped it, but I felt pleasure taking her there. In those days I took pleasure doing awful things."

Marbach kept silent. He felt that he understood what Leo was saying.

Leo continued. "Anna was so beautiful. But I felt pleasure the day I took her to Mauthausen. I lost my soul the day I took Anna to Mauthausen."

Marbach waited a moment, then said, "Leo . . . I probably could have been convinced back in 1938 that you had lost your soul, but whatever has happened, right now I know you have your soul. It isn't lost."

"There isn't much of me left."

"If you give me permission, I will bring Anna here. She'll tell you that she forgives you."

"Is Anna in Vienna?"

"She escaped from Mauthausen. She has a husband now. A fine husband. And she has a wonderful son."

"Thank God!" Leo made a long, groaning sound.

Marbach pressed firmly on the groaning man's shoulders and said, "Leo, I have to go. I will be out of town for a few days."

"But you'll come back!" Leo said in a pleading voice. The plea continued. "Tell me you'll come back and bring Anna. There are things I need to say to Anna."

"Yes. I'll come back and I'll bring Anna to visit you."

"Do you understand why I kept the Austrian Eagle all this time? It's because I wanted someone like you to be the one to throw it away. Can you understand that?"

"I understand. I'll take care of that piece of business for you."

"Good."

"I wish I didn't have to go out of town right now, but it is something I have to do."

I've been alone for a long *time*. I know how to handle *time*."

"Time?" Marbach picked up on the emphasis Leo placed on that word.

Leo said, "Do you remember . . . what some folk say about time on a mountain?"

"Time?"

"How time is measured on the mountain . . ." Leo's voice trailed off.

Marbach spoke the words he knew Leo wanted to hear. He spoke the words exactly as he had memorized them many years ago.

On the mountain, time is measured by the mountain. A second on the mountain can be an eternity. And an entire day can pass in just a few minutes. On the mountain, the pace of time is set by the mountain.

"That is right," Leo said eagerly. "In these hospitals, the hard thing to handle is time. The sentiment those words express has helped me keep my sanity."

Marbach wiped the wet cloth one more time on the ravaged face. It was time for him to move on. He grasped the clawed hand, picked up the Austrian Eagle and bade farewell.

CHAPTER THIRTY-TWO

After leaving Leo, Marbach went to see if his wife could be disturbed for just a minute. He could leave her a note about leaving Vienna for a few days, but he felt a great need to see her, even if only for a minute or two.

Permission was granted and he found Pammy sitting at her desk in her major's uniform. Her face reflected strain and weariness.

"What's the matter, sweetheart?" Marbach asked, speaking the English that came naturally to him when he was with his wife. He walked across the room, leaned down and kissed Pammy, held her face in his hands and kissed her again. She passively kissed him back.

Finally, he edged back and said, "For a medical professional you don't do a very good job taking care of yourself. Is your back . . ."

"You can give me a back rub tonight," said Pammy.

"I'm sorry. Not tonight. That's why I came here. I have to go on a short trip. I'll be leaving right away. I'll be gone for a couple of days. I'll explain about the trip when I get back. Right now, there's something you might like hearing.

I just had a meeting with Leo . . . Leo Lechner. Whatever he used to be, Leo is now a good person. I'll be dropping in on him again."

Pammy stood up. "Do you have to go on this trip?"

"Yes."

"Well, my awful back will just have to wait until you get back before it gets rubbed."

"It is a wonderful back."

"It has ugly shrapnel scars on it."

"I never see any scars. You don't understand, but believe me, it is absolutely true. When I look at your bare back, all I see is the precious back of the woman I love."

"You are sweet."

"I am grateful."

Pammy placed her arms around Marbach's neck. But just at the moment when tenderness might start becoming enjoyment, a clerk came into the office with some records to be checked. Marbach quickly stepped away from Pammy.

"I'm sorry, Major," the embarrassed clerk said, using the title major to address Pammy.

"It's all right," Pammy said, using her hands to straighten her uniform.

The clerk put the records on Pammy's desk and quickly left.

Marbach headed for the door, grasped the door handle, pulled the door open, turned, and said to Pammy, "I may miss your Sunday dinner. If so, I'll miss the good company on Sunday, but not the food. You can't cook a lick."

"Can't cook a lick? You stinker!" Pammy half-shouted, half-laughed after him as he left her office. "You bloody, rotten stinker!"

Out in the hallway, Marbach took only a few steps before he almost bumped into Millican.

"It sounds like Pammy is mad at you," the American said with a cheerful laugh.

"What's up?" Marbach asked.

"Sergeant Fay is taking the mail car to Salzburg. U.S. Army in Vienna delivers mail to and from Headquarters U.S. Army in Salzburg. There are a lot of GI patients in this hospital. I came here to pick up some of the mail from them. I just finished putting it in the car."

"I could use a car. I need to go to Innsbruck."

"Important business?"

"Yes."

"I'll tell you what, you can have the mail car after it stops in Salzburg. It'll have to make a couple of stops, so it'll be a five hour ride to Salzburg. But after that you can have the use of the car. I'll arrange for another car to bring the incoming mail our guys in Salzburg are holding for us."

"Can I have the car for a couple of days?"

"No problem."

"Thank you. That car will get me to Innsbruck several hours before the night bus."

"What night bus?"

"No time to explain now. I have to go and pick up Rolf and then I have to see about Father Anton. How crowded will this mail car be? Can I take some company with me?"

"It's a pre-war Chevrolet station wagon, one hell of a big vehicle. It can hold up to eight passengers comfortably. For the trip to Salzburg, we got a driver and Sergeant Fay. And we got a German. The station wagon can accommodate five more passengers with no problem, a couple more, if necessary."

"Who's the German?"

"His name is Klaus Becker. Anyway, that's the name he's currently using. I don't know much about him, but what I do know I don't like. I won't con you. This guy saw service with the Gestapo in France. He has been involved in black market activities and maybe some stuff with Nazi groups, but he's made himself valuable to CIC, gotten himself on the CIC payroll. A couple of months ago we had an arrest order with his original name on it—Klaus Barbie. Does that name mean anything to you?"

"Klaus Barbie? Well, I could check my files." That answer amounted to a lie. For Marbach deliberate deception was the same thing as a lie. His excuse for this deception was that he didn't want to say anything that might complicate getting the station wagon. He knew that Klaus Barbie's name hadn't shown up on public lists of Nazi war criminals. He wondered what would happen if and when Barbie's awful deeds became widely known.

"Do me a favor," said Millican. "Don't make a fuss with this guy if he gets obnoxious. Between you and me, I don't have any use for him, but he's on our payroll."

"All right."

"I'll have the mail car parked in front of the hospital about an hour from now."

"Thanks."

CHAPTER THIRTY-THREE

Marbach went into a telephone booth and dialed a number.

A moment later a familiar voice answered. "This is Police Detective Rolf Hiller."

Without identifying himself, Marbach went immediately to the point of his call. "Are you up to taking another trip?"

As always, Rolf was careful to avoid saying anything specific enough to be useful to uninvited ears that might be listening. "Are you talking about going where we might find those two characters we've been chasing?"

"You guessed it."

"What excuse do I give here?"

"Tell them you'll be gone for a couple of days, three or four at the most. Tell them you are under my authority."

"How do I find you?"

"A car will be leaving from outside my wife's office in about an hour."

After a moment of silence, Rolf said, "Someone left you a message. You had trouble with him and his father just prior to your departure years ago. Now he presents himself as a religious person. He's waiting for you in the printing shop."

There was no mistaking the deliberately obscured message. Rolf had communicated that Paul Neumayer, presenting himself as Friar Paul, wanted to see Marbach.

"I've got some time. I will go and see what he wants. He might have some information we can use."

"For our little trip, I already got my toothbrush packed. By the way, a friend of yours is here. I think he'd like to come along with us on our little trip."

"Put him on the line."

Less than a minute later, Zbik's familiar voice provided a tentative greeting followed by obscure words intended to eliminate any possible confusion about who was on the line.

"Are you up to going on an adventure?" Marbach asked.

"Of course," Zbik said. "I have been told a bit about what I imagine we are talking about. How long will I be away?"

"A couple of days. Who knows?"

"If I miss the Sunday dinner party, I'll catch hell from Anna."

"You don't have to come along."

"Try and stop me. I'm ready to go with just the clothes on my back. I'll borrow a razor."

"Tell Rolf to fix you up with some shaving gear and a change of clothes."

There was nothing more to say. The call was completed. Marbach hung up the telephone, stepped out of the telephone booth and hailed a taxicab to take him to the Franciscan Printing Shop within the French Zone in Vienna.

A few minutes later, acutely conscious of how quickly time was passing, Marbach walked into the customer service area within the shop. He had never before been in the Franciscan Printing Shop, but he didn't stop to ask any questions. He made a point of appearing to be a man who knew exactly where he was going as he walked to the rear of the customer service area and then went through a door into the work area. The fewer people who paid him any serious attention in this place, the better it would be.

Marbach was glad that no one seemed to be paying him any attention, but where was Paul Neumayer? He looked around. There were two friars, neither of whom was Paul Neumayer. In addition to the two friars there was a man in a suit and there were a half dozen men in overalls.

This was the Franciscan printing shop, but where was Paul Neumayer? He could be anywhere. This was a large building. He might be in a basement area, or upstairs in an attic.

Looking around, Marbach spotted a red sign identifying a toilet facility and decided that would be a suitable refuge for him while he examined his options. He went to the toilet facility, stepped inside, and availed himself of the stand-up toilet. When finished with the toilet, he walked over to the sink. He was ready to wash his hands when the door opened and a young friar entered, stared at him, looked embarrassed, and went into one of the three stalls where private toilet activity could be conducted.

For Marbach this was an opportunity too good to waste. There was one wash basin in the small toilet facility. He washed his hands, kept washing his hands until the young friar came out of the stall.

Marbach continued washing his hands. For a few moments the shy friar stood silently behind him, nervously tugging at the yellowish rope belt wrapped securely around the middle of his brown habit.

Marbach kept washing his hands, made a point of showing no sign of stopping.

Finally the friar said, "Excuse me, sir. I need to get some water on my hands."

"Don't let me block you." Marbach stepped to the side and began drying his hands. "I came to this printing shop to see Friar Paul. Do you happen to know where he is?"

"Friar Paul is in the delivery room. Just go out of here and keep walking straight ahead until you see a doorway. Go through the doorway and there are signs saying 'delivery room'. You can't go wrong."

Marbach bade farewell to the young friar, stepped outside the toilet facility, and followed the directions that took him to the delivery room.

The only person inside the delivery room was Paul Neumayer dressed in friar garb. Even after all these years, there was no mistaking who he was.

Marbach approached Paul Neumayer. There was immediate recognition. Paul Neumayer looked unsure of himself.

Marbach said, "You need fear nothing from me. I promised Father Anton I will protect you. Do you believe I will protect you? Do you believe I will do you no harm and that I will permit no harm to be done to you?"

Paul Neumayer fussed nervously before saying, "Father Anton was taken ill again last night. This morning he was taken to the hospital."

"What do you know about the Odessa papers?"

"The Odessa papers are why I left a message for you to come here. The papers were delivered here yesterday. A Russian woman named Natasha Yakovlevna picked them up. That caused Father Anton terrible distress. He told me to contact you. Advise you about what is happening. Father Anton has been admitted as a patient to the hospital."

"You should have contacted me immediately."

"I telephoned your office and left a message. I did that this morning. Isn't that what brought you here?"

"I haven't checked my telephone messages in hours. You and I have to get out of here. I have a safe place to hide you until this whole business is over."

"You despise me."

"What do you care what I think of you? I've given my word to Father Anton that I won't permit any harm to be done to you." Paul Neumayer looked miserable. "I am betraying my father and I am betraying brothers who wear the same garb I wear."

"We have to get out of here. Are you ready to go?"

Continuing to look miserable, Paul Neumayer said, "My father is in Innsbruck."

"What else can you tell me about your father and Innsbruck?"

"Adolf Eichmann, Otto Skorzeny and Dr. Emhardt are also in Innsbruck."

"I think we should go somewhere and talk."

"Father Anton told me to stay in this printing shop until the Odessa business is finished."

"Is there anything you told him that I might not know?"

"Do you know that this printing shop has started making up phony Red Cross identification cards?"

"Red Cross identification cards?" Marbach shook his head. He hadn't known about that.

Paul Neumayer said, "The travelers on Odessa who have Red Cross identification cards will be less likely to be questioned as they move from one relay house to the next."

"What else can you tell me?"

"This printing shop is also making phony passports."

"Phony Red Cross identification cards and phony passports?"

"Yes."

"Is there anything else you can tell me? Take your time. You are being very helpful."

"I have told you everything I know. May I ask? Can I go with you to Innsbruck?"

"Well, I can't deny you could be helpful for what I need to do in Innsbruck."

"Does that mean I can come with you?"

"What I am doing is calculated to cause grief for your father."

Paul Neumayer's face filled with agony. "I know. But Odessa is evil and maybe I can be of service. I have much to atone for. Can I come along?"

"Yes. Come along. I can use the help you'll be able to provide."

CHAPTER THIRTY-FOUR

It didn't take long for Marbach and Paul Neumayer to get to the hospital. On the street across from the hospital they spotted a U. S. Army station wagon surrounded by several men.

One of the men standing near the station wagon was Rolf, who was trying to carry on a conversation with Sergeant Fay. The American couldn't speak any German, let alone Viennese-German, and Rolf didn't know much English. Zbik and Max were standing off to the side. A man who apparently was Klaus Becker was standing alone, an isolated figure next to the station wagon.

Marbach asked Fay, "Can you handle a mob like us?"

"No trouble. This station wagon can hold a dozen in a pinch. What we got here is eight of us: me, the driver, Klaus Becker, and the five of you."

The 1939 all-wood Chevrolet station wagon had "USA" painted in large white letters on each side. There was a spare tire on the roof.

"When do we leave?" Marbach asked.

"There's nothing keeping us here. I'm ready to go whenever you're ready."

"Let's go," Marbach said.

"Let's go," agreed Fay.

Everyone got into the Chevrolet station wagon and the mail run to Salzburg began.

One block down the street, MGB Sergeant Petrova was sitting in a Russian truck. She had three men with her. "Follow them," she said to the driver.

As her truck pulled out, a second Russian truck followed her lead.

Petrova stiffened in her seat as the American car picked up speed, made a quick turn, and vanished from sight.

"This is hopeless," Petrova said. "Let's go pick up the one named Anna Peszkowski."

CHAPTER THIRTY-FIVE

"They're nowhere in sight behind us," Fay said when it was clear that the Chevrolet station wagon had left the Russian trucks far behind. He was in the middle of front seat beside the driver, Corporal Plunkett. Next to the door in the front seat was Max. The wood-paneled station wagon had three rows of seats. In the middle row were Zbik, Klaus Becker, and Paul Neumayer in his friar's garb. In the back row were Marbach and Rolf.

"It looks like we've lost them," said Marbach from the rear of the vehicle, speaking English to Fay, pitching his voice loud enough for the American to hear. "But why are the Russians chasing after us? I can't imagine they would try to stop an American Army car. It wouldn't be worth the trouble your country could make for them."

"The Russkies are sometimes hard to figure out," Fay said.

"Yes," agreed Marbach.

A man sitting in the middle row of seats turned around, faced Marbach, and, speaking German, identified himself. "My name is Klaus Becker."

Marbach politely exchanged greetings. He knew that Klaus Becker was really Klaus Barbie. He wondered what the full story was on Klaus Barbie, but right now there were more important things to think about.

"Herr Becker works for CIC," Fay, sitting in the front row of seats, said in a voice loud enough to be heard by Marbach sitting in the back.

Klaus Barbie, using the name Klaus Becker, was in his mid-thirties, short, stocky, with a large head on which was planted a broad-brimmed hat. He had a personality that was vaguely boorish.

Marbach asked the man identifying himself as Klaus Becker a question in English, using his hands in a series of movements to indicate that speaking English was a courtesy to Fay. "Why are you going to Salzburg?"

"I do not stay in Salzburg," came the reply in halting English. "I go to Munich. Then a train to Frankfurt . . . There is American business requiring my attention in Frankfurt."

In his halting English, Klaus Becker continued. He said that it was very important for him to be in Frankfurt as soon as possible.

"Will you be going to the Schmeling fight next week?" Marbach asked, making small talk in English. "The fight will be at the Frankfurt Civic Stadium next week. Max Schmeling's opponent is a young fighter named Werner Volmer. I've seen young Volmer fight . . . he has courage, but no experience."

"Max Schmeling is old," Klaus Becker said, doing his best with English. "No good for fight. Past forty years."

The driver of the Chevrolet station wagon, Corporal Plunkitt, kept his hands high on the steering wheel as he joined in the conversation. "Imagine Max Schmeling fighting again. If I was in Frankfurt, I'd go see it. I remember the two fights he had with Joe Louis . . . God, that was a long time ago."

"The Nigger Joe Louis is beneath contempt," Klaus Becker said in a distinctly coarse voice.

Corporal Plunkitt, staring hard into the rearview mirror, made a declaration. "Watch your mouth, Kraut."

Fay came alert and said to Corporal Plunkitt, "I agree with your sentiment, but drop the word Kraut."

"I do not understand," Klaus Becker said.

"Let me put it this way," Fay said, "if you bad mouth the champ—Joe Louis—I'll personally see to it that you finish this trip with your nose poking out the back of your head."

In the back seat, Marbach leaned over, placed his hand across the side of his mouth, and whispered to Rolf a translation of what had been said by Fay.

"Americans are usually a puzzle to me," Rolf whispered in reply. "But these two I like."

In the middle row of seats, Klaus Becker fussed awkwardly. "I withdraw my words," he said.

"Glad to hear that," Corporal Plunkitt said.

For a long while, there was casual conversation, none of it important.

Finally, Marbach used English to say to the driver, "Tell me, Corporal Plunkitt, who are you rooting for in the World Series?"

"I'm strictly a Dodger fan," Corporal Plunkitt replied. He pushed a cigarette into his mouth while expertly wheeling the station wagon around a slower moving vehicle. "We're gonna roll right over them Yankees. That's the way it's gonna be."

After that, during the long ride to Salzburg, at the wheel of the station wagon, Corporal Plunkitt did a lot of defending of his beloved "bums," the Dodgers.

At approximately midpoint in the journey, Corporal Plunkitt was relating one of his many stories about the Brooklyn Dodgers, the team he regarded as the greatest bunch of ballplayers in the world. Corporal Plunkitt's English was expressed in the present tense with peculiar connections between verbs and nouns.

Marbach, although experienced in American English, was having difficulty understanding the corporal.

"Back in July of '38, I'm sittin' in my seat at Ebbets Field. As usual, yours truly is in Section 6, Row 23, right on the aisle. A glorious day . . ."

A few minutes later, Corporal Plunkitt concluded that story with the words: "What matters right now is that the Dodgers are gunna murder the Yankees in da series."

"My wife agrees with you," Marbach said, finally hearing a sentence he was confident he could understand.

"Yeah?" Corporal Plunkitt looked over his shoulder. "Well, I guess some Austrians are following the series."

"My wife is American."

"Yeah? You don't say."

Fay leaned over and said to Plunkitt, "The police inspector's wife was at Anzio. You were there, Plunkitt. Ever hear of Major Pamela Green? With the British?"

"I don't keep track of . . . say, uh, yeah, I heard of Major Green. Of course, I heard of her. Say, Herr Marbach, are you really Major Green's husband?"

"I most certainly am."

"Well, I'll be . . . I mean, well . . . that woman doctor with the British. I remember hearing she was American, but didn't believe it."

"Yes, she is very much American," Marbach said.

"Well I'll be . . . well, I will be."

There was more talk about Marbach's wife as the army mail car moved at a fast speed toward Salzburg. The station wagon got stopped at check point after check point. It took almost five hours to complete the trip from Vienna to Salzburg.

CHAPTER THIRTY-SIX

After the Chevrolet station wagon arrived at the truck depot in Salzburg, Marbach spent a few minutes with Rolf, Max, and Zbik talking about the trip they would be making to Innsbruck. Then he went and found a lavatory.

He was leaving the lavatory when he encountered Corporal Plunkitt.

"Look . . . your wife is Dr. Green," Corporal Plunkitt said. "Well, I guess she's Dr. Marbach now . . . well, look, maybe you could you tell her something."

"Of course."

With an earnest face, Corporal Plunkitt said, "Could you tell her Homer made it."

"I will be glad to tell my wife that Homer made it."

"Homer's my buddy," explained Corporal Plunkitt. "Some of us was mixed up with the British after Anzio. Homer got wounded. Just a little, not too bad, but at first he thought it was bad. It's sometimes hard to tell at first how bad you're wounded. Anyway, your wife tended Homer. She told him he was going to make it. Homer told me those were the best words he ever heard. He's back in the States now, but . . . well, that British Army doctor meant a lot to Homer. And to lots of us guys. I remember seeing her once. She sure was something to see. She impressed lots of us guys. Not just Homer . . . eh, well, she sure impressed me."

Marbach nodded. "I appreciate what you are saying."

Corporal Plunkitt continued. "It'll tickle Homer to hear from yours truly that I talked with the British Army doctor's husband, that I made a connection with the British doctor."

"You might let Homer know that the woman doctor in the British uniform is as American as any of you Yanks."

"Yeah . . . ain't that something?"

"I insist that you meet my wife. And when you meet with her, I'm sure she will write a personal note for you to pass along to Homer."

The American corporal was unsure of himself. "Why, sure, anytime . . . are you kidding?"

"If your army doesn't know how to find me, just call any district of the Vienna police. There'll be no problem contacting me if you're serious about getting a note from my wife to pass on to Homer."

"Say, that'll be great. Homer'll get a big kick out of that."

"That is a commitment from you to me. I will be disappointed if you don't honor your commitment to meet my wife."

"You bet . . . gosh, that'll be great."

Marbach walked away. It was time to find Sergeant Fay and get on with things.

He found Fay standing in front of an American apparatus into which one delivered coins and received back soft drinks.

"I was told to let you have the mail car," Fay said in the only language he could speak. He held out a bottle of Pepsi Cola.

"Thank you. I have some change for the Pepsi in my pocket." "Forget it. My treat."

"I thank you."

"No big deal."

"Is the car ready?"

"It's ready. Look . . . I'd like to come along."

"Come along?"

"To Innsbruck."

"There could be trouble."

"Millican—that is, Captain Millican—said you were into something. He didn't tell me what. Nobody tells me nothing."

"If you don't know anything, why do you want to come along?"

"Maybe I got a hunch. Maybe I'm just restless."

Marbach stared at Fay while putting a question. "Do you know what Herr Becker's name used to be?"

"Sure. Klaus Barbie. So what? He was a Nazi, but lots of these guys were Nazis."

"Klaus Barbie was a real big Nazi."

"I didn't know he was a real big Nazi."

"One of the people we're going after in Innsbruck is named Dr. Heinrich Emhardt.

"That name don't mean nothing to me."

"Dr. Emhardt is a wanted war criminal."

"That's good enough for me. Let's go get him."

"Some high level Americans are trying to get him into your country. He has great science skills wanted by your country."

Fay took his time before asking, "How bad a stinker is this Dr. Emhardt?"

"His victims at the Dora Camp were too many to count. In addition, he has countless numbers of victims in other places."

"Dora was enough to damn his soul."

"Maybe you better stay here. You are U.S. Army CIC. There could be trouble for you."

"I saw Dora. And some of the other places. Giving any guy a free pass for what was done in those places is wrong. It's wrong even if the guy is a big shot scientist who can help the U.S. build important weapons. Don't worry about trouble for me. Let me come along. I can handle any trouble the army might end up throwing my way."

"Well . . . most certainly we could use your services."

"Then there's no more to be said."

"I am happy to have you join us. What about Corporal Plunkitt? Is there any chance of taking him along?"

"No chance. He's under orders. He has to take another mail car back to Vienna."

"I like Corporal Plunkitt."

"Yeah. He's a damned good man."

"We could use some more weapons. Maybe a couple of American rifles and some automatic hand guns."

"You can forget about automatic hand guns."

"Absolutely no chance?"

"None at all. Believe me. There's real tight security in this place."

"Can you bring your own weapon?"

"Yeah, I can bring my .38."

"I wish you had a Colt .45, a much more formidable weapon."

"What I got is a .38."

"Ah, the Commando .38."

"No, the .38 Police Special."

"I wish you had a Colt .45." Marbach smiled. "I wish I had a Colt .45." He laughed for a moment. "I wish I had a dozen fine rifles and a Colt .45."

"What you got is me and my .38. Say, what are you packing?"

"An Enfield revolver," Marbach said. Then he added, "I wish I had something besides this Enfield."

"Well, don't expect me to trade with you. I'm keeping my .38"

CHAPTER THIRTY-SEVEN

MGB Major Gorshkov was sitting glumly in a chair he didn't like. He didn't like the chair because it was too comfortable. Right now, he didn't want to be comfortable. Being uncomfortable helped take his mind off how frustrated he was. He was frustrated because countless informants had come to MGB with information about Dr. Emhardt and Natasha Yakovlevna, but after reviewing their statements, he had found nothing that looked helpful.

The buzzer on Gorshkov's desk sputtered. He connected to the speaker, and his heavy eyebrows lifted when he heard that Sergeant Dotnara Petrova was outside.

"Tell the sergeant to come in."

Petrova entered the office, found a chair and sat down. She fussed with her hands.

"Don't worry about not catching Police Inspector Marbach." Gorshkov said. "It couldn't be helped. Nobody is criticizing you."

"I picked up the woman named Anna Peszkowski."

"It is good that you picked up the Yid."

"No, Comrade Major, she is an Aryan. Her husband is a Jew." Gorshkov wondered if Petrova was correct about

Anna Peszkowski being an Aryan. More important, he was bothered by Petrova using the word "Jew" instead of the word "Yid." High-level officers in MGB never hesitated to use the word "Yid." Gorshkov thought that Petrova probably ought to be advised to use the word "Yid." It was hazardous in MGB to appear to be reluctant to use that word.

Gorshkov folded his hands together and became thoughtful. Finally, he said to Petrova, "Anna Peszkowski may prove useful when we have Police Inspector Marbach in our hands. He has feelings for her. Our records show he was once her lover and that he is still a frequent visitor in her home. The husband of Anna Peszkowski is a pitiful excuse for a man. He lets his wife's former lover be a regular visitor in his home."

Petrova said, "The one named Anna Peszkowski is now in the custody of Sergeant Tolbukhin. I don't think Sergeant Tolbukhin should be allowed to handle women prisoners."

Gorshkov stood up. He believed it was important to keep Petrova from making trouble for herself. He spoke firmly. "Comrade Sergeant Tolbukhin may sometimes be crude, but he has made an impressive record for himself. High level comrades have praised him in official reports."

"Sergeant Tolbukhin is a beast!"

"No," Gorshkov said forcefully. "Comrade Tolbukhin is not a beast. He is a valuable MGB agent. You . . . you must be cautious what you say about him."

"I cannot be silent about Sergeant Tolbukhin."

"Are you worried about this woman prisoner? You shouldn't be. She has no information to yield that will require very much of Tolbukhin's attention."

"Sergeant Tolbukhin takes enjoyment doing brutal things."

"You are a brave comrade, but you let foolishness make you forget your duty."

"Sergeant Tolbukhin behaves like a beast."

Gorshkov didn't like hearing such foolishness. For him, long ago it had been clearly established that sometimes comrades have to be tough. He decided that Petrova needed to be edu-cated before she attracted the attention of someone who might cause serious problems for her.

"I think it is time for you to learn a thing or two about our work," Gorshkov said. "Come with me."

"Where?"

"We are going to visit the belly of this fine palace. We are going down to where the prisoners are kept."

Gorshkov led the way out of the office. As he walked down a hallway, he glanced over his shoulder. Petrova was carrying herself rigidly. He knew she was trying to conceal apprehension, trying to look confident. He told himself that Petrova had courage, but she was squeamish. He believed the squeamishness could make trouble for her, that she had to learn to appreciate the role that personal toughness was playing in the struggle for the glorious new Soviet world.

Gorshkov led the way down steep stone stairs. He involuntarily winced as they passed a room from which children's voices could be heard, very young children, many of them crying. Keeping defensiveness out of his voice, Gorshkov said to Petrova, "Those cries are from children. Hearing those voices has an amazing effect on some of the prisoners. They seem to think they can hear the sounds of their own children. There are many things you need to learn about our work. You served in the war. We are still in a war. A different kind of war, but still a war. We must be strong and tough."

At that moment, Gorshkov realized Petrova had halted behind him. He stopped and glanced around. She had a troubled look on her face.

"This is part of our work," Gorshkov said, then faced forward and resumed walking. He was relieved when he heard Petrova move up close behind him.

Gorshkov searched for words that might help Petrova. "There are things I don't like, but that I accept. The worst thing is to show weakness."

There was no reply from Petrova.

Continuing to walk forward, Gorshkov recollected times in his life when he had been involved in doing bad things that had to be done. He believed that when bad things have to be done, the thing to do is put aside fear and squeamishness and direct yourself to what you have to do. He was convinced that the ones who bring the greatest burden on themselves are those who think too much when they have to do something messy, or crude. You don't like doing things you sometimes have to do, but when it is something that needs to be done—when it is your duty—you get on with doing what you have to do.

Gorshkov knew that what he was telling himself was true, but he began wondering if he had made a mistake, if maybe there wasn't some better way to teach Petrova what she had to learn. The problem was that it was too late to turn back now. Besides, there was a part of him that enjoyed seeing Petrova looking vulnerable. He told himself that he would never take advantage of her vulnerability, but he had to admit there was a certain enjoyment seeing her looking so terribly unsure of herself.

It didn't take Gorshkov and Petrova long to get to the area where the adult prisoners were kept. The outside door clanged shut behind them and—mercifully—they could no longer hear the cries of the children. There was only the eerie silence of a jail and the muffled sound of shoes on the cement floor.

Gorshkov led the way quickly past a series of cells. He headed for the women's section with Petrova trailing behind him. When they came to the cell where Anna Peszkowski would be found, he looked back at Petrova one more time, then stared at the closed door, used his fingers to open the spy hole on the door and peered inside. He expected to see the prisoner looking a little put upon after being in the hands of someone like Sergeant Tolbukhin, but what he saw caused him to slam the spy hole shut and take a step backward.

"Sergeant Tolbukhin is a fool," he said in a husky voice. He stared at the closed door.

Petrova stepped forward, jerked open the spy hole and stared at what was inside.

"Open the door," she shouted, her eye still at the spy hole. "Get the door open. I'm going in there."

Gorshkov was Petrova's superior officer, but he knew he couldn't refuse. He knew with a terrible certainty that he would be forever a foulness in the eyes of Dotnara Petrova if he used the authority of his rank to keep her from going inside.

"There's nothing to be done here," he said, his voice a plea. "I never would have taken you here if I'd suspected . . . Come, let's go. I promise you I will deal with Tolbukhin."

"Open the door!" Petrova demanded.

"Let me handle this."

"Open the door!"

Gorshkov lifted the steel bar that secured the door and made a final, feeble entreaty. "Petrova," he said, please . . ."

Petrova grabbed the cell door, pulled it open, and entered the cell.

Gorshkov remained outside. He assumed Petrova would find the naked, bloodied woman was dead.

After a few moments, he heard odd sounds from within the cell. He hesitated, braced himself, and went inside.

Petrova was holding the prisoner's head in her arms. The prisoner wasn't dead. She was muttering something into Petrova's ear. The prisoner's naked body was blood streaked.

Gorshkov stared at the nakedness.

Petrova spun her head around. "This woman must be taken to a hospital," she declared, her voice low and thick.

Overwhelmed by shame, Gorshkov helped Petrova take the woman to the hospital located a couple of floors above the area where prisoners were held.

CHAPTER THIRTY-EIGHT

Wearing her military uniform, Pamela Marbach walked quickly down a hospital corridor. An emergency case had been brought to the burn center. That was all Pammy knew: another emergency case.

She walked quickly past a female Russian sergeant sitting on a bench. Pammy was aware that the Russian woman was staring at her anxiously, but it wasn't unusual for her to get looks like that in hospital corridors. Farther down, on a separate bench, sat a Russian major with his head lowered.

Continuing down the hospital corridor, Pammy entered the room where the emergency case was waiting. A medical assistant stepped away from the bed on which a patient was lying. The medical assistant was one of the young British soldiers recently assigned to the burn center. The usually calm young man seemed to be unsure of himself. "This is bloody awful, Major. The Russians brought her here."

"Get control of yourself," Pammy said. "We can't help burn victims if we get emotional."

"This isn't a burn victim. It's somebody you know. She asked for you."

"Not a burn victim? What's going on?"

"Pammy! Oh, Pammy!" It was Anna's voice. She was the patient lying on the bed.

The medical assistant stood almost at attention as he said, "Some Russians brought her here." There was a pause, then words were spoken in a very low voice. "She's taken a pretty bad beating and . . . she's been raped."

"Anna . . . oh, my precious Anna." Pammy put her arms around Anna and held her tight.

"A Russian woman brought me here," Anna sobbed. "She did that for me. She helped me." Anna tightly clutched at the sheet covering her body.

Pammy kissed Anna's face. "I will take care of you."

"Don't tell Zbik," Anna cried, holding tight to the sheet. "I don't want him to know about this."

"Zbik is a good man," Pammy said. "But I won't tell anyone anything without your permission."

"Take care of me, Pammy. Please take care of me."

"I will take care of you." Pammy placed her hands on both sides of Anna's face for a few moments. Then she lifted the sheet covering Anna's body and began her examination.

An hour later, after leaving Anna under sedation, Pammy left the room and walked wearily down the corridor.

"Please." That single word spoken in German brought Pammy to a halt. It was the Russian woman sergeant who had spoken the German word.

The Russian woman sergeant had agony in her eyes as she continued speaking German. "I am so sorry for what happened."

The Russian major, sitting on a separate bench from the one the Russian woman sergeant was sitting on, stood up, then with resignation sat back down.

"Thank you for bringing her to me," Pammy said in German.

The Russian woman sergeant mumbled a reply Pammy wasn't able to understand. A crying sound was released by the Russian woman sergeant.

Pammy drew the crying Russian woman into her arms and spoke German words that seemed to help.

The Russian major, sitting on his separate bench, watched the two women. He tried to understand how it was that things had turned out this way. He wanted to cry out with shame, but managed to keep silent.

CHAPTER THIRTY-NINE

F ar away from the hospital, in another part of Austria, a Chevrolet station wagon was moving fast. Rolf was behind the steering wheel. Beside him was Fay. The American was wearing his U.S. Army jacket with sergeant stripes on the sleeves. Sitting alone in the middle row of seats was Paul Neumayer wearing his friar's garb. In the rear seat were Marbach, Max and Zbik. The conversation was in German. Not Viennese-German, just ordinary German that everyone in the station wagon except Fay could understand.

"We'll beat that bus to Innsbruck," Rolf said.

Marbach looked around at the others. "Let's check our weapons."

Fay, unable to understand German, saw what the others were doing, guessed what had been said, and began checking his .38.

Marbach said to the others in the vehicle, "The American Sergeant Fay has a fully loaded .38. As for myself, like Rolf, I have an Enfield. For both of us, all six chambers of our Enfields are loaded."

"I have a Luger," said Max.

"Me too," said Zbik.

Fay shifted his head slightly. He had heard his name spoken mixed in with German words he couldn't understand. He turned away and stared out the car window.

"Do you have extra shells, boss?" Rolf asked Marbach.

"I have a box with two dozen shells."

"Are you going to share?"

"Here." Marbach provided Rolf with twelve shells.

"We could use a rifle or two," Max said.

"I wish I had my Radom VIS 35," Zbik said. "I left that most excellent of all pistols back in Poland."

"To hell with any hand gun," said Max. "Even that Polish VIS 35. I used to carry one of those, but what I'd like to have right now is an American tommy gun."

For a few moments, there was laughter in the car. Fay had no idea what was causing amusement for the others, but he joined in the laughter.

As the laughter died down, Marbach decided to bring up a personal concern that he felt a need to talk about.

"Something unusual happened this morning at the hospital. I'd like to talk about it. Today I visited with Leo Lechner. I know what you men are going to say, but . . . well, I am going to see him again."

Rolf didn't like what he was hearing. He clutched the steering wheel tightly.

Max shut his eyes.

Paul Neumayer, not recognizing the name "Leo Lechner," shifted in his seat, looked from one man to the other.

Zbik also didn't recognize the name, but, like Paul Neumayer, he realized that it was a name of significance to others in the station wagon.

Max opened his eyes. "See Leo again? What for? Leo is excrement! He was always excrement."

Marbach knew Max was saying what he would have said before his meeting with Leo. In reply to Max, he said, "I know what Leo used to be, but he has changed."

Max made an angry gesture. "Just because Leo got fried like a cinder doesn't mean it is all right to feel sorry for him. What about the victims—all those victims? The victims Leo was personally responsible for? Count them, Karl. Count them one-by-one. Only after you get through counting all of Leo's victims do you have the right to forgive him."

"I know . . . I know."

Max continued his diatribe. "Years ago, back before the war, I made the mistake of thinking Leo wasn't so bad. A big, friendly guy, I thought. The last time I saw big, friendly Leo he had a smile on his face while shoveling people into a transport bus to Dachau. The man is excrement."

Marbach knew he didn't have the right to forgive Leo, that Max was right about that. But he didn't believe it was a matter of forgiving. He knew that Leo was a genuinely contrite man who wanted to put an evil past behind him.

Rolf, at the wheel of the vehicle, stared straight ahead.

Marbach wished he hadn't got this started. This wasn't the time or place for him to have brought up how he felt about Leo.

"Shame on you," Max said. "Feeling pity for excrement like Leo."

"It isn't pity." Marbach regarded that as the truth.

"Make a damned fool out of yourself if you want to," Max said, "but don't ask me to forgive Leo. I can't forget Leo's victims."

"I know."

"Shame on you for pitying him."

"I told you it isn't pity. I know what Leo was like and I know what he did. I know how bad he was . . . but he's changed."

"Leo sure has changed," Max said. "From what I hear, he doesn't have much of a face anymore. Or much of anything else, either."

There was silence in the car.

Fay didn't know what the others were arguing about, but he wished the arguing was over and done with.

Finally, Zbik spoke up. "Is there anyone on the bus watching Frau Emhardt?"

"A colleague of mine is doing the watching," Max said.

Rolf said, "It's a long time until morning. We're at least six hours ahead of the bus, even with our detour to Salzburg and all the delays."

"When you get tired, I'll drive," Marbach said.

"I'll pull over," Rolf said. "You can start driving right now. When we get to Schwaz, the parking lot of the church in the center of town will be a good place for us to set up temporary camp."

"That sounds good to me."

CHAPTER FORTY

I t was early in the morning when the station wagon driven by Marbach arrived at the small Tyrolian city of Schwaz, a short distance from Innsbruck, less than an hour from the Italian border. He steered into a market place, then drove down a short street to a parking lot behind a small church before bringing the station wagon to a halt.

"Here we are, gentlemen," he said after turning the motor off.

Rolf, who had been asleep, stirred into wakefulness and said, "I sure would like a cup of coffee."

Zbik, who had also been asleep, rubbed his face and leaned forward in his seat. "Where . . . where the hell are we?"

"At church," Zbik said.

Rolf spoke in the language all of those in the station wagon except Fay could understand. "Karl, we can't all of us go charging inside. There's too many of us. Why don't you and I and Zbik go in there and check things out?"

Marbach agreed, got out of the station wagon and inhaled deeply the clear, fresh, early morning mountain air. "Breathe that Alpine air," he said to Rolf and Zbik as they exited the vehicle and walked up beside him. Paul Neumayer stood apart from the three men.

Rolf stood still, took a deep breath, and nodded to Paul Neumayer, who agreed that the Alpine air was wonderfully invigorating.

Marbach, Rolf and Zbik walked out of the parking lot, then up several cement steps leading to the small church. Marbach pulled open a heavy wooden door and with the other two men entered the church and looked around inside. A few steps off to the side was a marble bowl filled with holy water. All three men advanced and, one after the other, dipped their fingers into the bowl, blessed themselves, and then stood facing the interior of the church. The pews were empty. An elderly priest, standing with his back to them, was at the altar. It was either too early or too late for morning Mass.

Marbach, Rolf and Zbik genuflected, then stepped forward and walked down the middle aisle toward the altar. Their feet clomped heavily on the church floor.

The elderly priest looked over his shoulder, blessed himself and went to deliver a greeting. He was tall and white haired. He said, "I greet you, but spare me a moment. I will go and remove my vestments, then we can go to the rectory and talk."

A few minutes later, no longer wearing vestments, the priest joined his visitors in the rectory.

"Could you gentlemen use some breakfast?"

"We have some friends with us," Marbach said. "We drove all night from Vienna. Is it possible for our friends to come in here, perhaps shave, freshen up, and maybe have some of that breakfast you were talking about?"

"Of course."

"Is Father Gallo here?"

"I am afraid he has gone off to try to help a troubled family. He isn't expected to be back until tomorrow. There is a new priest here, but he is off doing some chores. I'll introduce you to him when he returns."

Marbach said, "We have some friends outside in a car."

"You and those outside in a car will need to freshen up and have some breakfast."

After saying that, the tall, elderly priest went outside and brought in the ones who had remained in the station wagon.

It didn't take long for all the men to get freshened up and start eating breakfast.

CHAPTER FORTY-ONE

I t didn't take long to finish breakfast. Marbach pushed his plate away and talked to Rolf. He wanted Rolf to find out if there was any news about the bus. Rolf agreed to go to the bus station and see what he could find out.

Marbach decided Rolf might need some back-up, so he asked Sergeant Fay to go along with Rolf. Fay couldn't speak any language but English, and Rolf couldn't speak English, but Marbach was sure they would be able to work well enough together to get the job done. Fay was wearing his U.S. Army jacket with sergeant stripes on the sleeves, but Marbach found another jacket for Fay to wear.

After Rolf and Fay left, it was quiet in the church kitchen. The elderly priest faced Marbach and said, "I just received a telephone call. I have to go the friary."

"The relay station for fleeing war criminals," Marbach said, pointedly offering a correction.

"Yes," the elderly priest said in a sad voice. "The friary is a relay station, one of the places of refuge for Nazis fleeing from Austria into Italy."

Marbach pressed the point. "The friary that is supposed to be a holy place is being used for something very unholy."

"Yes," the elderly priest said. "But if I go there now I may be able to learn something that will help clean up the unholiness."

"Do you want company?" Marbach inquired.

"Trust me," the elderly priest said. "It is best if I go alone. Some of the people in the friary are sympathetic to the Nazis."

"We will wait here for you," Marbach said.

At that moment, a young priest appeared. He was the new priest. He had a timid manner.

The elderly priest provided conventional introductions, then left to go to the Franciscan friary that was now a Nazi relay station.

CHAPTER FORTY-TWO

Marbach was sitting at a table with Paul Neumayer and the young priest. They were talking about nothing important, just making idle conversation. Paul Neumayer didn't have anything to say and eventually began nodding off. Finally, his head dropped almost to his chest. In that instant, he came fully awake and shook his head.

"You look exhausted, Brother Paul," the young priest said to Paul Neumayer. He assumed he was addressing a genuine friar.

"I guess I need some sleep," Paul Neumayer replied.

The young priest said, "There is a fine bed upstairs you can use."

"You don't have to show me. I can find the way," Paul Neumayer said. He got up from the table, directed a nodding motion to Marbach and the young priest and went upstairs.

Marbach sat at the table across from the young priest, who fussed nervously with his hands for a few minutes before saying, "Herr Police Inspector, this is terrible for Brother Paul. I have been told about his father."

Marbach didn't say that Paul Neumayer wasn't a friar. Instead, he said, "Yes, it is terrible for him."

Timidly, the young priest poured Marbach a cup of coffee and then one for himself.

"Do you know anything about other relay stations around here?" Marbach asked.

"Yes."

"What can you tell me?"

"In addition to the one here in Schwaz, there is one in a house in Innsbruck and another one in a house in Neustift."

"Three relay stations clustered this close together," Marbach mused. "I wonder which of them might operate for the new ratline called Odessa."

"I don't understand."

"I am trying to figure out how we might find the ones we are chasing."

"No one has told me who you are chasing."

"Adolf Eichmann and Dr. Heinrich Emhardt."

"Eichmann is an evil one. I never heard of the other person."

"Dr. Emhardt is an evil man."

"What about Brother Paul's father . . . ?"

"We'll be picking him up, too. He is mixed up in this."

Looking distressed, the young priest asked, "Does Brother Paul know about your plans for his father?"

"Yes, he knows. He knows and it was his choice to come along."

"Have pity on him. Please . . ." The young priest's voice trailed off.

"I have pity for him, but it was his choice to come along."

"I just don't know . . ." The young priest had pain in his eyes.

Marbach took a breath, almost spoke, but kept silent.

Timidly, the priest said, "I think these men you are chasing will try to climb over the Dolomites into Italy. I don't think they'll try to go by motor car from here into Italy."

Marbach agreed with the observation made by the young priest. He said, "You are probably right. In their shoes I think I would try to climb over the mountain."

"I sometimes climb," the young priest said.

Marbach was surprised to hear that. The timid young priest didn't look like a climber.

The young priest said, "My climbs usually begin around Neustift. I just do short climbs. I don't like to climb too high."

"During any of your climbing, have you encountered those who use the Dolomites to escape from Austria into Italy?"

"Yes."

"What can you tell me about those people?"

"There are a lot of refugees. Many lost persons."

"Tell me about the National Socialists."

The priest's youthful face looked troubled. "A few days ago, on one of my walks, I came across a farm where I encountered Colonel Count Neumayer. Yes, the colonel count: Friar Paul's father. He used to spend a lot of time around Innsbruck; I recognized him. We talked. He is a frightened man, very vulnerable."

"He identified himself?"

"I addressed him by name. As I said, he has long been a prominent person around here. There was no way he would know me, but I recognized him."

"Were there any other people around the colonel count?"

"One local lad showed up while we were talking. I knew him from years ago. Now the lad is a Werewolf, one of those Nazi guerrillas."

"Do you know other Werewolves?"

"Of course."

"Is there anything else you can tell me about your meeting with former Colonel Count Neumayer and the young lad who has become a Werewolf?"

"I don't know anything more."

"It might happen that I will ask you to show me where this farm can be found."

"I hope you won't, but if you do, I will show you."

"Do you know what ratlines are?"

"Of course. Some call them ratlines, but they are mostly escape routes for those fleeing the Soviet."

"Allow me to correct you. There are many legitimate refugees using the ratlines, but the purpose of the ratlines is to aid fleeing Nazi war criminals."

The priest had a confused look on his face. After a few moments, he said, "I don't know . . . I just don't know."

"I am one of those trying to close down the ratlines. Those ratlines are a way for National Socialism to continue to influence things in this troubled world."

"But the war is over. National Socialism has been defeated."

"National Socialism has been defeated, but it still exists. In the years to come, National Socialism may once again become vigorous. That will depend on how many of the worst National Socialists manage to escape and at some later time come back and spread their evil."

"All I see are victims."

"National Socialism is a virus that feeds on cruelty. I hate cruelty cruelly."

"Hatred is always wrong."

"Not hatred of cruelty. A good woman taught me to understand that. She introduced me to the philosopher Montaigne. He coined the words "Hate cruelty cruelly.""

"I am only a simple man."

"I think I could use a little sleep."

"There are several good beds upstairs."

"Anything will do."

Marbach went upstairs and found a bed. He believed that when you are doing certain types of work, you grab sleep where and when you can, even if might last for only a few minutes.

CHAPTER FORTY-THREE

When Fay returned from the bus station Rolf wasn't with him. Fay provided a silent greeting to Zbik and Max.

Zbik gestured upward with his thumb and Fay understood. He went upstairs and found Marbach asleep in one of the several beds.

"Wake up," Fay said, giving Marbach a small shove.

Mumbling in Viennese-German, Marbach came awake, shook his head, saw where he was, sat up, and asked Fay in English what was happening.

"I am back. Your friend Rolf found something else to do. He went off on his own."

"What did you learn at the bus station?"

"The bus is slow. It is still at least two hours before the bus will arrive."

"Let's get some coffee."

A few minutes later, Marbach and Fay were sitting with Zbik, Max, and the young priest in the church kitchen drinking coffee when the elderly priest returned from his visit to the Franciscan friary.

"It is dangerous for you gentlemen," the elderly priest said in German. He repeated himself in English for the benefit of Fay.

The elderly priest continued talking in English, addressing himself to Marbach and Fay. Max shrugged. He didn't mind not understanding what was being said. Zbik leaned forward. His wife had talked him into taking a course to learn English, so he was able to understand most of what was being said.

The elderly priest stared at Marbach and Fay. "The French army just raided the Franciscan friary."

Marbach and Fay exchanged glances.

The elderly priest had concern written on his face. "There was some shooting. I wasn't able to get close enough to learn anything, but the French have control of the friary. It is a certainty that the French will be coming here soon."

"We better get out of here," Marbach said.

At that moment, Paul Neumayer came into the kitchen and said, "There's a telephone call. I think it is Rolf. Odd, but he wouldn't speak his name. He got very brusque when I asked who was on the phone. Anyway, Herr Police Inspector, the call is for you."

"Where is the telephone?"

"Come. I'll show you," Paul Neumayer said.

Marbach followed Paul Neumayer to a small room, picked up the telephone, and said into the speaker, "Hello."

"It's me," Rolf said at the other end of the line. He provided no further identification.

"You better get back here," Marbach said. "There has been some poking around in the place of local holiness."

"I know. That's why I called."

"What more do you know?"

"I talked with some people who told me that the ones of interest to us weren't picked up. They got away."

A momentary pause.

"Anything else?" Marbach asked.

"Our former boss has joined the group." That was all Rolf needed to say to Marbach. Back in 1938, Stephan Kaas had been their boss when he was Commander of Vienna Kripo.

"Is anyone going after the ones who ran away?"

"Yes. A lot of American soldiers are on the chase. They are putting up road checks from here to the mountains. The soldiers should be showing up here soon."

"You better get back here."

"Don't you want to know what else happened?"

"Tell me."

"The bus from Innsbruck got stopped by some impolite people outside of Schwaz. Very clearly, the impolite people are the ones of interest to us. Oh, something more, a Russian woman whose name you know was taken into the warm arms of the impolite people."

"Fay and Rolf just showed up here," Marbach said. "They didn't hear about that."

"The people I talked with just learned about it a few minutes ago."

"It is time to move on. It'll save time if you don't come back here. Let me know where to pick you up,"

The reply that was provided would have baffled an eavesdropper, but it enabled Marbach to know how he would be able to find Rolf.

CHAPTER FORTY-FOUR

Former SS Major Kaas was at the wheel of a car speeding toward the border. Beside him, the only passenger in the car, the Russian wife of Dr. Emhardt, a woman who carried identification as Natasha Yakovlevna, was struggling to appear fully in control of herself. Kaas was impressed with the Russian woman's dark, heavy eyebrows. He favored women with eyebrows like this Russian woman. The eyebrows punctuated a face that was exceptionally feminine.

"That was a lot of excitement," the Russian woman said.

"Yes," Kaas said, wondering if he should address the Russian woman as Frau Emhardt.

"Are you taking me to my husband?"

"That's where we are going. Your husband is at a farm up ahead. We use the farm to coordinate our activities in this area."

"Perhaps we could stop somewhere so I can look my best for my husband."

"We've been lucky, so far. It's best to not take any chances," Kaas said, casting a glance at the Russian woman.

As always, he evaluated women in terms of usefulness and attractiveness. This Russian woman was useful to him and he found her highly attractive.

"You are correct," the Russian woman said. "What I said was foolish."

"Are you up to a climb? A climb across the Dolomites to Italy?"

"Can't we go by motor? Is it necessary to climb?"

"If we go by motor, it will be necessary to use the Brenner Pass or the Reschen Pass. At those places there are many inspection points. It would be folly to try to get past those inspection points."

"Then we climb."

"Is Dr. Emhardt up to a climb?"

"My husband knows how to climb. So do I."

Kaas glanced again at the Russian woman. His pleasure having her in the car with him increased.

CHAPTER FORTY-FIVE

M ax, at the wheel of the Chevrolet station wagon, was confused by the instructions coming from the young priest sitting behind him in the middle row of seats. "Are you sure you know where we're going?" he asked over his shoulder, making an effort to keep irritation out of his voice.

"Yes," the priest said in a cautious voice. "We are going to a farm where I believe we will find those we are chasing."

"That is the place for us to go," said Marbach.

"Yes," the priest said, shyly nodding his head.

Max glanced at Sergeant Fay sitting beside him. The American had put on his army jacked with the sergeant stripes on the sleeves. There was no reason for the American to not be wearing his uniform, Max told himself. He considered the American to be all right even if he couldn't speak anything but English. Max stared into the rearview mirror. The priest was sitting beside a friar in the middle row of seats. In the rear seat were Marbach, Rolf and Zbik.

Max focused his attention on what he could see through the windshield. Somewhere up ahead was Neustift, a village in a deep valley surrounded by high mountains.

Almost half an hour later, Max brought the Chevrolet station wagon to a halt.

The priest said in his timid voice, "We are near the farm. Just a little way down that road to the left. We are very—"

At that moment, there was an interruption.

The interruption came in the form of a young man with a rifle who edged out from behind a tree and moved up to within a few feet of the station wagon.

Max put an amicable look on his face as he rolled down his window.

The youth with the rifle spoke in an angry voice. "Who are you?"

Two more youths ran up to the other side of the car, both of them holding hand weapons. One of them shouted, "I see an American uniform. Kill them! Kill them!"

In the next instant, all three youths began shooting. Thudding sounds could be heard as bullets hit the outside of the station wagon.

Max grabbed for the weapon secured under his belt, but it was bundled up, hard to retrieve.

While Max struggled to get his gun into his hand, Fay, sitting beside Max, pushed open the door on his side of the car, rolled out onto the ground, got to his feet and began firing his .38.

In a parallel movement, from the back seat, Rolf followed Zbik out of the rear door, both of them looking for targets.

Fay killed one youth. Zbik killed another.

The youth with the rifle was making a series of awkward jerking movements in an attempt to pull his rifle bolt back.

Looking around, Rolf was relieved there was no one left to shoot. The youths had to be killed, but, still . . . they were very young.

Marbach leveled his Enfield at the youth with the rifle. "Drop your weapon," he ordered.

Helplessly, the youth stared for a moment, then dropped the rifle, a Mauser Gew 98.

Marbach filled his voice with menace. "Where is Eichmann?"

"I . . . I . . . I don't know." The youth looked terrified.

"Tell me where Eichmann is or be damned."

The youth's voice was a choking sound. "I won't tell you."

Far off in the distance shots were being fired.

The young priest said, "Those are warning shots. Someone is giving a warning to the ones staying in the farm."

Marbach stared thoughtfully at the young priest. He concluded that the priest might be timid, but he seemed to be pretty good at figuring things out.

"Everyone back in the car," Max shouted.

"We might have use for this rifle," Marbach said, picking up the Mauser dropped by the youth who was now visibly trembling.

"Don't kill me," the frightened youth pleaded.

"Nobody's going to kill you," Marbach said. "Get running."

The youth stared at Marbach for a moment, then turned and ran away.

"One of them is getting away," shouted Max.

"Forget him," Marbach said. "Shooting him won't accomplish anything."

A few moments later, with everyone back inside, the station wagon left the scene. Max was behind the wheel. The bullets fired into the station wagon had hit at least one tire, making the vehicle difficult to handle, but Max was a competent driver.

CHAPTER FORTY-SIX

While the station wagon drove toward the farm, far in the distance clouds of dust could be seen. A half dozen bicycles carrying Werewolves were fleeing from the farm. There was also a car moving away at a high rate of speed.

When the station wagon got to the farm, everyone jumped out.

"We'll have to stop chasing for a while," Marbach said. He gestured at the station wagon. "We have some repair work to do. We have a punctured tire and a ruptured radiator."

"We better get the car into that barn," Max said in the German everyone but Fay could understand. "At least we'll have cover if the Werewolves come gunning for us before we can get the car fixed."

A few minutes later, inside the barn, the Chevrolet station wagon was up on a large wooden block when bullets began hitting the walls of the barn.

"Cover the windows!" Marbach shouted.

The men placed themselves at the windows. Each of them strained to see what there was to see.

"Can you see any of them?" Rolf addressed his question to no one in particular. He added, "How many are there?"

"At least three or four on this side," Zbik said.

"Five, maybe six on this side," Max said.

"See if you can pop off some of those Werewolves," Rolf said to Marbach. "The rest of us will see about getting this damned car fixed."

Fay, unable to understand what anybody was saying, joined up with the ones working on the car, contributed his mechanical skill, made himself useful.

CHAPTER FORTY-SEVEN

I n a car moving at high speed, Kaas pushed his foot down harder on the accelerator. He was impressed by the warning system at the farm. There had been enough time for him to round up everyone, get the car loaded and go driving off. The vitally important Odessa papers were safe, stuffed into a secure place in the trunk of the car. For Kaas that was what mattered most: keeping the Odessa papers safe. Of the others in the car, he despised Eichmann, had only contempt for Dr. Emhardt, and didn't like Colonel Count Neumayer. He didn't like the one who was a former Colonel Count, but it suited his purposes to identify the man as though he was still a colonel count.

Kaas glanced at the Russian woman, Frau Emhardt. She was the only one he deemed worthy of any of his attention. But infinitely more important than the Russian woman were the records containing information essential to keep Odessa functioning.

Kaas held tight to the steering wheel when the car hit a rough bump in the road. From the back seat, Colonel Count Neumayer gave out a shout. "I think you ought to drive more carefully."

Reluctantly, Kaas eased up a little on the gas pedal.

Eichmann hunched down in his seat and said, "Was this flight really necessary? One car approaches the relay station and we flee like frightened chickens. Can't the Werewolves protect us from the occupants of one car."

"It was a U.S. Army car," said Dr. Emhardt. This is the French zone. American military don't drive idly around in the French zone. Whenever one of those American cars shows up, there is always big trouble."

"Americans are assassins!" shouted the Russian wife of Dr. Emhardt.

Kaas clasped the steering wheel while speaking in a voice calculated to sound calm and reassuring. "Not far from here is a place where we will be getting out of this car. We will go on foot up the mountain."

Colonel Count Neumayer leaned forward in the back seat. "Climb the mountain? Is it really necessary to climb the mountain?"

Dr. Emhardt's Russian wife said, "My husband and I are ready for the climb."

Dr. Emhardt nodded reluctant agreement.

"I will do the climb," Eichmann said.

"I will try," Colonel Count Neumayer said in an anxious voice.

Almost half an hour later, Kaas stopped the car. Nearby was a meadow. Beyond the meadow were some pine trees. Beyond the pine trees were the Dolomites.

"My love, my Heinrich," the Russian woman said in German to Dr. Emhardt. She added additional German words of endearment.

Kaas thought it would be nice to hear Dr. Emhardt's wife speak sweet words to him. He was still thinking that as he gave instructions to get the car unloaded.

When the unloading was finished, with the others helping, Kaas pushed the car to a steep slope. With one final shove, the car went crashing down onto rocks far below.

Eichmann appeared to be having second thoughts. He stared upward at the mountain and said, "Look how awful it is. It's a giant battlement."

"We must climb this battlement," Dr. Emhardt's wife said. Dr. Emhardt nodded agreement.

Kaas checked his pack. Inside were the Odessa papers. They were heavy, but he wasn't tempted to ask any of the others to help lug them around. There would just be questions. After taking a moment, without saying a word to Eichmann or any of the others, he lifted the heavy pack onto his back and started walking on a path that stretched upward to the mountain. The others followed him.

A few minutes later, at a place where the path leveled off, the group being led by Kaas passed first one crucifix sticking up in the ground and then another.

Dr. Emhardt's wife slowed her pace. When she was sure her husband wasn't looking, she furtively blessed herself.

Kaas, glancing back over his shoulder, observed the Russian woman blessing herself. More and more he was finding her to be a fetching sight. But after a moment of reflection, he focused all of his attention on the business at hand. He looked upward, adjusted the heavy pack, and hitched his weapon high on his shoulder. The weapon was a Kar 98, a reliable carbine. Beside him, he saw Eichmann was carrying a Schmeisser. The Schmeisser was a useful rapid-fire weapon, but he wouldn't be inclined to trade weapons if a trade was offered. The Kar 98 was more than just a useful rapid-fire weapon.

A quick walking pace brought the group to a place where serious mountain climbing would begin.

After a short pause, the upward climb began. Kaas in the lead, the others trailing behind.

An hour later the party had climbed up to a broad mountain ledge where Kaas called a halt. "I think we're safe, but we can't count on the weather. I think we ought to keep going, but it's up to you others if we take a rest."

There was agreement. Even Colonel Count Neumayer agreed. The group would not take a rest. The upward climb would continue.

CHAPTER FORTY-EIGHT

While Kaas and his group were climbing the mountain, back at the farm all shooting suddenly stopped. After waiting a few minutes, Marbach edged out of the barn to find out what was going on. Those who had been doing the shooting had fled, and the reason for their flight was one French policeman in a blue uniform riding a bicycle, a very ordinary bicycle. The French policeman's kepi—a visor cap with a round, flat top—was pushed back on his head at what any independent observer might think was a rakish angle.

Marbach recognized the French policeman, stood still and waited while the Frenchman pedaled over to where he was standing.

Two expressive eyebrows lifted upward on the Frenchman's forehead. He addressed Marbach in Viennese-German.

"Karl Marbach! Greetings, my friend. Whatever was the shooting all about?"

"Henri Sampeyre, you have rescued us."

"I guess that makes me a hero," Sampeyre said with a laugh.

There was a vigorous hand shake between two friends who were unexpectedly meeting in a strange place. After completing the hand shake, they clasped arms around each other.

Finally, Marbach stepped back and said, "I know I'm under French authority, my friend. A short explanation for what you have encountered is that I and my friends were set upon by Werewolves. We are in pursuit of Adolf Eichmann and an important Nazi scientist. We intend to capture those two and, maybe even more important, we intend to capture documents that will make it possible to close down a new Nazi ratline."

"Adolf Eichmann, you say, and a new Nazi ratline."

"Yes. The ratline is very new and very ominous. We have an American military car. We intend to use the car to help us shut down the new ratline."

"You have an American military car?"

"Yes, inside the barn."

"I'll call in a general alert—if you agree. Is there a telephone around here?"

"Yes, by all means call in an alert. As for where a telephone is, I don't know. You might check the farm house."

"Yes," Sampeyre said. He paused for a moment, then headed for the farm house.

A few minutes later, after having called in a general alert, Sampeyre entered the barn, faced Marbach, smiled, and said, "I trust you will kindly tell me what is going on here."

Marbach provided Sampeyre with relevant details about Eichmann, Dr. Emhardt, and Natasha Yakovlevna. Then he told what he knew about Odessa, about the records for the new Nazi escape route.

When Marbach was done, Sampeyre said in reply, "Most certainly those you have been chasing will not try to drive to Italy. If they do, our inspection points will seal their fate. I suggest we assume they will soon leave their car and do a climb from Austria to Italy."

"There's a good place for climbing not far from here," the young priest said, timidly intruding. "If they know about it, that's the choice they will make. It's the best place anywhere near here to cross over from Austria to Italy. They will be able to end up very close to Cortina on the Italian side."

Sampeyre addressed Marbach. "I do, of course, insist on joining with you on this chase. There is, however, a point of protocol."

Most definitely there was an important point of protocol: who was going to lead the chase?

Marbach said, "We are in the French zone and you are the better climber. When you give an order, I shall obey."

"Good," Sampeyre said. He paused a moment and looked at the others. "Is that all right with the rest of you?" He said that in German, not Viennese-German, but ordinary German.

"All right by me," Rolf said.

"And me," Max said.

"Me also," Zbik said.

Paul Neumayer and the timid young priest also agreed.

"And you Monsieur Sergeant?" Sampeyre said in German to Fay. "Do you agree to follow my orders?"

"What?" Fay asked. He had given up trying to understand what was going on.

Marbach said in English to Fay, "Monsieur Sampeyre is now in charge. Do you agree to follow his orders or do we leave you behind?"

Fay nodded his head up and down. "Are you kidding? Of course, I agree."

"Good," Sampeyre said. Without understanding the words spoken by the American he could tell by the head nodding that agreement had been expressed. He turned and said to the men assembled around him, "Now, my first order. Let's get the station wagon fixed so we can promptly get on with chase."

"The station wagon is ready," Rolf said. "The American did most of the mechanical fixing."

"We better find some climbing gear," Marbach said. "We're going to need it."

"There must be some gear around here," Sampeyre said.

Marbach gestured. "Over there are some bins that look promising."

Sampeyre went to check what was in the bins. Upon opening the first bin, he uttered an exclamation of satisfaction at the collection of gear inside. Quickly, he began perusing. Pitons, karabiners, even hammers got his close attention. Some items were discarded, including hemp rope. "We will use the nylon rope," he declared.

"Nylon rope? Why not hemp?" Marbach wasn't sure about nylon rope.

"We will use nylon rope," Sampeyre said decisively. And we will take only Italian pitons. To hell with German pitons made of tool steel."

"Where do we find gloves?" Marbach asked. "I don't see any gloves."

"Around a farm there must be gloves," Sampeyre said. "And extra trousers and shirts."

Poking around, it didn't take long to find gloves and some clothes. There were also parkas, woolen coats with hoods.

Sampeyre was pleased to find for himself an extra-long parka. He used the French word "cagoule" to assert his ownership. He put on the "cagoule" and was pleased to find that it fit him well.

Fay didn't understand anything being said, but he didn't bother Marbach with any questions. He just copied the others while selecting what to wear.

"Let's get the climbing gear loaded into the back of this very large American car." Sampeyre said. "And then we will get on with the chase."

CHAPTER FORTY-NINE

T he chase was ready to get started. Zbik got into the driver's seat and, when everything was ready, he drove the Chevrolet station wagon at a high rate of speed down a muddy road, and then onto a narrow macadamized road that led higher and higher into the mountains.

While keeping his foot pressed firmly on the gas pedal, Zbik cast a quick glance at the American sitting beside him, then stared straight ahead while he listened to what was being said by the others in the station wagon.

Sampeyre, sitting in the third row of seats, was saying that the Marshall Plan proposed by the Americans would never work and that Democratic Socialism was the only rational answer to the Soviet threat.

When Sampeyre finally finished his spiel, Max, sitting in the middle row of seats beside the young priest and Paul Neumayer, started talking about what he did as a private investigator, but the other passengers quickly indicated a lack of interest and Max soon stopped talking.

Clasping the steering wheel tightly, Zbik turned his head slightly when Sampeyre, sitting in the back of the station wagon between Marbach and Rolf, said, "This leg of mine won't be a problem once we start climbing. It never bothers me when I am climbing. In fact, climbing seems to get the stiffness out. My leg only bothers me when I can't stretch it out from time-to-time."

"I have a leg that bothers me a lot," Marbach said. "I got a bullet in it during that other war, the one that began in 1914."

After saying that, and realizing the American was being excluded from the fellowship of the others in the car, Marbach repeated in English to Fay what he and Sampeyre had said about their legs.

"I got a real bad leg," Fay said in reply. "Got it messed up in Italy. Almost lost the damned thing."

Marbach told the others what the American had said.

Sampeyre rubbed both of his legs and said, "My injuries have always been in the mountains. Never in police work and never in war."

Rolf said to Sampeyre, "All the war you've seen and you never got wounded?"

"I have no wounds from war," Sampeyre replied. "Only from mountain climbing. I have never had even a small injury during war. When this most recent war started, I was serving with French mountain soldiers, the Chasseurs Alpins. They were fine men, very good men. Anyway, in 1940 my troop was sent to fight in Norway and then, after the defeat, a lot of us fled back to the Somme. It was a rout, but I never got any slight injury. I ended up in Italy with no injuries, not even any bad bruises."

Marbach chose this moment to address a question to Sampeyre. "What do you think ought to be done with those Russians who joined up with the Nazis, joined up because they hated Communism, wanted to be free from Communism. Now lots of them are being rounded up wherever they have ended up in Europe and they are being sent to where they will face Soviet justice."

Sampeyre didn't mince words with his reply. "They took a stand with Nazism, the great evil of our time. I don't have any sympathy for them. Let them all be returned to Russia. That is the best thing. It is what they deserve."

Marbach shook his head. "I don't agree. It is wrong what is going on, all the countless numbers of Russian men, women and children being sent by the Allied forces to death, torture and slavery in Russia."

Max scowled. "It is a mistake to have pity for the Russians who are being returned to Russia. I hate the Communists, but they were fighting the Nazis. Those Russians who are now being returned to Russia allied themselves with the Nazis."

Rolf joined in the talk. "In the fall of 1944, I was in northern Italy when the Nazis opened the area around Tolmezzo as a refuge for General Vlasov's troops. Those Russian troops had their women and children with them. We were told there were two hundred thousand in all. At first, I had no feeling for those Russian people in Italy, but as time passed the ones I got to know I always liked."

Zbik held tight to the wheel of the station wagon as he said, "I was born and raised in Poland. I have never seen any Russians I liked."

Marbach spoke with studied deliberation. "Two years ago I saw what was being done to Russians fleeing Russia. I saw them being rounded up. The British . . . the Americans, the French, too, gathered them up. Gathered them up and put them in trucks and shipped them to where they would face Soviet justice. There were people who cut their throats rather than be sent back to Russia. I saw a Russian woman deliberately throw herself under one of the moving trucks. That's an awful way to get yourself killed. I was told she did that because she didn't have a knife."

Max snorted angrily. "They placed themselves in service to Hitler. I have no pity for any of them."

Marbach didn't back off. "A lot of good Russians saw Hitler as their only chance to free themselves from the Soviet."

"Shame on you!" Sampeyre shouted at Marbach.

As the argument became more heated, Paul Neumayer and the timid young priest exchanged anxious looks.

From where he was sitting in the rear of the station wagon, Marbach was able to see that up in the front seat Fay was curious about what the shouting was all about. Marbach leaned forward and, despite the distance that separated them, provided an explanation to the American.

Fay listened, took a moment for reflection and said over his shoulder to Marbach, "I'm on your side. I served under General Kennedy when he accepted the surrender of eight thousand troops from General Vlasov's army. He gave his word they wouldn't be turned over to the Soviets and he kept his word. He was ordered to turn them over to the Soviets, but he didn't turn that bunch of Russians over to the Soviets. There's talk he is going to be court martialed. Maybe that's going to happen. Lots of folk say it ought to happen. But ask me and I'll tell you General Kennedy is one hell of a good man."

Marbach told the others what Fay had said and the argument got louder.

Sampeyre, Zbik and Max united angrily against Marbach and Rolf and Fay. The timid young priest and Paul Neumayer kept silent.

While the argument continued, the Chevrolet station wagon moved steadily upward into the mountains. Soon they were high enough up for there to be snow on the road.

It was then that something outside the station wagon caught Max's attention. He made a pointing gesture and said, "It looks like someone sheared those trees off."

Everyone in the car peered out of one side of the station wagon or the other. On both sides, trees could be seen that had been knocked down. The broken trees hadn't been uprooted. They looked like they had been snapped off, torn away leaving stumps barely a foot or two above the ground.

"There was much snow last winter," the priest said. "In the Spring and in the Summer came the avalanches."

"I don't see the debris an avalanche would have left," Rolf said with doubt in his voice. He didn't know much about mountains, but it seemed to him that if an avalanche had knocked down the trees there should be debris lying around. He saw very little debris. Only a lot of tree limbs lying beside broken tree stumps.

"The avalanche didn't come this far," the priest said in his timid voice. "But the avalanche pushed the wind this far and the wind did the rest."

"Wind did all this?" Max shook his head. That didn't seem believable.

"Yes," Marbach said. He'd seen this sort of thing before. "The wind did it."

Before more could be said, Sampeyre, who was peering through a window, said, "We better stop here. This is where those we are chasing started climbing the mountain. You can see the signs they left."

Zbik brought the Chevrolet station wagon to a halt and one after the other the men got out of the vehicle and looked upward. They saw continually changing patterns of colors emerging and dissolving across the face of the mountain. There was gold and gray and, mixed up with those colors, shifting blends of black and purple and red.

"My God!" Max exclaimed, his face filled with awe at what he was seeing.

The priest blessed himself.

Each of the others responded in his own way to the power, strangeness and beauty of what they were seeing.

Sampeyre was the first one to find something else to do. He opened the rear door of the station wagon, fussed around, did some tidying up.

Going off on his own, Zbik quickly spotted tire tracks, then an abandoned car. He shouted to the others, "Their car is down there. They dumped it down there before going up."

Sampeyre stepped away from the station wagon and used his eyes to trace a journey all the way to the top of the mountain. Deeply moved by the intense, irresistible energy of upwardness possessed by the mountain, he whispered, "Ensemble éternel."

Marbach moved up beside Sampeyre and said, "The best chance we will have is if we can get up above the ones we are chasing."

Sampeyre nodded. "Yes. I was thinking the same thing. Once we get above them we can use fire power to keep them from going back down. We have that Mauser rifle. It is a good weapon for killing at a distance."

Paul Neumayer, standing nearby, spoke in a voice filled with anguish. "Do you have to do killing?" His father was with the ones they were chasing.

Sampeyre stared at Paul Neumayer, looked at the friar garb the young man was wearing, and said, "Killing is always terrible, but we have to stop this evil thing called Odessa. If these people surrender that is all right, but if they don't surrender they must be killed."

"Yes," Marbach said. "We have to stop Odessa."

"We better start climbing," Sampeyre said. "If we climb all day today, maybe into the night, then cross over, we will be on top of them and we will be able to keep them from going back down, or sideways, or anywhere. They will belong to us."

The priest said in his timid voice, "There's a way for us to give them a rude surprise by early this afternoon."

"By this afternoon . . . ? Sampeyre stared intently. "Tell me more."

"There's a tunnel that goes almost all the way to the top of the mountain."

"A tunnel?"

"Yes," the priest said. "I discovered it by accident. It is an ammunition shaft that was built during the war that ended in 1918. The tunnel has a marvelous ladder. It is very safe. I have climbed that ladder several times. During the first of the two terrible wars the tunnel was used to move ammunition from the bottom of the mountain up to the top where there were cannons. One can move much faster using the ladder than by climbing up the mountain. Much, much faster."

"Where do we find this marvelous tunnel of yours?" Sampeyre asked.

The timid voice answered, "A fifteen minute drive from here is a pile of ice. We will have to cross the ice to get to the mountain, but once we get to the mountain I will be able to show you how we can quickly get to the entrance of the tunnel."

"Let's get on with it," Sampeyre said. "Let's find this marvelous tunnel."

CHAPTER FIFTY

When Sampeyre gave the order to get inside the Chevrolet station wagon there was a lot of running and shoving. At a strategic moment, Fay managed to push ahead of Zbik and plant himself in the driver's seat. Marbach and Rolf jumped into the front seat beside him. Zbik angrily settled for a place in the middle row of seats with Sampeyre and Max, while Paul Neumayer and the young priest placed themselves in the back row of seats.

As soon as everyone said they were ready, Fay started driving. The priest, from the rear of the station wagon, provided instructions that Marbach passed on to Fay.

For Fay the driving was easy enough, taking instructions was easy enough, but he didn't know what was going on or why. He glanced at the sergeant stripes on his sleeves and told himself this was like the army: other guys call the shots and what you do is go with the flow.

A quarter of an hour later, the station wagon came to a halt and the eight men got out of the vehicle. They stared at the lake of ice stretched out in front of them.

"This looks like more than just some ice," said Max. "It looks like a glacier."

"We can cross it," said Sampeyre.

Max jumped out of the station wagon and walked around to the back of the vehicle. He rolled down the rear door and looked inside. There were almost a dozen ice axes in the rear of the station wagon.

Sampeyre walked over, took his time, finally selected a long-handled ice axe. Marbach, Rolf, Zbik, Paul Neumayer and the priest each took his time selecting an ice axe.

Fay couldn't tell one ice axe from another, so he just grabbed the first one he laid his hand on. Then, while the others examined their ice axes, Fay stared lamely at the one he had chosen.

Marbach had been watching and he knew what was bothering Fay. "You have a perfectly good ice axe. Now we will collect the necessary gear and get on with things. We'll need rope and carabiners, good double-locked carabiners made of steel. And we'll need pitons. Come, friend, it's time to load up."

Fay clapped Marbach on the shoulder.

Marbach smiled at Fay, then moved off to one side and knelt down near a clustering of edelweiss, Alpine flowers. "This edelweiss is a good omen," he said to Fay. For the benefit of the others, he repeated what he'd said using German.

Comments about the edelweiss—unintelligible to Fay—were made by Rolf and Zbik.

"We better start moving up," Sampeyre said. "Getting across this ice shouldn't be too difficult as long as we watch where we put our feet."

Standing alone, Fay looked around. The ice was covered with a blanket of snow and there was a thin mist. He cocked his head. There was the sound of insects: crickets were chirping.

"What's with all these insects up here on this ice?" Fay asked Marbach.

"Up here it is winter, but not far from here it is summer. Those insects must have gotten blown here by the wind. Don't be surprised at anything you see from this point on. We are in the Dolomites and the Dolomites aren't just the grandest mountains in the world, they are the strangest."

A few minutes later, after watching Marbach and the others fuss with their rucksacks, the backpacks, Fay copied what they were doing until he saw them begin attaching crampons—metal spikes—to their boots. He said to Marbach, "I don't think I'll need those. I can get across this ice without wearing those damned things."

After Marbach translated to Sampeyre what Fay had said, the Frenchman said angrily, "Tell him that if he is going with us across this ice, he will use crampons."

"I heard. I heard," Fay said. He didn't need to understand the words to know that Sampeyre was insistent that crampons would be used.

Marbach walked over, knelt down and helped secure the crampons to Fay's boots. When that was done, he said, "These will be hard for you to get used to at first, but you'll be all right. Just remember to keep your legs wide apart and put your feet down flat with all the points of the crampons going in at the same time. With each step you take, try to bring your feet up cleanly and put them down hard. It's important to not make any sudden jerking movements. One more thing, keep your pack as high on your shoulders as you can. And the most important thing: if you think your crampons are coming loose—if you have any trouble at all—call out for help. From this point on, the only disgrace is to fake anything. Especially don't fake not needing help when you need it. You will just make it worse for the rest of us if you don't ask for help as soon as you need it. If you goof up, don't be embarrassed, but if you fake anything—anything at all—that will be unforgivable. To make mistakes is honorable as long as you don't fake anything."

"I understand," Fay said. He wasn't faking. He did understand. He was ignorant about mountains, but he knew about combat. That meant he knew better than to fake things when he was the novice in a dangerous place.

Marbach finished securing the crampons, looked up and grinned. Fay grinned back.

CHAPTER FIFTY-ONE

S ampeyre did one final check of each of the men. He checked their parkas, rucksacks, tied-off trousers, boots, and, finally, their crampons. Then he pulled tight his own parka—his cagoule—and the trek across the ice began.

The eight men headed toward where the mountain was stretching upward into the sky.

Probing with his long-handled ice axe, Sampeyre led the way along the flat surface. Each man was linked to the others by a rope that was never allowed to hang slack. Sampeyre kept up a steady forward movement. Whenever his long-handled ice axe detected softness in the solid ice, he shifted direction, but only slightly.

There was one critical problem. The air was saturated with water vapor and that was causing an enervating lassitude to afflict the men. They complained among themselves about how they felt. Because he couldn't understand what the others were saying, Fay didn't understand why he was feeling so much aching tiredness, but he kept plodding forward.

Halfway across to where they were going, knowing that the fatigue afflicting all of them made it sensible to take a break, Sampeyre pushed the handle of his ice axe into the ice and maneuvered his backside into a comfortable position that left him half-standing, half sitting on the axe head. The other men also used their ice axes as seats. All except Fay, who was too tired to do anything but lie on the ice.

"We don't have glasses to protect our eyes," Sampeyre said. "The sun does mischief playing off the ice. It is best to avoid looking around too much. Anyone who goes blind will have to be left behind." The Frenchman paused a moment, then took a jar from his jacket, rubbed some of the contents on his face and passed the jar to Marbach who took the jar in his hand and examined it. The jar advertised itself as containing woman's face cream, an expensive brand of woman's face cream.

Marbach said to Sampeyre, "It is good to have this face cream. It will provide protection against the sun and help with the snow that the wind keeps blowing in our faces. But I must ask, do you always carry around such an excellent brand of women's face cream?"

"A fortunate accident," Sampeyre said, allowing his French accent to trump German words. "It was originally planned as a present for a woman I met in Hallstatt. If it hadn't been for this adventure, I would be spending this evening with that fabulous female creature. I can only hope the lovely woman will accept a lame excuse from me for giving her no notice that I will not be able to show up tonight."

"I wish just one time a woman—any woman—would accept a lame excuse from me," Marbach said.

Everyone laughed, even Fay, who had no idea what had been said.

A few minutes later it was time to move on. But the men went only a short distance before they encountered a dark snow patch more than ten feet wide, stretching about fifty feet from one end to the other. On both sides there was broken ice and water. Going around the bridge didn't look safe. The best thing to do was walk to the end of the snow patch.

Sampeyre led the way, probed forward, poked his ice axe into the snow patch while giving a slight tug to the rope being held by Max, who was standing directly behind him. There was no thud or tinkle to suggest a hollow surface, but Sampeyre knew it was best to be cautious. He quickly but carefully got to the end of the snow patch.

When ready, he rolled up some rope, held one end tossed the roll to Marbach.

Marbach caught hold of the rope, moved up close beside Fay, and said to the American, "Tie the rope around your waist and don't let it go slack while you move to the end of this patch."

Fay did as he was told.

Marbach was next. He tied the rope around his waist, didn't let it go slack while he carefully made his way to where Sampeyre and Fay were waiting.

After that, always keeping the rope tight, the friar walked the snow patch, then the young priest, then Rolf, then Max.

Zbik was going to be the last one to come across.

"Keep the rope tight," Marbach shouted.

"Be careful, Zbik," Sampeyre shouted. "I have a bad feeling. We've put a lot of stress on this snow patch."

With the rope secure around his waist, Zbik started across. He was half-way to safety when the snow surface broke away. There was a crashing sound, a hole opened up and Zbik dropped out of sight. Although held by the rope, he disappeared into icy water.

Without exchanging words, Max joined with Sampeyre and working together they hauled Zbik out of the icy water.

Soaking wet, Zbik lay for a moment on a firm blanket of snow, then slowly rose to his feet. "Thank you, friends," he said.

One after the other, the men stepped forward, shook Zbik's hand and clasped his shoulders. Then the danger was put in the past and movement across the ice resumed. There was a lot of mist, but, to the relief of everyone, no more snow patches.

It didn't take long to get to a place where there was no more mist. The upward poking mountain was clearly visible, not a stone's throw ahead of them.

Everyone stopped. Fay looked off to the side. On the ice, a short distance away, a sky-blue butterfly, making a futile effort to free itself, was fluttering in the snow.

While the others exchanged glances, Fay stood still for a moment, then walked off to the side several steps, reached down and slowly used the warmth of his bare fingers to melt ice until the sky-blue butterfly got free from the ice and flew out of sight into the mountain air.

"Imagine a butterfly up here," Fay said with awe in his voice.

Sampeyre stared at Fay. He told himself the American was a fine fellow, even if he couldn't climb much and didn't speak a civilized language.

Sampeyre made a futile effort to see if he could catch a final glimpse of the sky-blue butterfly. It comforted him to think that, with luck—a kindly wind—the butterfly might be able to make it to safety. Sampeyre liked thinking about the butterfly making it to safety.

CHAPTER FIFTY-TWO

The eight men trekking across ice were very close to the mountain. All they had to do now was get to the end of a stone bridge, a string of solid rock a half dozen feet wide, stretching out from the mountain for a distance of about fifty feet. On each side of the stone bridge there was emptiness, vast engulfing nothingness. When the men got to the end of the stone bridge, there would be a climb up the mountain.

With rope trailing behind him, Sampeyre went first. He stopped one time in the middle of the stone bridge and, before moving on, stared down into the emptiness below.

One-at-a-time, the other seven men followed. Each of them held tight to the rope. None of them stopped in the middle and looked down. Instead, unlike Sampeyre, they kept their eyes straight ahead as they crossed the narrow stone bridge.

After everyone was across, the group collected together close to where the mountain began stretching upward. There was no conversation. Sampeyre scratched his head as he sized up the situation. He felt the mood of the men was too subdued. He reflected for a moment, then said, "We must declare our victory over emptiness." He stared hard at Marbach, then at each of the other men and, finally, at Fay, who didn't understand what had been said, but, clearly was ready to do whatever might be expected of him.

"We must look down into the emptiness," Sampeyre said. "We must stare down into the icy white soul and do some cursing!" He walked over to where the stone bridge ended, leaned forward and delivered a loud French curse. A faint echo could be heard.

Marbach and the others moved over to where Sampeyre was standing. They all leaned forward, looked down and began howling and cursing. Fay, with a puzzled look on his face, joined in the howling and cursing. Even the priest uttered a loud curse expressing defiance.

As though in reply to being cursed, the emptiness screamed back. A series of echoes came bellowing up from below.

Laughing loudly, Sampeyre turned his back and walked away. "Come, comrades," he shouted over his shoulder. "We have let the emptiness know what we think of it. We don't care what it says to us in reply. Let us turn our backs on what is being howled up at us as we walk away."

Like a small squad of soldiers united in celebration of a battle won against a powerful enemy, the men, laughing loudly, followed Sampeyre. They marched the last few steps to the mountain where they stood facing upward-stretching limestone.

Sampeyre looked around and said to the men, "I want to see if it is possible to spot those we are pursuing." He walked over to a small ledge in order to get a better look up the mountain.

Standing on the small ledge, he stared upward and, after a moment, said, "I can just barely see them. They're far above us, but if that tunnel is around here and if it lives up to its promise, it shouldn't take us long to get comfortably above them. Then we'll grab them up like little birds."

"Let's see what this tunnel looks like," Marbach said.

With an eager look on his face, the priest led the group to a nearby boulder. Behind the boulder was a large hole, a couple of feet high. "Inside that hole is the tunnel," said the priest.

Sampeyre, standing beside Marbach, told Rolf, Zbik, Max and Paul Neumayer to remain outside while he and the others would go inside the tunnel.

Sampeyre, Marbach, the priest and Fay went inside the tunnel. They got down on their hands and knees and started crawling. Leading the way, Sampeyre crawled forward. He crawled forward, ever forward.

After about five minutes of crawling, the four men emerged into a jagged open place. It was too dark to see very much until the priest lit a rag-topped torch he had brought along. The torch made it possible to see that they were in a cave room and directly above them was a large tunnel. There was a wooden ladder leading up the tunnel and a wire cable hanging downward.

The priest said, "The tunnel goes almost to the top of the mountain, but at intervals there are exits. I never counted them. Each of the exits is about twenty meters above the one below. The third exit up there will most certainly get us above those we are chasing. I must admit I have never enjoyed mountain climbing and I didn't like crossing the ice, but I have always very much enjoyed climbing up this tunnel."

"Get moving up that ladder," Sampeyre said to Marbach. "I'll bring the others in here. Get yourself and the American and the priest up to that third exit. We'll be quick behind you."

Marbach secured his rucksack and the Mauser on his back, hung a heavy coil of rope on his shoulder and started up the ladder.

As he moved upward, stones broke loose within the tunnel and tumbled downward.

About twenty minutes later, Marbach had made his way up to the third exit. He promptly dropped the rope down to those below.

Sampeyre retrieved the rope, fixed his eyes on Fay, checked the American's rucksack, grabbed his shoulders, gave him a good-natured hug and shoved him toward the ladder.

At first, all went well for Fay. But half-way up his right leg, the one that had been wounded, began to shake. The shaking became uncontrollable and he had to stop climbing.

From up above, Marbach sized things up. He shouted, "Going up a ladder is tricky for some kinds of legs. I've got you by the rope. Don't worry about falling. Maybe if you stretch that leg out and push your foot onto one of those ledges, you can get your leg to stop shaking."

Fay edged down a bit, stretched out his leg and pushed his foot down onto a small ledge. After a couple of minutes, the trembling stopped.

"I think it's all right now," Fay shouted.

"Whenever you're ready, try climbing on up," Marbach shouted.

Fay made it the rest of the way up to where Marbach was waiting.

Marbach smiled at Fay, then dropped the rope down into the tunnel.

"I'm glad that's done," Fay said, nursing the leg that had begun shaking again.

"That leg of yours could be a problem."

"Yeah."

"I have to stay here and help the others. Why don't you go outside and see what the situation looks like?"

Fay left the tunnel. Nursing his leg, he made his way out on a wide mountain ledge, walked carefully to where it was possible for him to see down the mountain. He quickly spotted the Eichmann group far below, studied the situation for a minute or two, then went back inside the tunnel and said to Marbach, "That Eichmann bunch is way down the mountain. It'll take them at least an hour to get up here."

"Does it look like they will be coming right up to this place, or will they be going off to one side or the other?"

"They're directly below us. My guess is they'll be climbing right up into our arms."

"Good," Marbach said. While saying that his concentration was on the man coming up through the tunnel: Paul Neumayer.

A few minutes later, Paul Neumayer scrambled out of the tunnel, went outside, and stared down the mountain. One of the tiny figures climbing upward—given the distance, no telling which one—was his father.

CHAPTER FIFTY-THREE

fter all eight men had come up the ladder, Zbik went to where he could keep watch on the group climbing up the mountain while Marbach and the others made themselves temporarily comfortable in an accessible mountain hut. Like countless other huts scattered from one end of the Dolomite Alps to the other, this place of refuge was provided with food, liquor and cigarettes.

Three lanterns kept the hut well lit. Marbach squatted on the floor, chewing on a piece of chocolate. Sampeyre stood in the middle of the hut holding a coil of rope in his hands. Max chewed on an apple while reading an Innsbruck newspaper someone had left in the hut two weeks ago.

"We'll have to leave money and post a message thanking those who supplied all this," the young priest said in a voice that seemed to have lost much of its timidity.

"Is this hut stocked by the Alpine Club?" Max asked.

"Of course. All these huts are Alpine Club huts," Sampeyre said. "Their poster is on the wall over there. It says this is Alpine Hut AG 137."

Rolf, chewing on cheese, had a contented look on his face.

"I could use some whiskey," Max said. Even under primitive circumstances he managed to look and sound dapper.

Thunder began clapping in the distance. A mountain storm was coming.

Zbik poked his head into the hut. "Never much warning for weather changes in the Dolomites." After saying that, he came all the way inside and found a place to sit down.

Immediately, a flash of lighting totally lit up the inside of the hut. A moment later, there was an especially loud clap of thunder.

"That bunch climbing up here are in for a hard time," Marbach said.

"This storm might finish them," Zbik said.

Paul Neumayer put his face in his hands.

The priest didn't say anything. His head was lowered. He was praying.

After more loud thunder, the mountain storm attacked in full fury. Powerful gusts of wind hurled with full force upon the hut. There was lightning and thunder.

When the lightning finally stopped, a violent assault of large hail stones began. After a few minutes the hail stopped and a light snow began falling.

The light snow fell for several minutes until the short period of peace was interrupted by a powerful clap of thunder.

The hut shook.

A window broke.

And then there was silence.

CHAPTER FIFTY-FOUR

After the storm passed, Paul Neumayer was the first one out of the hut. He walked a couple of dozen paces, stopped, and stared down the mountain.

Quickly, the others rushed up and stood beside him.

"I don't see anything," Rolf said.

Sampeyre stared downward. "A lot of mist . . . wait a minute."

With startling suddenness, the mist cleared.

Paul Neumayer exclaimed, "They're alive! There's five of them. They must have found a cave, but they aren't coming up. They're headed back down."

"We've got to stop them from going down," Marbach said as he unslung the Mauser rifle and peered down the mountain. "It's a shame they aren't closer. From this distance, with them in those clothes, I can't tell which one is the woman."

"Take your shot," Max said. He gestured with his finger. "Hit the one farthest off to the left. That ought to make the others back off to the right. There's no way they can get down from over there on the right."

Marbach lay down on his stomach, leveled the rifle and took aim.

"Oh, please . . ." Paul Neumayer gasped. "You are going to kill my father."

Marbach kept aiming.

Sampeyre said to Marbach, "Get on with it."

Marbach continued aiming.

Paul Neumayer put his hands on his face. Then, in a quick move that caught everyone by surprise, he rushed forward and jumped on top of Marbach, causing the Mauser to fire a wild shot.

Marbach clutched the Mauser to his chest as he stood up. Paul Neumayer got to his feet and covered his face.

Words trailed out of his mouth. "My father. My father."

Max stepped forward and delivered a punch that knocked Paul Neumayer down.

Rolf edged over to a place where he could look down the mountain. While continuing to look downward, he shouted to the others, "That round caused them to back off to the right. All of them. It looks like they found a cave. They're going inside."

Lying on the ground, Paul Neumayer stared up at Max and made a crying sound. "I am sorry. I am sorry."

In a defensive voice, Max said to Paul Neumayer, "I had to hit you."

At that moment, Sampeyre yelled, "We've got company."

"Where?" Marbach shouted.

"Come over here and see for yourself. There's a bunch of strangers down by the entrance to the tunnel."

Everyone trotted over to where Sampeyre was standing.

For a few moments, everyone stared downward and no one spoke. More than two dozen men were clustered down below near the entrance to the tunnel.

"It's a small army," Sampeyre said. "And it is clear they've found the entrance to the tunnel."

Rolf expressed dismay. "Where are the French? Who won the war, anyway?"

"We are defeated," said Sampeyre. "There is no longer any chance to get the Odessa papers."

Yes, thought Marbach, most certainly the Frenchman is correct. This is defeat.

"There is defeat," said Sampeyre, "But we must not be broken by the defeat. We can't get the Odessa papers, but we may be able to avoid capture."

Zbik shook his head. "What's wrong with staying where we are? We can fight them off."

Marbach explained, "The ones down there are Werewolves. That's for sure. And you can bet they are heavily armed with automatic weapons. The only thing for us to do is climb."

The priest said, "We don't have to climb. We still have the tunnel. We can use it to climb to the top of this mountain and then climb down the other side."

Sampeyre shook his head. "We can't go up any higher using the tunnel. There'll be rifles firing up that tunnel in a few minutes. Anyone in that tunnel will be shot to pieces."

"I agree," Marbach said. "We can't use the tunnel, but we can keep the Werewolves from using it to quickly climb up here. If they get up above us, we will be trapped."

Max said, "We must tear the tunnel up."

Sampeyre smacked his hands together. "First, we will tear up the tunnel. Then we will get started with the climb we are going to make that will take us up to the top of this mountain and down the other side."

CHAPTER FIFTY-FIVE

With Sampeyre in charge, the men set about preventing any pursuers from making use of the tunnel. They tore down the wire cable and dropped heavy stones. They kept tossing down stones until it was obvious that the ladder was useless.

"They are not going to give up chasing us, but this will put them hours behind us," Sampeyre said. "Now we are going to have to do some serious climbing." He had a length of nylon rope in his hands and was using his elbow and the palm of one hand to wrap the rope in a coil. "We have to go up to the top of this mountain and then down the other side. Any questions or comments, Monsieurs?"

Max shook his head. He had nothing to say.

"It's a shame about the Odessa papers," said Marbach.

"A bitter shame," said Rolf.

We'll go up," said Zbik. "We'll go all the way to the top of this mountain and then climb down the other side."

"Agreed," Sampeyre said. He finished coiling the nylon rope and grasped the coil with his hand.

"I am used to the hemp," Marbach said. "But nylon is what we have."

"Do you really prefer hemp for the high climb, Monsieur?" Sampeyre asked.

"Hemp is all I have ever worked with."

"I, too, once liked the hemp," Sampeyre said. "But things change. Now there is the nylon. The nylon is good when there is climbing over ragged rocks and, more important, it is much lighter than hemp."

Marbach shrugged.

"I have always liked hemp," Rolf said.

Sampeyre stared at Marbach and Rolf, shook his head and said, "The nylon keeps its strength even when it becomes wet. And the nylon stretches. The hemp doesn't stretch. When you see the nylon stretching, you should not be concerned. The stretching means the nylon is better than the hemp. Believe me, Monsieurs, the nylon is better."

Max was dubious. "I don't know." Like Marbach and Rolf, he had never before used nylon rope.

Fay, sitting on the ground, stared at the nylon rope. All rope was the same to him.

Paul Neumayer had a miserable look on his face. He said to Marbach, "I am so sorry."

"That was your father I might have killed, Marbach replied. "There isn't anything more to say. I wanted to take the shot and you stopped me. I do not hold against you what happened. That's in the past. Only one thing matters. We have to work together from this point on."

Zbik, who had been quietly watching, stepped forward and put his hand on Paul Neumayer's shoulder.

Paul Neumayer looked at Zbik. He didn't say anything, but he had gratitude in his eyes.

Sampeyre said, "We are going to climb upward and I am going to be fussy about the belay."

Marbach looked up at the forbidding cliffs above them. "I expect you to be damned fussy about the belay."

"Put on your rucksacks," Sampeyre said. "I will go first. When I find a good place, a solid position, I will use the rope to belay the man who follows me. The last one up will be the American. He is the least experienced. Karl will be above him."

"Agreed," Marbach said.

"Tend to the American closely," Sampeyre said to Marbach. "He is going to need help with that leg of his."

While Sampeyre shifted his attention to Zbik and began talking about climbing technique, Marbach walked over to where Fay was sitting.

"You are going to be a climber," Marbach said.

"I guess so," Fay answered.

"Listen to me. The instructions are simple. I will tell them to you and you will repeat them back. Are you ready?"

After receiving a confirmatory nod, Marbach crouched down and faced Fay. "We will be doing the belay. What that means—as far as you are concerned—is that all of us are secured to each other by the rope. The rope keeps us from falling. Only one man moves at a time. Each time you are ready to make an upward move, you must wait for my permission. When you're ready shout to me in your American language the word 'climbing.' If you think there is too much slack on the rope, shout to me the American words 'up rope' If you need the rope tighter shout 'tension' And when you are in a safe position, call out, 'off belay.' Can you remember all that?"

"I'm no mountain climber," Fay said testily while getting to his feet. "And I've got a bum leg. Maybe I ought to stay behind."

Marbach didn't reply to that. Instead, for the second time, he told Fay to repeat the instructions.

Fay shrugged. "When I'm ready to climb I shout 'climbing.' If I think there is slack in the rope, I shout 'up rope.' And there is some more."

"Tell me all of it."

"If I want the rope tighter, I call for tension."

"Good. And what do you say when you are in a safe place?"

"Off belay."

"That is good. There is something more you need to learn." Marbach laughed softly so the American would know that what was about to be said was intended as humor. "If you think you're going to fall, call out 'Prepare for fall.' And if you find yourself falling be sure to yell to me 'falling.' Can you remember that?"

Fay laughed good-naturedly. "Go to hell."

Marbach placed his hands on the shoulders of the American. "There is one very important thing I must say to you. Fear cannot be overly indulged where we are going. Fear must be kept in its place. If fear for you becomes serious, focus on what you are doing. Focus on the feel of the rock, the pull of the rope. Think about what you are doing and how you are doing it. And think about what you are going to do next. Think! And think! And think! Always keep thinking. Thinking is good for keeping fear from becoming too serious a problem."

"I got you," Fay said with a grin.

"Remember that the mountain can kill you, but if you are not afraid when you die, the victory belongs to you."

Before there was time for reply, Sampeyre walked over.

"We are ready," Marbach said to Sampeyre in German.

Sampeyre replied in German. "Tell the American that when he does the climb with us he is our brother, and we will watch after him. And he must do the same for us."

Marbach passed on to Fay what Sampeyre had said.

Sampeyre stood watching Marbach and Fay for a moment, then turned, walked a few steps away, faced the other men and said in the German everyone but Fay could understand, "Pay attention! The American is coming with us. That is settled. He is part of our brotherhood. He is a good man, but I expect more from you than I do from him."

Sampeyre had more to say. "The belay doesn't do your climbing for you, but when it works, it keeps you secure. I will try to make sure it works, but don't misunderstand. The purpose of the belay is not to haul you up. You are expected to climb."

When Sampeyre walked away, Rolf stepped up close to Max and said in a low voice, "I think maybe this Frenchman knows his business."

Max whispered back, "I would prefer the hemp to this nylon rope, but I am beginning to think maybe this Frenchman knows what he is saying. Anyway, like you and the others, I will do things his way."

"It will be rough for the American," Rolf whispered.

"He looks like a good man," Max whispered in reply.

Standing a few feet from Rolf and Max, hearing what they had said, Marbach faced Fay and said, "I am jealous of you. Yes, I am. You are about to learn the belay. I wish we could exchange places. Such a grand thing it is to learn the belay."

Sampeyre had been watching Marbach and Fay. He walked over to them and said to Marbach, "Be sure this American understands that he must avoid getting exhausted. And that he knows it is no disgrace to be inexperienced."

"Yes."

"And be sure to tell him that the mountain won't tolerate deception and neither will I. If he gets in trouble, he is obligated to call for help."

"I already told him that, but I will tell him again."

CHAPTER FIFTY-SIX

On the climb up to the top of the mountain, the inexper-ienced Fay several times asked for help. Usually Marbach did what needed to be done, but sometimes one of the others provided the needed assistance.

The important thing was the climb. Whenever there were traverses to the right or to the left, Sampeyre moved Fay to the middle of two climbers, Marbach on one side and Rolf on the other. The two skilled climbers guided the untrained American.

At several places, it was necessary for Sampeyre to drop down and find a better way up, but, finally, all eight of the climbers got to the top of the mountain where they found a broad, flat area covered with snow. Quickly, a space was cleared that was large enough for all eight men to sit. The rucksacks and other gear were placed off to the side.

Sitting beside Fay, Marbach said, "You are doing good. You learn quick. Give me a few days and I could make a competent mountain climber out of you. How is your leg?"

"It's all right," Fay said.

Marbach stood up and walked in deep snow to a place where he could peer down the mountain. He spent two or three minutes peering downward before walking back to where Fay and the others were waiting.

He stood in front of Fay and repeated his question about the leg.

"The leg hurts, but it isn't too bad," Fay said. "If it was a bad problem, I'd tell you. I know the rule about not faking things."

"Why don't you get the graspa out of my pack?" said Marbach.

Fay stood up. "Graspa?" He didn't know what that was.

"You don't know about graspa?"

"Never heard of it."

"It's time you learned. Check my pack. You will find a bottle. Inside the bottle is graspa." After saying that, Marbach sat down. He stared around at the other men who had heard the word "graspa" and were eagerly smiling. They knew that graspa was brandy, mountaineer brandy.

Fay went to where Marbach had laid his pack, shoved a hand down deep and brought out a bottle.

"Graspa is what I need," Marbach said as Fay approached with the bottle.

"Graspa," said Sampeyre enthusiastically.

"Graspa," Rolf said with exuberance.

"Graspa," Max shouted, clasping an arm around Zbik, who echoed in a loud voice what Max had shouted.

"Graspa," Paul Neumayer said softly.

"Graspa," the priest whispered.

While connecting with each repetition of the word "graspa,"

Fay struggled to get the top off the bottle. When he finally succeeded, he held out the bottle to Marbach.

"First, yourself," Marbach said.

Fay lifted the bottle to his lips and took a couple of swallows.

"My God Almighty!" Fay managed to say while trying to stop coughing. "That's good stuff. I never drank anything like that in my life."

Fay passed the bottle of graspa to Marbach who drank one swallow, then passed the bottle to Sampeyre, who took one swallow, sighed heavily and passed the bottle to Rolf. After a couple of lusty swallows, Rolf passed the bottle to Max, who drank two modest swallows, one after the other, and passed the bottle to Zbik, who took one deep swallow and passed the bottle to the priest. After swallowing thirstily, the priest passed the bottle to Paul Neumayer and blessed himself. A moment later, the priest blessed himself two more times.

Fay made a whistling sound. "I never drank any brandy like that before. That's real potent stuff."

Marbach said, "Graspa is made from the vine stalk after the grapes have been removed. It is said to be a miracle drink. I do not say it is true, but some men swear they have seen graspa bring to life mountaineers, some of whom had been lying dead in snow for a dozen years or more."

Fay laughed. "I can almost believe that."

The eight men drank graspa and talked among themselves. Fay wondered if the powerful graspa was somehow making German sound intelligible to him.

"Why didn't anybody ever tell me about graspa before?" Fay said. "It sure has banished my fatigue. I feel all over alive. Totally alive. I'll bet graspa does bring people back from the dead."

Marbach smiled. "The way you feel . . . is it because of the graspa or is it because of the great height we've reached?"

"Maybe both," said Fay.

"Some people say that at the top of the Dolomites there is no sin," said Marbach.

Fay grinned. "Whether it is the graspa or being on top of a Dolomite mountain, I feel sin free."

Shifting to German, Marbach said to Sampeyre, "You're a mountaineer. Do you believe there is no sin up high in the Dolomites?"

"Many good mountaineers would disagree, but I agree with the French writer Francois Mauriac who says that when you have climbed up high enough on a mountain it is impossible for you to nourish evil thoughts."

Marbach repeated to Fay what Sampeyre had said.

Fay said, "I don't know if it's the graspa or being way up here on the mountain with you and these others, but right now I feel sin free."

"Drink some more graspa," Marbach said. "It will fortify you for the climb to come."

"What's the rush? It's getting dark. Besides, we're safe up here, aren't we?"

"We are safe until tomorrow morning. Then this mountain top will be a trap. Those pursuing us have powerful weapons. By tomorrow they will block any downward moves by us—on any side of this mountain." Marbach pointed to a nearby peak that was higher than the one they were on. "How long do you think it will take them to get some marksmen over there. When that happens what will become of us?"

Fay peered at the nearby mountain peak. "Just one marksman over there who has a rifle with a telescopic sight and we wouldn't have a chance."

Marbach said, "I have a feeling that there will be no absence of sin for those who will soon be on top of that mountain."

Sampeyre got to his feet and stood facing the men. "There is no choice. We must do a downward climb at night."

"It is going to be difficult doing the downward climb," Max said. "It would be hard enough doing it in day light and the worst thing is that the weather is changing."

Sampeyre said, "Yes, the weather is changing. It is going to turn bitter cold. Drink more graspa. Graspa is good for keeping the cold out."

Rolf said, "We are drinking graspa together at this place on top of the whole world. And all of us are Alpines."

"Yes," Sampeyre said. "All of us are Alpines. Each and every one of us. We disagree about some things, even about important things, but while we are filled with the Alpine spirit our disagreements do not matter. All that matters is that we Alpines are bonded together."

Marbach looked at Fay and said, "Monsieur Sampeyre says that all of us are Alpines. Very specifically, that includes you."

"I'm just a novice."

"If Monsieur Sampeyre says you are Alpine, then you are Alpine. It's official."

"Well . . . all right. I am Alpine."

"You are Alpine, but you don't know what the word means."

"It has to do with the Alps," Fay said defensively. "These Dolomite Alps."

"You are wrong," Marbach said. He continued like a pro-fessor addressing an uneducated student. "Alpine doesn't stem from the word Alps. It derives from two Greek words. The words are 'once more' and 'drink.' The drink is graspa. An Alpine is one who is filled with the spirit of graspa. It is a holy thing to be filled with the spirit of graspa."

"All right, I am Alpine," Fay said, "I sure do like the feeling."

A few feet away, Rolf poked around in his rucksack and pulled out a large supply of bacon rind. "Gentlemen, pull off your shoes and socks. And take off your gloves."

"Yes," Sampeyre said. "It is going to be cold and the bacon rind will help."

The men rubbed bacon on their bared feet. After putting their shoes back on, they rubbed bacon on their hands and on their faces.

"The downward climb is going to be tough," Max said.

The priest expressed his concern to Sampeyre. "How can we climb in this darkness?"

Sampeyre said. "We have torches. Our torches are kerosene rags tied to the ends of pieces of rope. We will light our torches when we need them and it will be possible to see what we need to see."

Zbik grinned. "I wish I could be as calm as the rest of you Alpines about doing a damned downward climb at night."

With a laugh, Max moved over beside Zbik and said, "If we go to folly, we go to it with grace and courage."

"And the spirit of graspa," the priest said in a voice filled with confidence.

"The spirit of graspa," said Zbik in a prayerful voice.

Sampeyre held rope in his hands. "We will now begin what I call *the going down of the rope.*" He stared at the men around him. "You are good men, all of you. Come, you Alpines, let's get on with what we are going to do. We will be bonded together while doing *the going down of the rope.*"

"Yes, we will be bonded together while doing *the going down of the rope,*" said Marbach.

Sampeyre knelt down and hammered a sharp-pointed piton into limestone rock. At each blow, there was a sold, ringing sound. "That is the best limestone rock in the world!" he declared.

"Yes, that is a truly grand sound," Zbik said.

"Up here where we are now the limestone looks like marble," Sampeyre said. "It is like marble. But down below some of it will be red. The red limestone breaks away and crumbles. We must all of us look out for the red places. It will be hard to see the red places in the dark. Those red places are bad places. Light from torches will help you to seek out the red places. And when there is no light from torches, there is moonlight. The moon has come out. Whenever you find a red place warn the rest of us."

Sampeyre looked around. A lot of things were different on a downward climb compared to an upward climb. On the upward climb, he, the best climber, had been first. On the downward climb, he would be last. The poorest climber, the American, would be in the middle. A strong climber was needed to go first.

"The first one on the rope will be Rolf," Sampeyre said. "Then Max. After Max goes the friar. And then the priest. And then Zbik. Then the American. And then Karl. I will be the last."

"I better get ready," Rolf said.

Sampeyre pulled Marbach off to the side. "The American has learned quickly, but be sure he knows everything he needs to know about climbing down this mountain."

"May I take the last place on the rope?" asked Marbach.

"I will be the last one on the rope," Sampeyre said.

Marbach nodded. They both knew that on this downward climb the most dangerous place belonged to the last one on the rope, the one above all the ones below.

Marbach and Sampeyre stood together and watched while Rolf moved up to the jumping off place, took up a length of rope, twisted it expertly, made two loops, put his feet into the loops, pulled the rope up and made a seat for himself. He was ready to start down.

Sampeyre moved forward, faced Rolf and spoke words of encouragement. Rolf nodded, took a moment, then stepped backward into darkness and dropped out of sight.

Keeping himself relaxed, Rolf did a small dance on the sheets of stone until he had descended a distance that he estimated was about three times the height of a tall-peaked church. He didn't think it was odd for him to have the image of a church in his mind while measuring distance in the Dolomites.

Rolf steadied himself on a ledge and beckoned for those above to join him.

One after the other, those at the top of the mountain started down. It didn't take long for all of them to join up with Rolf on the ledge.

Sampeyre, the last man down, looked upward and pulled expertly on the rope. As the rope tumbled down, everyone stood clear.

After that, everything was repeated, one pitch after the other. After each descent, there was a brief rest. But never for long.

"Time to move on," Sampeyre kept saying. Always after saying that he lit a torch at the end of a piece of rope and dropped it down to see what lay below.

At one place of rest, more than a dozen pitches down the mountain, while standing on a very small ledge, Max rubbed his arms and complained that it ached.

"You have hangover of the muscles," Sampeyre said.

"And you have hangover of the brain," Max said with a grin.

CHAPTER FIFTY-SEVEN

While Sampeyre and the seven men with him were doing the going down of the rope, on the other side of the mountain, down at the very bottom, a couple of dozen Werewolves gathered around Stephan Kaas, Adolf Eichmann, Colonel Count Neumayer, Dr. Heinrich Emhardt and Dr. Emhardt's Russian wife.

Kaas took charge. First, he quieted Werewolf chatter about the tunnel that had been rendered useless, its ladder smashed by rocks dropped from up above. Then, in a firm voice he declared that there was chasing and killing to be done. The words he spoke and his manner of speaking brought forth shouts of enthusiasm from the young Werewolves.

Kaas moved among the Werewolves. In what amounted to a short speech, he said that the Werewolves should do their best, be courageous, get necessary killing done.

After the Werewolves enthusiastically agreed to do their best, Kaas used a quiet but forceful voice to say that if any of them got captured they would disgrace themselves if they said or did anything that might reveal the identities of him, Colonel Count Neumayer, Adolf Eichmann, Dr. Emhardt, or Dr. Emhardt's Russian wife. Very deliberately, Kaas spoke the Russian name "Natasha Yakovlevna."

With their voices melding together each individual Werewolf affirmed that he would deny ever having seen Eichmann, Colonel Count Neumayer, Dr. Emhardt, or Natasha Yakovlevna.

After staring at the early evening sky, Kaas stood stiffly like a soldier at attention while the Werewolves separated into two groups. One group of Werewolves was going to chase up the close-by mountain and the second group would chase up a taller mountain near the close-by mountain. From the top of the taller mountain, rifles could be used to kill those who needed killing on the close-by mountain.

After the two groups of Werewolves left to start their nighttime climbs, one Werewolf remained behind for a few minutes. That Werewolf suggested to Kaas that refuge might be found for Kaas and those with him in a nearby hut where there was food and drink.

Kaas and the group with him followed the Werewolf to the hut. After bidding farewell to the Werewolf, they went inside the hut where they found American gear, American uniforms, some weapons and a lot of food, liquor and cigarettes. One very important thing inside the hut was a large radio.

The radio captured everyone's attention. It was on a small table. Eichmann pulled up a chair, sat in front of the table and fiddled with the radio while Colonel Count Neumayer pressed up close behind offering suggestions. Kaas sat quietly in a nearby chair nursing a glass of American whiskey.

The hut consisted of a single room measuring a dozen paces in length. At the mid-point of the hut, on a wire stretching from one wall to the other, several heavy blankets were hanging. The blankets provided privacy of sorts for Dr. Emhardt and his Russian wife. Soon, secure behind the heavy blankets they began giving noisy expression to their passion.

Kaas listened to the sounds of sexual passion. When the grunts and moans first started, he was amused, but that didn't last long. He soon began feeling angry. His mood was shared by Colonel Count Neumayer and Eichmann.

"How disgusting," Colonel Count Neumayer whispered.

"Awful," Eichmann murmured.

Kaas didn't say anything. He tried to tell himself that the wife of Dr. Emhardt was unattractive, but to his distress, he was finding her desirable. Her desirability fueled a rage that rose within him as he listened to the sexual sounds.

Ignoring what was going on behind the heavy blankets, Colonel Count Neumayer pressed up close behind Eichmann, who continued fussing with the radio, shoving the antenna in various directions and, again and again, pushing the transmission switch while cranking the call-up handle. A red bulb was glowing. That meant the transmission circuit was working. Everything was working as it should, but nothing was coming out of the radio except static.

"You aren't doing it right," Colonel Count Neumayer said.

"I am trying," Eichmann said.

To the distress of Kaas, from behind the heavy blankets came loud sounds from the Russian woman: "Uh . . . uh . . . oh . . . oh . . ."

Kaas bolted up from his chair, advanced a few paces toward the sounds of carnality, then abruptly stopped. He realized he would just make a fool of himself if he crudely interrupted love making. With a need to find a target for his anger, he turned on his heel and aggressively advanced to where Colonel Count Neumayer and Eichmann were standing in front of the radio. Pushing past them, he brought his fist down hard on the top of the radio.

Eichmann and Colonel Count Neumayer backed away while the strong, forceful Kaas jerked at knob after knob on the radio and hit switch after switch. It was reckless behavior, but sometimes recklessness pays off. The radio began to sputter and a voice speaking English could be heard amidst the static. "Radio Rome. This is Radio Rome."

All three men froze upon hearing those words.

After a few moments, Eichmann stepped forward, edged around Kaas, debated a moment, carefully selected one of the dials, twisted it, and the static disappeared. In that moment very clear words in English could be heard. "Radio Rome . . . This is Radio Rome. We are receiving. Over."

Eichmann stared at the switchboard. One switch was marked "send/receive" in English. He flipped the switch and spoke his fallible English. "Here is an Alpine group. Who is at Radio Rome?" Eichmann paused. Then, collecting his wits, he said, "Over."

A reply was quickly delivered. "This is Radio Rome. The U.S. Army in Rome. How can we help you? Over."

"Let me handle this," Colonel Count Neumayer said while reaching out his hand. He knew about radio connections like this.

Eichmann yielded the microphone.

Colonel Count Neumayer made use of highly competent English as he said into the microphone, "I am Colonel Count Neumayer. I speak my former title to make myself recognized. I am trying to contact U.S. Army Colonel Ralph Crider. I believe he is in Cortina. Can you arrange some sort of contact? This is important. Over."

"This is CIC relay. We can patch you to Colonel Crider."

Everyone stared at the radio. It wasn't simply the U.S. Army in Rome that had been contacted. It was CIC in Rome, U.S. Counterintelligence. Everyone listened closely as the voice on the radio addressed former Colonel Count Neumayer.

The voice on the radio said, "Colonel Crider will accept your call, Colonel Count, but he has no easy access to a radio. You can contact him by telephone. Or, if you want, I can pass messages back and forth. Over."

"Can I use this radio to contact Vatican City?" Colonel Count Neumayer spat the words out. "I need to talk with Bishop Alois Hudal. Over."

"I'll need approval . . ." There was static again on the radio, but it cleared quickly and a different voice came out of the radio: "This is Colonel Weiss. I have approved patching you through to Vatican City."

For a few moments there was nothing but a lot of loud static. Then a voice broke through the static to announce that a connection had been made with Vatican City. After that, a voice came on speaking Italian.

There was nothing but Italian spoken for a minute or two, then a voice came on speaking German. "I'm sorry, the bishop is in his office. He can't be disturbed. Over."

Colonel Count Neumayer became an energized force. "I guarantee the bishop will be disturbed if you don't see to it that my message is immediately passed through to him. Tell the bishop that Colonel Count Neumayer wants to talk to him about Odessa. I repeat. Colonel Count Neumayer wants to talk about Odessa. Do you receive? . . . Over."

Kaas paled visibly at hearing the word "Odessa" spoken so freely over a radio connection. He stiffened when a voice on the radio said, "Keep the line open. We're telephoning the bishop's office. This better be important. Over."

"I will wait," Colonel Count Neumayer said. "Over."

After a few moments of silence, the voice came back on the radio and said, "The bishop will be in the radio center in less than twenty minutes. Can you stay on the line that long? Over."

"I don't know how long this radio is good for. If we sign off, can you reconnect with us? Over."

The voice on the radio sounded almost desperate as it said to not disconnect.

There was no disconnection.

A little more than ten minutes later, without warning, a Slavic voice came on speaking German: "Bishop Hudal here. Am I in contact with Colonel Count Neumayer? Over."

A prompt reply was delivered. "Colonel Count Neumayer here. I am on the new escape route—Odessa. Over."

"Are you aware of security? Over."

"If we are captured security won't matter. Over."

"Where are you? Over."

"In the Dolomites. On the Austrian side, down at the bottom. There are people here of considerable importance.

In addition, there are a lot of important records. We are in danger of capture. Over."

"Be more specific about your location. Over."

After a small fuss, Colonel Count Neumayer the correct number: "Alpine Hut AG 137".

There was a long period of silence, then the Bishop's voice came back on the line. "I am instructed that help will be provided to you at your location within two hours. Over."

"We will be waiting. Over."

"My private telephone will be kept free all day for any contact you may need to make. You have done me . . . you have done the Church a great service. I salute you. Over."

"I salute you, Bishop. I hope to see you soon. Out."

Colonel Count Neumayer switched the radio off, then turned and faced the others in the hut.

Kaas nodded.

Adolf Eichmann smiled as he looked at the men standing around him.

CHAPTER FIFTY-EIGHT

High up in the Dolomites, Rolf, leading the downward climb, had made himself secure, was waiting for the others to join him on a narrow ledge when a clap of thunder erupted in the distance. That was bad news: another mountain storm was coming.

Not too far below him, Rolf spotted a cave. He signaled to those above him and soon all eight men were inside the cave.

A few minutes later, the storm attacked the mountain; flashes of lightning lit up the sky.

The storm lasted barely five minutes. When Sampeyre stuck his head out of the cave, he couldn't see anything but darkness. He shouted to those behind him, "Get yourselves ready."

After giving them time to get ready, Sampeyre did a quick check of each man, from cap to boots, then told Rolf to resume leading the way downward.

There was one quick downward pitch after another. Occas-ional patches of red limestone were encountered and carefully avoided. Sometimes pitons being pounded into limestone did not yield a solid ringing sound, but unless the sound was too dull, risks were taken.

"I don't like it here," Max shouted after one of the downward pitches left him in a bad place, at the same level as the others, but way off to the side.

"Over to your left," Rolf shouted.

Reaching over to his left, Max pounded in a piton and no longer was in any trouble.

"Drop a torch," Sampeyre shouted to Marbach.

"Here goes," Marbach called out as he touched a lit match to a bundle of oily rags tied to a short length of rope. He slowly lowered the flaming rags and began making a swinging motion. For a minute or two, by the light of the swinging torch it was possible for all of the men to see far down the mountain.

When satisfied that he had seen what he needed to see, Marbach pulled the torch up and put out the flames.

There was an exchange of cheerful shouts among the climbers and another downward pitch began.

And then another.

And another.

A half hour later, Sampeyre and Marbach were readying to complete yet another downward pitch, join up with the rest of the group waiting below them. Sampeyre was standing on what had seemed to be a safe piece of rock when, suddenly, it gave way and he started dropping down before there was any chance for Marbach to grab onto him.

Sampeyre was in a free fall, but in a matter of moments, his fall came to a jerking halt and he was able to steady himself by standing on a piece of limestone thrust aggressively outward. The rope that had become his life line was secured high above with a piton. He balanced himself precariously on the outward thrust of limestone and looked downward. He saw that the young priest, not far below him, was going to try to move out to a precarious place on a narrow ledge and pull him to safety. It was an act of courage that would put the priest in great danger.

Sampeyre was ready to shout to the priest to move back to safety when the situation suddenly became desperate. The rock beneath Sampeyre's feet broke away and he began pitching wildly, swinging round-and-round in open mountain space. The rope pulled him away from the mountain and slammed him back harshly against brutal mountain limestone.

Rendered nearly unconscious, Sampeyre swung wildly in the air for a few moments. As his mind cleared, he was able to see Paul Neumayer move up behind the priest. Young Neumayer was going to try to hold onto the priest who was going to try to grab onto Sampeyre. Both of them were taking a great risk. A bad jerk on the rope, the failure of a piton, and they would be pitched to their deaths.

Continuing to swing, Sampeyre used his legs to try to soften the blow as he slammed one more time against unforgiving rock. A few moments later, barely conscious, he was vaguely aware of being pulled to safety by two men who, his clouded mind told him, he had failed to respect even after the beginning of this climb when they had made various climbing moves that had earned them respect. He cursed himself for failing to see the worth in these two men until these last few moments.

CHAPTER FIFTY-NINE

In the dark of night, Sampeyre, in great pain, was lowered down the mountain in a makeshift sling. Slipping in and out of consciousness, his mind didn't begin to clear until he was laid on the ground at the bottom of the mountain.

Zbik clasped Sampeyre's hand, looked around at the others, then stared at the mountain, barely visible in the darkness. "This was an awful climb. I'm glad it's done."

Sampeyre came fully alert and spoke in as loud a voice as he could muster. "It was a good climb. Whenever terrible obstacles are overcome and climbers end up bonded together, the climb is a good climb."

"A good climb?" Rolf, standing nearby, stared at his bleeding hands. They all had bleeding hands.

In a troubled voice, Max said, "I messed up. I put pitons into red limestone."

Sampeyre said, "We all did that. In the darkness it was sometimes impossible to see the color of the limestone."

Zbik let go of Sampeyre's hand, carefully placed it on the Frenchman's chest. "Several times I pounded pitons when I couldn't even see the hammer in my hand."

Rolf said, "It was often impossible to see much of anything in the darkness."

Marbach pulled the bottle of graspa out of his rucksack, wiped clean the top, and offered the bottle to Sampeyre.

"Give me a lift," Sampeyre said.

Marbach knelt down beside Zbik, and, working together, they carefully pulled Sampeyre into a sitting position. Then Marbach held the bottle to the Frenchman's mouth.

Sampeyre took a swallow and handed the bottle back.

Continuing to hold Sampeyre, Marbach took a swallow and passed the bottle to Zbik.

Zbik took a drink and passed the bottle to Fay.

"The spirit of graspa," Fay said in German after taking a drink. He hadn't intended to speak in German. It just happened.

"One more time the graspa works its miracle," said Sampeyre.

Fay cocked his head. He understood what Sampeyre had said. He grinned.

Marbach said to the assembled group, "Take a rest. It's still pretty dark around here. Drink more of the graspa while I check things out. On the way down the mountain, I spotted the lights from a couple of farm houses. One of them is just beyond those trees over there. Maybe I can learn the best way to get to Cortina. I'll be back as quick as I can." He waved his arm and in the next few moments disappeared into the darkness.

"Zbik," said Sampeyre, still being held in a sitting position by Zbik. "where are the priest and the friar?"

Don't try to move," said Zbik. "They are here. It's just that they are standing where you can't see them."

The priest and Paul Neumayer moved into Sampeyre's line of vision.

"That was a foolish thing the two of you two did," Sampeyre said. "I say to the two of you that my debt is greater than I can repay."

The priest said, "I am glad you are safe." He looked confident, no sign of timidity.

Sampeyre said to the priest, "You're a good man." He paused a moment, then addressed Paul Neumayer. "And you, Friar Paul, you are also a good man."

"I am not a friar. I am a fake."

"Tell me what to call you."

"I am Paul Neumayer."

"You are a good man, Paul."

"Me? A good man? You don't know what you are saying."

"You are a good man. You are a good man who just finished doing a Dolomite climb with me and the others here."

"I do feel different, but I don't think I can be called good."

"Feel the good that is within you. Hold on to that good."

Paul Neumayer stared at Sampeyre. "You were good even before the Dolomite climb."

"Not as good as you think. I don't know if the Dolomite climb has made me sinless, but I intend to hold onto the good I now feel within me with all the strength I have. I expect you to do the same."

Paul Neumayer said, "I would like to spend more time in the mountains. I would like to spend a lot more time in the mountains in the company of Alpines."

Sampeyre nodded. "That would most certainly help you to hold onto the good that is now within you."

CHAPTER SIXTY

There was early morning sunshine when Marbach returned to where the others were waiting. He had a woman with him. The woman with Marbach was skinny; her small face appeared to be awkwardly featured. The garment she wore was torn and dirty.

In Marbach's hand was a large tin can filled with cold soup. One cigarette butt was what he'd paid the owner of a farm house for the cold soup.

Marbach explained to the men about the woman. He said that she regarded herself as Ukrainian. Not Russian, but Ukrainian. Marbach said that this Ukrainian woman had told him she would rather be dead than sent to Russia, that six days ago she was captured by Italians and an Italian mayor, a Communist, had exercised his authority under the refugee agreement with the United States and arranged to have the U. S. Army transport her to Russia. But she had managed to escape her American captors before they could turn her over to the Russians.

"Tell this woman she is safe with us," Sampeyre said when Marbach finished explaining things. "When we argued in the station wagon about Ukrainians who separated from the Soviet and were now available to be sent back, I said send them back. I thought I was right, but I was wrong. Now I say this woman will not be transported against her will to the Soviet. I say this woman is safe with us."

The others joined in quickly. Max and Zbik were loudly vocal expressing their agreement with Sampeyre.

Fay, confident he was able to understand what this was all about, told Marbach in forcefully phrased English to tell the Ukrainian woman that he would stand alongside the others to keep her safe.

Marbach faced the Ukrainian woman, spoke to her in Slavic words she was able to understand. "You are safe with us. All of these men agree we won't give you to the Americans or to the Italian mayor. For myself, I ask that you tend to this wounded man." He gave the Ukrainian woman the can of cold soup and pointed to Sampeyre lying on the ground.

"I will feed him," the Ukrainian woman said.

"Good," Marbach said. Then he walked over to where Rolf and Zbik were standing and the three men stood together and watched while the Ukrainian woman tended to Sampeyre. She fed him cold soup that he swallowed appreciatively.

It was obvious to the three men that the odd-looking Ukrainian woman knew about tending wounded men. After the soup was gone, she secured Sampeyre in her arms and whispered words in his ear that those watching could tell he appreciated hearing even if he couldn't possibly understand what he was being told.

Zbik said, "She is skinny, no looks at all. Even if she wasn't so skinny and dirty, she wouldn't have any looks, but I wouldn't mind being the one this woman was tending to."

CHAPTER SIXTY-ONE

Ten minutes later, the Ukrainian woman was still tending to Sampeyre when shouting voices of young boys could be heard far off in the distance. After a couple of minutes, two small boys approached. They immediately became quiet when they saw that they had encountered some people.

Rolf tried speaking an Italian greeting to the two boys, but it was immediately obvious they didn't understand what he was saying.

Marbach and Rolf shared a look of recognition. The boys were Ladins, a small ethnic group living in the Dolomites. Marbach moved toward the two boys while introducing himself speaking Ladin. They quickly replied in Ladin, a language different from Italian or Austrian, closely related to one of the Swiss dialects. Ladin was one of the several languages Marbach spoke with at least a minimum competence. He'd had a lot of contact with Ladins during the First World War.

Speaking Ladin, Marbach quickly learned that the two boys were brothers. One of them, aged ten, almost two years older than the other, was excited about a small rock—a crystal—he had found. It was small and flawed, totally worthless, except to a young boy.

Marbach asked in Ladin, "Does that crystal belong to you?"

"It is my crystal," the Ladin boy said with wariness in his voice.

"Of course, it is your crystal," Marbach said.

"All of you men look terrible. And the woman, too."

"We've had a hard climb."

"Here is the crystal. You can look at it, but you have to give it back."

Marbach accepted the crystal, held it up in the air, first in one direction, then another.

"Give it back," the Ladin boy said.

Marbach returned the crystal. "Thank you for letting me look at your crystal."

"Who are you?"

"My name is Karl Marbach. I am from Vienna. A Frenchman is here. He is the injured one."

"Who is the woman?"

"What does it matter?"

"Is she a Jew?"

"Does that matter?"

"Everyone says Jews are bad."

"Why don't you ask me if I am a Jew?"

"You are not a Jew. Jews are bad."

"Ah . . . even here. Come. We will have a talk."

Marbach led the two Ladin boys a few steps away from the others and talked with them.

CHAPTER SIXTY-TWO

Sampeyre leaned on the Ukrainian woman while struggling to get to his feet. When he felt ready, he said in German, "Come along, Monsieurs. We must move on." Looking around, he stared at Marbach who was still talking with the two young Ladin boys. He had no idea what they were talking about, so he called out, "Are those boys telling you how we can get to Cortina?"

"We aren't talking about Cortina."

"Then you are just wasting time."

"Give me one moment. I am writing something down."

Sampeyre was impatient. "It is time for us to move on."

"Here," Marbach said to the two Ladin boys. "I have written down on this piece of paper some of what we've been talking about. I wrote it in Ladin. Can you read it?"

The older of the two Ladin boys, about ten years old, said, "I am sorry for what I said about Jews. You have convinced me it is wrong for me to say or think that being Jewish means someone isn't as good as me."

Marbach said, "All of us are sometimes wrong. The important thing is to try to be right. A good person isn't always good, but a good person always keeps trying to be good."

"I will remember that."

"Can you read what I have written in Ladin on this piece of paper?"

"I have trouble reading."

"You and your brother must learn to read. Some day you must both read for yourselves what is written on this paper. In the meantime, all you can do is try to remember what I have told you."

The younger of the two Ladin boys said, "I remember what you told us. You said to hold up high the image of Janusz Korczak, a Jew, a Polish man. While telling us about Janusz Korczak, you said your friend over there is Jewish and Polish." The Ladin boy pointed at Zbik.

Marbach spoke to both Ladin boys. "Tell me what Janusz Korczak taught."

The older Ladin boy began reciting: "A child can make mistakes. A child is entitled to respect. A child can protest injustice. A child can have opinions . . . I don't remember the rest."

Marbach said. "You have to learn to read. Until you learn to read you must get someone to read to you what is written on the paper. You must get it repeated to you until you are able to remember all of the children's rights."

"Herr Police Inspector," Sampeyre said, unable to understand the Ladin talk. "You are holding us up."

Marbach said to Sampeyre, "I was telling these two boys about Janusz Korczak—about the statement of children's rights."

Sampeyre rubbed his jaw. "That is good. It is good for them to know the statement of children's rights. If you taught these boys some of the wisdom of Janusz Korczak, that is more important than me being in a rush to get out of here."

Marbach said, "Yes, it is, but now I'm ready to bid my young friends a fond farewell."

Sampeyre tried not lean heavily on the Ukrainian woman while he used a free hand to inspect his various injuries. A few moments later, when the inspection was finished, he laughed and said, "I take great pride in the climb we have just completed, *the going down of the mountain*."

Zbik said, "It was just a downward climb, but it does sort of leave me with a good feeling."

Sampeyre said, "What you feel is better than just a good feeling."

Zbik smiled. "Do you think I am sinless?"

Sampeyre spoke very directly to Zbik, but made his voice loud enough for all the others to hear, "Yes, I think you are sinless. Climbing up and down the Dolomites purged you of sin. Right now you are sinless."

The Ukrainian woman was confused by talk she couldn't understand. Marbach smiled at her and explained in her Slavic language about sinlessness and climbing up and down mountains.

The skinny, awkwardly structured face brightened for a moment.

Sampeyre stared at the face of the dirty, skinny Ukrainian woman. It pleased him to look at her face. He believed it was a good face, even if a little unusual.

"Well," Marbach said while staring at the mountain, "I don't know if it is sinlessness or if I just feel better than I have felt in years. I've got a good feeling even though we have failed. We didn't capture Dr. Emhardt or Adolf Eichmann.

And we didn't get the Odessa papers. This is total, absolute, complete failure, yet I have a good feeling."

Marbach shook his head and began laughing.

All of the men joined in the laughter, including Fay who was sure he understood everything Marbach had said.

The two Ladin boys, even though they had no idea what had been said, also joined in the laughter. They laughed while rushing up to Marbach, laughed joyfully while they clasped their arms around him.

The Ukrainian woman watched as the laughter continued. She stared intently while Marbach stood apart from the other men, his arms around the two young boys, the three of them laughing and pointing up the mountain. She was still watching when the man she knew was named Zbik walked over and hugged the man named Marbach. She continued watching while Zbik knelt down and hugged each young Ladin boy in turn.

Moved by what was going on around her, the Ukrainian woman fixed her eyes on her edelweiss, her precious mountain flower. Then she stared at the Frenchman.

Sampeyre stared back at the Ukrainian woman. He wanted to say something, but they didn't have a common language. Reluc-tantly, he turned away and said to the others that it was time to move on.

He led the way while the Ukrainian woman held her arm around his waist, helped him take some of the strain off his body. The others fell into place behind Sampeyre and the Ukrainian woman.

The two Ladin boys waved at Marbach, kept waving long after he was out of sight.

CHAPTER SIXTY-THREE

In a hotel room in Cortina, CIC Colonel Ralph Crider was trying to make a telephone connection with Bishop Hudal on a secure line. It took a while, but finally, the connection was completed. After exchanging preliminary greetings, Colonel Crider said, "I'm glad you understand English. That makes it possible for me to tell you on the telephone what I hope I will soon be able to tell you face to face: your people pulled off a great rescue; Dr. Emhardt is safe. I will personally be taking Dr. Emhardt and his wife to Milan later today. From Milan they will be taking a plane to their new life in the States."

Stephan Kaas, a look of satisfaction on his face, was sitting near Colonel Crider.

Millican, the only other person in the room, had a drink in his hand and an uncomfortable tightness in his gut. He knew that smarter people than him had decided that Dr. Emhardt was vitally important to the security of the U.S. He accepted what he had been told: that in a world of atomic bombs, the services of people like Dr. Emhardt might keep cities in the U.S. from becoming cinders. But Millican's gut was registering distress.

Colonel Crider continued his telephone conversation with the bishop. "Your people saved Dr. Emhardt. They also saved Stephan Kaas, who's sitting beside me right now. And there are a couple of others who got saved. One of them is former Colonel Count Neumayer. Just for the record—records are important—who was the man who wanted to go to Italy instead of coming to Germany?"

Colonel Crider frowned as he listened to the answer. Finally he said, "You don't know the name? Well Stephan Kaas is here. Maybe he can tell me the name of the guy."

Stephan Kaas lifted his head.

Colonel Crider laughed as he said into the telephone mouthpiece, "Say, let me share some of the news at this end. The Frenchman and the Vienna cop have been seen here in Cortina with some friends of theirs. There's nine of them in all. Eight men and a woman. The woman has been described as looking like some kind of refugee."

Millican realized that "Vienna cop" meant Karl Marbach. The tightness in his stomach got worse.

Colonel Crider finished the telephone call. "Thank you, thank you, Bishop. I hope to see you soon in person. I plan on going to Rome in a couple of weeks . . . Thank you, Bishop. Goodbye."

Colonel Crider hung up the telephone.

Millican looked up. Kaas was standing in front of him offering a fresh drink.

"No thanks," Millican said. He didn't want any contact with Kaas.

Colonel Crider said to Kaas, "I need to have the name of the guy who was with you and Dr. Emhardt."

Determined not to speak Adolf Eichmann's name, Kaas said to Colonel Crider, "It was a classic chase scene. Not much talk. If that extra guy identified himself by name, I didn't catch it. There are lots of escaping war criminals. He might be one of those. Or he could be just a jerk. Frankly, he didn't seem half bright."

Colonel Crider said, "Don't worry about it, but if you get any clues, let me know. As soon as you feel up to it, get back to Munich. I've got the one who calls himself Klaus Becker hidden away in a house there. Klaus Becker, Klaus Barbie, whatever his name, he's a guy who has shown that there are important services he can perform for us."

"I am prepared to leave immediately," Kaas said.

"Klaus Becker is a guy who gets things done," Colonel Crider said. "He has made himself useful. We need him if we're going to keep German scientists out of the hands of the Russians and bring some of the important ones into the States."

"I will watch after Herr Becker for you," Kaas said. "Have no concern."

Millican connected with the names Klaus Barbie. He had read the highly classified record on Klaus Barbie. He realized that some pretty bad Nazis were going to be excused for their misdeeds because of their potential usefulness, but it was awful thinking that one of those was Klaus Barbie.

Millican shifted uneasily in his chair. He could hear church bells pealing outside the hotel, calling the faithful to early Sunday Mass. He recalled from years ago the sound of church bells in St. Colman's parish in Cleveland. Sometime . . . maybe not too long from now, he would be able to take Sally and the kid to Mass at St. Colman's.

Colonel Crider said to Kaas, "You're a good man. The war is done and past. I say to you, Herr Kaas, that I am proud to know you."

"The honor is mine," Kaas said to the American colonel, who nodded approvingly and replied, "I am going to Milan later today. I gotta wave goodbye to Dr. Emhardt and his wife. A plane is taking them to the good ole U.S.A. I sure wish I was going with them."

"One of these days I hope to go to America," Kaas said.

"About this Sergeant Fay . . ." Colonel Crider said, letting his words hang in the air.

"Fay?" Millican hadn't meant to speak the name aloud. But having caught the attention of Colonel Crider, he continued. "How does Sergeant Fay figure in this? I haven't been briefed on anything that's happened. I just got to Cortina an hour ago."

Colonel Crider spoke aggressively. "Sergeant Fay is in league with the Frenchman and the Vienna cop. When he shows up I want him put where he won't enjoy himself too much. I want him moved to a file job in Frankfurt. Sergeant Fay is finished in CIC. Do you hear me, Captain Millican?"

"Yes, sir," said Millican. He was convinced there was nothing else he could say.

Colonel Crider said to Millican, "I'm not taking any disciplinary action against Sergeant Fay, but that's just because we can't afford to do anything that might open this matter to the public. Still, I don't want him enjoying himself too much. When is his enlistment up?"

"I'm not sure . . ." Millican shifted uneasily in his chair.

"The sonuvabitch," Colonel Crider snorted. "Be sure all our guys know they'll score points if they make Sergeant Fay very uncomfortable."

Millican's stomach felt like a tight knot, but he told himself that anything he might say at this time would just be futile.

Colonel Crider gulped down his drink, then looked reflect-ively at his empty glass. "Imagine!" he said. "A frog mountain climber and a Viennese coffeehouse cop thinking they are good enough to come out on top of us in a match of brains and guts. Well, we showed them. We beat them. We will beat dogs like them every time . . . because we're tougher and smarter."

"True," Kaas said.

Millican silently ground his teeth.

Looking around, Colonel Crider lifted his glass. "Let us toast ourselves, gentlemen."

Kaas didn't hesitate. "Toast," he said cheerfully.

Millican knew there was no way he could avoid joining in. "Toast," he said.

"Toast," Colonel Crider said before drinking from his glass. After putting down the glass, he said, "That Frenchman—that skirt-chasing mountain climber—what are his politics?"

"I don't know," Millican said.

Colonel Crider shook his head. "I'll bet that lady's man is a Communist. I'll bet the frog is a Communist."

Kaas nodded agreement, mused a moment, then said, "That may also explain Police Inspector Marbach. His wife is a Jew. I wouldn't be surprised if Karl Marbach and his wife were both Communists."

"I'll bet you're right," Colonel Crider said. "They gotta be watched. I'm gonna ask our guys to do a full check on that Kike wife."

Kaas echoed approval using the German word "Yid," equiv-alent to the English word "Kike."

For Millican it was awful hearing Pammy spoken about this way. He found it especially troubling to hear the jerkoff colonel suggest that Pammy was a Commie. Calling people Commies these days could bring them a lot of trouble. It hurt Millican that he couldn't say anything in Pammy's defense, not without bringing an incredible amount of trouble on himself. And, in the end, he told himself, nothing he could say would help Pammy.

The church bells continued ringing.

"I think we deserve medals for what we pulled off," Colonel Crider said. "We got Dr. Emhardt." He sighed, then continued. "But there'll be no medals for us. Everything's gotta be kept secret. Still, there's one consolation. Even if no one ever learns what we did, we can take pride among ourselves for what we've done."

Kaas pursed his lips, spoke slowly, thoughtfully. "The Frenchman and the Vienna cop are in town and there's a Russian refugee with them."

Colonel Crider scowled. "A Russian refugee?" He gestured turned toward Millican. "Put out an order to pick up the Russian woman. The U.S. has an agreement with the Russians to pick up their people and pitch them to Russia. The higher ups have put a high priority on that. The Russians can have her. Sergeant Fay can't be picked up. That would lead to complications. We'll leave all of them alone, except for the Russkie woman. We'll pick her up and leave all the others alone."

"Yes, sir," Millican said. He had a feeling of total futility.

Colonel Crider smiled warmly at Kaas.

Kaas smiled back cheerfully.

With a satisfied look, Colonel Crider turned slightly and looked out the hotel window. There was a mountain in the distance. "That sure is some sight," he said. "That mountain looks like a naked woman waiting for someone to jump on her."

"I agree," Kaas said, laughing lustily as he got to his feet and poured more liquor into the colonel's glass. Remaining on his feet, he gestured toward the mountain that was highly visible through the window, and offered a toast: "Here's to the naked woman . . ."

Colonel Crider completed the toast: ". . . waiting to be jumped on."

Millican took a deep breath and joined in the toast. He told himself that even if you don't like what you are doing, when you get orders you obey them. Besides, making a fuss wouldn't help anything. It wouldn't help Fay and it wouldn't change anything for Pammy. Millican took relief from the thought that in a couple of months a furlough was coming up for him. A real furlough back in the States. That was something to look forward to. A Sunday morning in Cleveland, taking Sally and the kid to Mass.

CHAPTER SIXTY-FOUR

wo U.S. Army MPs in a fast-moving jeep spotted the group they had been searching for and exchanged a shout of triumph. The jeep came to a halt a couple of dozen feet from the eight men and the woman. The two MPs sitting in the jeep felt good. Along with a dozen other MPs in a half dozen jeeps, they had been trying all day to find this bunch.

One of the MPs gestured toward the tower. "What is that thing?"

The second MP gave a perplexed look. "I don't know. Maybe some sort of church. That ain't important. This is the bunch we were told to find. There's the sergeant. He's supposed to be a good guy. The important one is the Russkie woman. God, look at her. What a dog! No looks at all and I'll bet she hasn't bathed in a year."

The first MP nodded his head. "The woman is the one we're supposed to pick up. We're supposed to leave the sarge and the others alone."

"Yeah."

The two MPs got out of the jeep and walked toward the eight men and the woman. They didn't take their rifles.

They had handguns tied to their waists. One of them had a Kodak box camera hanging around his neck. They stopped when they got within a few feet of the eight men and the woman.

"Hey, Sarge," said the MP with the camera hanging around his neck. "How're yuh doing?"

"I'm doing all right," said Fay. "We're here to see the memorial."

"Is that piece of rock a memorial?"

"Yeah."

"Hey, Sarge, the rest of you guys are all right, but we gotta take the Russkie woman. She's gotta come with us."

Marbach moved up beside Fay. Speaking his best English, he said to the MPs, "I am Vienna Police Inspector Karl Marbach and this woman is under my authority."

"The hell she is," one of the MPs said. Quickly, both MPs started to pull out their holstered guns, but Marbach got his weapon out first and pointed it at them. While the two startled MPs watched, all of the men surrounding the woman pulled out guns, including Sergeant Fay.

"I insist that both of you drop your guns onto the ground," Marbach said to the two American MPs, who stood stiff and straight for a moment before dropping their weapons on the ground. Marbach made a nodding motion toward the woman and said to the MPs, "We have told this woman she is safe with us."

"This is crazy," one of the MPs said, "All we want is the woman. Let us have her and you guys can go wherever you want."

Marbach spoke firmly. "You can't have the woman."

One of the MPs turned toward Fay. "Sarge, if this doesn't stop right here and now there'll be bad trouble for you. I'm talking Leavenworth time."

"We told this woman she would be safe with us," Fay said. He knew the consequences for him. He was, after all, still in the army. But he had climbed up and down a mountain in the company of the men standing around him now and he had joined in the pledge to help keep the Ukrainian woman safe.

Rolf walked over to the two MPs and picked up their guns. He also took the Kodak camera one of the MPs was wearing around his neck.

Zbik headed over to the jeep, found two rifles that he expertly stripped apart. He tossed the pieces in various directions, then pulled up the hood of the jeep and jerked free a couple of wires.

Looking around, Marbach said, "Before we leave here, I'd like to go inside the bell tower. It'll only take a minute." Without another word, he headed toward the bell tower.

While Rolf and Max and Zbik kept their weapons aimed at the two American MPs, Paul Neumayer, the priest, the Ukrainian woman, Fay and Sampeyre followed Marbach into the bell tower.

After getting inside the bell tower, Marbach and the five people with him looked around. Names of Austrian and Italian fallen soldiers were linked together on granite panels. The names belonged to soldiers—Austrian and Italian—who had fought against each other and died on the Dolomite front during the war of 1914 to 1918.

Marbach reached out his hand and touched one of the names chiseled on granite rock. After that, he touched a second name placed beside the first name, and spoke the names of the two fallen soldiers: an Austrian soldier and an Italian soldier. Then he moved around and spoke other pairs of names chiseled on the granite panels. He spoke one name after another: an Austrian name followed by an Italian name. After speaking each pair of names, he paused for a moment.

Sampeyre stood at attention while Marbach spoke the names of soldiers from the two opposing armies who had fought each other and died and now had their names chiseled side-by-side on granite panels.

Finally, Marbach paused for a moment.

Sampeyre said in a soft voice, "Surely there isn't another memorial like this anywhere in the world."

The Ukrainian woman didn't say anything. She couldn't understand what Sampeyre had said, but she knew she was in a holy place, as holy a place as a cathedral.

Fay had stopped practicing his religion many years ago, but at this moment, on impulse, he touched his forehead with the fingers of his right hand, dropped the hand downward, then touched his left shoulder and his right shoulder.

After standing for a few minutes in silence, the six people walked out of the bell tower and joined the three who were still holding weapons on the two American MPs.

Sampeyre edged over and whispered in Marbach's ear, "Our very fine American friend can get into a lot of trouble for this. There is no need for that to happen. We might create some confusion here, fix things so he could say we had our guns on him all the time. To make it convincing, one of us could give him a convincing punch or two."

"Yes," agreed Marbach. "No point for this fine man to bring the wrath of the U.S. Army down on his head." He turned away, walked over to where Fay was standing and whispered in clear English, "You are American Army. There's no reason for you to get into trouble over this. You and I could share some angry words and I could punch you. Then we could roll in the grass a bit. If we are convincing enough you will be able to spare yourself a lot of trouble. All you'll have to do is tell your superiors we had guns on you all the time and that your gun was empty. I'll say a few things that will make that sound convincing."

"I read you," Fay said in a low voice. "That'd probably work, but unless you tell me I am not really Alpine I want to stay joined up with you guys. I'd like to be a partner with those of you who are going to keep the Ukrainian woman safe."

"There'll be a big price for you to pay," whispered Marbach.

Fay spoke in a low voice. "I came out of the war feeling numb. I did my duty, but it left me feeling numb. Right now, I feel all over alive. I want to hold onto the feeling of being all over alive."

Marbach understood. He said, "You are Alpine."

The Ukrainian woman stepped to one side and moved back toward the bell tower. She laid down her edelweiss at the entrance, then placed her thumb, index and middle finger on her forehead, moved them down her body, then onto her right shoulder and, finally, over to her left shoulder.

Sampeyre moved up close to the Ukrainian woman and per-formed the same ritual, only not in the manner of the Orthodox Church. He did it the way he had been taught as a youth. He touched his four fingers to his forehead, moved them downward, then to his left shoulder and finally to the right shoulder.

When he finished blessing himself, Sampeyre looked at the Ukrainian woman. She returned his look with a smile. The smile seemed to transform her awkwardly structured face. Distinctly feminine features emerged.

Max, standing by himself, looked at the Ukrainian woman. He had known many beautiful women in his life, but at this moment he thought that if he had his choice of any woman in the world to look at it would be this Ukrainian woman.

Zbik held the Kodak box camera in his hands. The sun was beginning to set. There was just enough time for one quick photograph. After a photograph was taken the eight men and one woman would head for safety in Italy. With things the way they were it would be foolish to go to Germany or Austria.

Marbach spoke to the Ukrainian woman in her language. He asked her to stand very still for a moment. Just before the picture was taken, he said, "Don't worry, Ludmilla, you are going to be safe."

Sampeyre realized that the Ukrainian woman had been addressed by her name. It was the first time he'd heard her identified by name.

Fay, standing apart from the others, didn't understand what Marbach had said to the woman, but he realized she had been identified by her name. He whispered the name to himself: *Ludmilla*. Such a marvelous name, he thought. He was grateful he was one of those helping to keep this woman safe. Sooner or later there would be a price he would have to pay, but he knew he would never have any regrets for the choice he had made.

Zbik raised the camera and took the picture.

After the picture taking was done, Sampeyre looked at the woman standing beside him. She was smiling and the smile was lighting up a face filled with femininity. From the days of his youth, he had always had a proclivity to favor surface allure over deep down femininity, but that was in his past. The climb up and down the Dolomite alps had changed him. He was profoundly aware of the powerful femininity of the Ukrainian woman. He knew right down to the core of his being that from this moment on there would be one woman in the world for him. He was bonded to this Ukrainian woman for the rest of his life, or for as long as she would have him. If she rejected him, he would have to find a way to handle the rejection.

He stared appreciatively at the Ukrainian woman and was grateful when she smiled back.

"Yes," she said in German. Sampeyre hoped this marvelous woman was affirming the bond he felt for her. He expressed his love by speaking her name with reverence: "Ludmilla."

THE END